To Sally

The Secret Clinic on Downtown Broadway

Gloria S Walker

ISBN: 978-1-64316-054-2

Cover Photo by Another Believer [CC BY-SA 3.0 (https://
creativecommons.org/licenses/by-sa/3.0)], from Wikimedia Commons.

                                                        Viejo Press

During yesterday's march in Washington a special poster was held high among the others. It was of Anne Thompson, a Portland abortionist during the forties and fifties. Her courage in the face of unfair laws and an all-male court system earned her a permanent place in American women's history. She was there for us before the pill and Roe v Wade.

After the Supreme Court decision in 1973, most of us believed our fight was won. Sadly, this is not true. Once again, her face rises above the crowd, reminding us of what life was like during a time when abortionists were arrested for helping women exercise an essential freedom: The right to choose.

Reaction to an article covering a march of more than 500,000 abortion rights supporters in Washington, D.C. on April 25, 2010.

Chapter One

December 8, 1941

Lauren sat at the kitchen table studying for a physiology exam. In the background she heard the rise and fall of a sport-caster's voice. Her grandfather was listening to a playoff game between the Brooklyn Dodgers and New York Giants.

The game stopped and Lauren alerted. Someone was making an announcement, but static made it difficult to hear.

Within seconds her grandfather yelled, "Come quick!"

She ran to the living room. But before she could ask what was happening he thrust out his hand hushing her.

"We repeat: The White House just announced a Japanese attack on Pearl Harbor. Stay tuned to WOR for further developments – broadcasted immediately as received."

"Pearl Harbor! The Japanese?" Lauren squinted, confused, and waited to hear more, but the static took over.

Her grandfather nodded, "Yes, the Japanese have attacked our base… The phone rang, cutting him off as Lauren ran back to the kitchen and grabbed the receiver, "Ben, you've heard".

"Yeah, and I need you here. I'm about to tell Mom where I'm heading in the morning."

"What! That's too soon. Your mom will have a fit, and I…"

Ben interrupted, "Mom already is, and I haven't even told her where I'm going. And you, of all people, know it isn't too soon."

He was right. They had talked about his enlisting from the time Germany invaded Poland.

"But…" Lauren stopped. She needed time to think. "Wait. Don't tell her. Oh my God, Ben… I'll be there in minutes. I'm leaving now."

She put the receiver back but didn't move. It occurred to her that the world – her world – had just changed and wouldn't ever be the same.

After minutes she walked back into the living room and saw that her grandfather was at the closet, putting on his old Navy pea coat.

"I'm reenlisting." Lauren shook her head in disbelief. "It's been years since you were in the Navy!"

"You're right. It helped me grow up and needs me now."

He buttoned his jacket as he headed for the front door. Then stepping outside, he waved for Lauren to come. "Neighbors are gathering out front." He walked toward them and raised his voice, "You'll be heading to Ben's. Tell him to choose the Navy."

Lauren wanted to stop him – tell him to wait, talk to her, things were happening too fast. But he couldn't hear her and she mumbled, "Ben already has."

She pulled her red hair into a pony-tail, applied lipstick without a mirror, and put on her coat as she left. Neighbors were crowding the sidewalks. She zigzagged past them heading for Bens' house – two blocks away. Their excitement was palpable.

"It's time for action." "Our boys in Honolulu were taken by surprise." "We'll return it ten-fold." Yamamoto, Hitler, Mussolini – explosive words, with epithets in instant play. Mothers expressed concern for their sons and husbands. Fathers, themselves eager to volunteer, knew what was expected of their sons.

Lauren hurried. She thought how Sundays were always special at Ben's house, but this would be like no others – except in one way: Mary would be in charge.

Coming to America, pregnant with Ben, Mary had kept her allegiance to Ireland. She and Joe were proud of their heritage. But Mary defined it. She bragged that the Irish enjoyed a comic mixture of tragedy and wit. She also said they had a tempestuous nature that eliminated the dullness that was common in their English cousins. Mary Sullivan made certain that her children recognized what it meant to be Irish – often proving it through humor and theatrics.

And Sunday was the best day to accomplish this. After Mass, she insisted that the family stay home together. Enticing them, she prepared brunch that included an egg casserole, fruit salad, crumpets, homemade jams, and pies that she rolled, filled, and placed in the oven within minutes.

Lauren liked being included.

But today as she approached the door there was no spicy scent of apple pies. Then before she rang the bell, Mary flung the door open, her face full of outrage. She often turned commonplace into high-drama, but today she was reacting to what was dreadfully uncommon.

"Hello, Lauren. 'Tis a bad day. Ben, my oldest, wants to leave this home; and his brother, with little need for a razor, wants to do the same." Mary had never attempted to lose her accent, preferring an expressive Irish brogue to the flat sound of Oregonians.

Lauren looked past her to Ben. She knew how difficult this was for him, but there was warmth in his smile as he listened to his mother. As usual, everyone's attention was on her. This was her family – her audience, whom she loved to entertain. But this morning she wasn't looking for laughs; there was fear behind her words.

"'Tis not a time to be smiling, Benjamin O'Sullivan." Her husband had eliminated the "O" when they arrived in America, but Mary retrieved it on occasion.

She faced Lauren. "Talk to him. Get some sense into him. This is not a time to play soldier." Her face was grim. "We should have stayed in Ireland. They know the price of war, and would be careful about siding with England."

"Sorry, Mum, but you know I've seen this coming – expected it – all of us: Jon, Dad, Lauren. And so have you. We each know what we have to do."

"Don't include me in this. I was hoping you'd all have better sense. But you're all tetched in the head – each of you, except Lauren." Mary looked at her. "She doesn't want you to go. Tell him."

Lauren faced Ben and spoke softly, "He knows, Mary."

There was nothing more to say. Lauren walked to the table and poured herself a cup of coffee, then sat next to Ben. He reached for her hand and squeezed, and her eyes filled with tears.

"There," Mary said. "Look at Lauren, Ben. See what we are feeling. Oh my God – see her tears. There will be many more."

"Mum, stop." Ben rose. "We're going for a walk."

Lauren stood, surprised that Mary didn't respond. She knew there was no arguing with her, and Ben seldom tried. But today it was much more than an argument; Mary's fears were deep and well founded.

As Ben and Lauren walked toward the door, he tossed words, "Think about it, Mum. How would you feel if they found me 4-F? Rejected, I'd be the only man left home on the block."

"Great. If you and Jon were 4-F, I would be feeling great."

"Not a chance. Who told us that God's protection was in a good Irish stew? And you've made hundreds of good Irish stews. No one in this family could be 4-F."

Ben enlisted in the Navy on December tenth, and nine days later he was on a train headed to Camp Pendleton. After he left Lauren kept busy at school – wishing she could fast forward her studies and enlist as a nurse. They had each talked of joining-up and stopping Hitler. Now it didn't seem right that he was gone and she was still home.

Surprising her, his letters weren't focused on Europe. Nor did he write about the rigors of boot-camp. Instead he wrote detailed letters about the war in the Pacific. And typical of Ben, he knew more than Lauren learned from newspapers and radio. Especially about what was happening in the Philippines. The Japanese appeared to be winning!

For a long time, Lauren and Ben had believed that America should join the war against the Nazis. They never questioned that the United States would turn the war around and become the victor. Now, Ben was writing about the war in the Pacific, and he described Americans as over-confident – even arrogant.

He wrote that thousands of Americans and Filipinos were dying. He added, "I know I'm doing the right thing. But my reasons are different now. We have no choice but to fight – Japan attacked us; the axis needs to be stopped. But I no longer believe that fighting is a moral prerogative; it's much more basic. If we don't fight and win, our world as we know it will be reshaped."

Lauren and Ben had been friends since early grade school and started dating when they were sophomores. By the time he enlisted they knew they would get married – but talked about waiting until the war was over.

When Ben came home from boot camp he wanted to move the

date earlier. Lauren agreed, and they decided it would be on his next furlough. But for now, they would spend a weekend at the beach, just the two of them.

They told Mary and Joe that they were taking off. And showing no surprise, Joe suggested they drive his 1929 Ford, and Mary packed them a basket of food.

Attracting stares, they walked on the beach holding hands. After twenty weeks at Camp Pendleton, Ben looked taller, tanner, and as his father had noted "a hell of a lot tougher." Lauren was vibrant – her long auburn hair tossed by wind, and cheeks flushed by the chill air.

Months earlier Lauren might have described herself as happy. Now everything was equated to war and his leaving. Happy was too simple.

Late afternoon they gathered drift-logs and built a fire. Lauren had tucked a bottle of wine and a blanket into her bag. They sat leaning against a log, sipping the wine and enjoying the snap and crackle of the fire. Within the hour it turned to embers, and they watched the sun dip behind gold waves.

Now dark, she smoothed out the blanket and they lay next to each other. As they kissed she pulled the straps of her swimsuit from her shoulders, and gently guided as he ran his lips from the curve of her neck to her breast. Tingling, she pulled him closer and whispered for more.

Later, as she lay with her body touching his, she wondered if anything in life could ever equal the pleasure and warmth she felt.

It was close to midnight when they returned to the cabin. They showered and then walked to the twin sized bed. Lying, bodies entwined, Lauren thought how she could never love anyone as much as she loved Ben. And he, his voice soft, said, "I'll love you forever."

In the morning he turned onto his back, and she lay close to him–drowsy and happy.

But he didn't move, and after minutes she asked, "Are you all right – I mean…"

He spoke slowly. "I am. But I can't shake this feeling. And I know I'm not alone – some of the guys talk about it." He was quiet, and then mumbled, "It's just a feeling."

"No," Lauren said, frightened. "Don't think it." She put her fingers on his lips. "Don't."

When he didn't answer, she sat up and read his expression.

"Ben, don't go. Stay with me." She bent down and kissed him.

His words didn't go away. She was haunted during their drive home, and the feeling grew stronger through the week.

Then, as she and his parents stood at the train depot surrounded by young men in uniforms, she saw tears in Ben's eyes.

And before he stepped onto the train, she whispered, "Don't go."

Lauren hadn't noticed Mary's expression until now. She looked frantic. And as Ben disappeared into the crowded train, she cried, "No."

As the train started to move, faces filled the windows, eyes searching, frightened and sad. Finally, they saw Ben. He had made his way to the back of the train and waved to them until he was out of sight.

Chapter Two

Lauren stepped from the elevator and headed down the long hallway, then stopped. The taste of vomit filled her mouth. Spotting the arrow to the ladies' room she ran, pushed the door open, made it to the stall and bent over the toilet. Perspiring, gagging, spitting – there was no relief. Finally, she pulled herself up, went to the sink and wiped her face with a wet paper towel. Then, determined, she walked back into the hall.

But when she got to the clinic she paused before pressing the buzzer.

A tall woman, almost her own height, opened the door. "Lauren Martin?"

"Yes. I called yesterday."

The woman smiled. "I'm Carol, the one you spoke to. Come in."

Lauren stepped into the office and thought how it conveyed homey comfort, as if to detract from her reason for being here. A crystal vase of fresh roses sat on Carol's desk, and a deep green philodendron twisted up a windowsill and along the edge of the ceiling. On the wall behind the desk there was a calendar with a Norman Rockwell watercolor – a boy and his puppy. The month and year were in large print: June, 1942.

Lauren sat, queasy and unsure, ready to leave – to walk back out of the room but told herself she couldn't. Looking for a distraction she noted the magazines on the table next to her: Readers Digest, Good Housekeeping, Redbook, and Hollywood – with a picture of Betty Grable on its cover, dressed as a WAC and smiling like the leggy pinup girl she was.

Lauren picked the magazine closest, Good Housekeeping, and flipped to a full-page ad titled, The New Patented Equalizer. It had a photograph of a woman in a sleek evening gown, being watched by a shy pubescent girl. Its statement was discreet:

This year – some five million young girls between the ages of 10 and 14 will face one of the most trying situations in all the years of young womanhood.

This year – some five million mothers will face the most difficult task of motherhood. Thousands of these mothers will be too timid to meet this problem – and it will pass, but with what possible unhappiness...what heartbreaking experience.

To free this task of enlightenment from the slightest embarrassment, the Kotex Company has had prepared a simple, understandable story booklet called "Marjorie May's Twelfth Birthday".

Some problem! Lauren thought. She shoved the magazine back with the others, then checked her watch. It was nine, straight-up. If Dr. Karriden was going to be late, she would leave.

As if reading her, Carol looked up from the papers on her desk.

"I know that coming here hasn't been easy. The doctor will talk with you in a minute. She tries to schedule so that waiting time is minimal."

As if on cue, Dr. Claire Karriden entered the room and Carol left. Lauren had seen pictures of her in The Oregonian, usually accompanying well-known Portlanders to clubs or the race track. Captions never referred to her as an abortionist. Instead she was described as the glamorous or sophisticated Dr. Karriden.

But looking at her now, Lauren thought how "professional" best described her. Her jacket and flat shoes were white, and her dark hair was pulled into a bun. The word pretty didn't fit; she was striking. And there was an easy strength about her. However, instead of feeling more assured, Lauren felt uncomfortable.

Then, with a warm smile, the doctor reached out to shake Lauren's hand. "I'm Claire Karriden."

Lauren's handshake was weak; she wanted to have the abortion and leave.

The doctor pulled up a chair and sat facing her.

"I know you're nervous. That's something I wish I could help with. I can't, but I can tell you that you're not alone. Most women are nervous when they come here, and for good reasons. It's important that I learn your reasons. They will help us make decisions carefully – while in limited time."

Lauren was bothered by the doctor's voice: Low, with a deep throaty edge, it reflected far more self-assurance than her own. And her use of "us" was disturbing. It wasn't the doctor's decision.

"Why do you want an abortion?"

Lauren shot her a look. This doctor, confident and poised, was going to make this situation even more difficult than it already was.

Dr. Karriden waited for an answer.

Lauren thought how she wasn't about to discuss reasons; not with her or anyone. But as minutes passed, it hit her that she might have to leave without having anything done.

Annoyed, she sighed and repeated, "Why do I want an abortion?" Then, looking directly at the doctor, she asked, "Is that necessary to know? I'm here. Do I need to spell out reasons?"

"Yes. It's important to talk. Have you talked to anyone about this?"

"No." Lauren's answer was curt. Ben was 6,000 miles away. "I just want this pregnancy to disappear."

Dr. Karriden looked resigned. "All right, let's go slowly. How old are you?"

"Almost nineteen," Lauren's voice was a monotone.

"Graduated from high school?"

"Yes. I'm …" Lauren stopped; she hadn't come here with the intention of talking about her life.

"You're what? Working? Attending college?"

"What difference does that make? Do you have a preference?" Lauren stopped – she wanted to leave but couldn't. "Look, it was hard for me to come here. I'm sick, tired, worried, and most of all… oh never mind."

Dr. Karriden was unruffled. "Miss Martin, I'd be surprised if you said it had been easy to come here. Abortion is a relatively simple process, but its impact can be enormous." She paused, giving emphasis to her words, "With that in mind, you have the choice of leaving; but if you stay we're going to talk."

Lauren studied her. This assured doctor had made it clear that she was in charge. And then Lauren sighed, recognizing that this was probably good. Besides, it made no sense to fight her when, in fact, she needed her.

"I've finished a year of nursing school and am planning on returning in the fall. For the past month I've been aware that this won't happen if I don't see you. Not just school, but so much else in my life. My friend and … I mean, Ben, the father of…" She stopped and took a deep breath. "Ben left for Guadalcanal in March. We plan on marrying when he comes home on leave. I - well - I don't want this to be… don't want us to start with… At the same time as…"

Her words fizzled, and she looked at the doctor for help, "Quite honestly, I don't know what I want."

"And I can't help you with that. But before your decision is made, let's find out if an abortion is even an option. Let's start with some dates. Making this easy, do you know the date of conception?"

Lauren felt her face grow warm.

"Yes, I know the exact date. March 20th." Reading the consternation on Dr. Karriden's face, she added, "You're right. It's been three months."

"What symptoms are you experiencing?" I'm assuming your periods stopped. What else is happening?"

"Constant nausea – but worse in the morning. I get no relief."

Dr. Karriden nodded. "You're in nursing school and know the symptoms. Are there changes in your breast?"

"Yes. They've grown and are painful. I'm pregnant. And as I said, I know my dates." She looked at her, pleading, "I'm hoping you'll do the procedure today.

The doctor looked doubtful. "You're right on the line. It's my policy to never do surgery when the fetus is past the first trimester, because of its advanced stage of development, as well as your health."

Lauren looked at her with disbelief. "Doctor Karriden, I know exactly when Ben and I were together. I can't be more than three months pregnant. We weren't together before or after March twentieth. It's now June seventeenth. I've waited till the last minute, but you just said that you do abortions up till the second trimester."

"Yes, and as you know, you're on the line. I don't like to accept patients this close to twelve weeks." She looked weary. "This is because I assume you've been struggling with your decision, or you wouldn't have waited this long."

"That's true. But Doctor, I cannot have a child right now. Not only because I want to finish nursing school. But when Ben and I marry, I want us to start right – share in having our child. I want him to be with me through the pregnancy and birth. I want him to know our child and be part of everything that's important in our lives.

"Doctor, everything will change if I have this baby – all of my plans. I have thought and know what needs to be done. Please help me."

Claire Karriden was quiet for a minute, and then said, "You don't have much more time to decide, as I won't contradict my rules. When I see as much ambivalence as you're showing, I usually put off surgery."

Claire pressed her lips together, deciding, "Tomorrow is Saturday, and it's another busy day around here. But I'll see you first thing in the morning – seven o'clock. You go home and think hard. If you arrive in the morning we'll proceed. If you don't, I'll assume another choice was made."

Lauren boarded the bus heading toward Ben's house, where she usually spent Friday afternoons. She plunked onto the seat and stared through the window, thinking of what had just happened – she had begged to get rid of Ben's baby.

She tried to push the thought from her mind but knew what had to be done and there wasn't more deciding time. She'd be at the clinic early…

Interrupting her thoughts, the bus swerved, avoiding an old woman who had stepped into the street.

"Stop!" Lauren mouthed. Then as the bus continued down the road, the word stayed in her mind. Stop. She squeezed her eyes shut; tired, but her thoughts didn't stop.

Bring a baby into a crazy world with no assurances…I can't…

She rested her head against the bus window, wanting to sleep. But as happened during the past month, a memory came to her. One she had almost forgotten was now as clear as when it first happened. It took place in Montana, 1926, when she was four.

Lauren saw a shadowy scene. Her mother stood in front of the house where they had lived: she was slim, and her pale dress and long red hair flowed together in the dusk of evening before she disappeared. Lauren remembered her own screams as she stretched toward the back window of the car, begging for her grandfather to stop and take her back home.

Now, as she sat on the bus, Lauren thought of several years back, when she had found old documents in the attic. There was a picture of her mother. Lauren had been struck by her beauty and touched when she recognized her own resemblance – with her red hair and fair skin.

Looking for more, she had searched further through her grandfather's papers. She found her birth certificate. In the space identifying her father, someone had typed "unnamed."

Chapter Three

The teenager had freckles and eyes that seemed irrepressibly happy. Mary watched with protest as he parked his bike and walked toward her. She tried to call Joe, but her voice caught in her throat. He didn't need to be called. Having seen the Western Union insignia on the boy's cap, he was coming up behind her.

Joe signed for the telegram as the boy mumbled that he was sorry and said something about his brother being 'over-there.' Joe took the notice and with his arm around Mary's shoulders they walked inside. It was several minutes before he unfolded the yellow paper and whispered Ben's name.

And, with a sound reminiscent of the moment Ben was born, Mary cried out.

Within the hour Joe tried to contact Jon. But this was difficult because he had shipped out from San Diego three weeks earlier. Joe was assured by the officer in charge that a furlough would be arranged for Jon. But Joe didn't feel assured; he was frightened, having no idea where Jon was headed.

Mary phoned the nurses' dorm, but Lauren wasn't there. Then she remembered that it was Friday afternoon, and Lauren was probably on a bus headed for their house.

The bus stopped one block from Ben's house. Normally on a day as clear as this, Lauren would feel invigorated as she walked to his house – his family and her future. But today she wanted to turn back.

Her decision was growing more difficult. And now she had to face

Mary. One thing was certain; she wouldn't mention Dr. Karriden. Mary would never know.

Lauren picked up her pace as she climbed the stairs to the front door. Then, before she knocked, the door opened and she saw the expression on Mary's face.

"What?"

"Ben," Mary cried, "Our Ben..."

"What? Ben is injured? Oh my God. What?"

Mary's words mingled with tears, "Ben's dead."

"Lauren squinted, "What? What are you saying? He can't be, he..."

Mary reached for her. "Oh Lauren, I know..."

Lauren felt the dampness of Mary's tears, and pulled away. This had to be a terrible mistake. She stepped through the door and saw Joe. He was sitting on the couch and stared at her, not speaking – his eyes were filled with stark pain.

Joe had always been a man of few words, whereas Mary never kept a thought to herself. His being home early – seeing his face – Lauren winced; then walked to the couch and sat next to him.

His voice was weak and Irish brogue thicker than usual. "Ben loved you, Lauren."

Shaking her head, denying the past tense, Lauren answered, "And I love Ben."

Mary also shook her head, acknowledging Lauren's denial. Then, wiping her eyes, she walked to the chair across from them and sat with her head bent.

Lauren thought everything was surreal, and mumbling she begged God, "This isn't true. Tell us it's not." She wiped tears from her cheek, It's not true. Please, please show me it isn't true. Bring Ben... She tried to muffle tears, but they filled the room.

Then Mary spoke; her voiced turned harsh. "Look at us!"

Lauren looked up and read her expression. It was anger and aimed at Joe.

"Look at Lauren. And look at us now – like we hadn't known. We should have stopped him from going. More than that, we should never have left Ireland. I carried my Ben to this country to be born a citizen and look what has come of it. And Jon, who should be in school – where is he?"

Joe glared at Mary and got up. His lips pressed together, holding thoughts tight, he walked to the cabinet and pulled out a bottle of Jamison's. Uncorking it, he took a swig as he returned to the couch.

Mary glared back. "That's right! Try to numb this day away – as if it could be done-with."

He took another drink.

Lauren watched – amazed. She had always believed that Joe, who was usually quiet and reserved, enjoyed Mary's strong opinions; that he was proud of her spirit. Today there was nothing to enjoy about her words: they were cruel and harsh.

But Lauren sighed – Mary was right. She had begged Ben and Jon not to go.

Now, instead of backing off, Mary's eyes flashed, "All morning I've been remembering the day – not even six months ago – when Ben told us he would enlist."

She turned to Lauren, and her voice softened, "Oh Lauren, do you remember that day? Of course, you do. We should have done more, said more – stopped him."

Lauren nodded, agreeing. "But none of us could have done that, Mary. Ben had been ready to join up for over a year. He believed Roosevelt should have declared war sooner."

She started to say more – to defend Joe but was stopped. For the first time since she had heard about Ben, she felt overcome by nausea. The acrid taste of vomit hit and she put her hand over her mouth.

"Excuse me, I..," she mumbled, while rushing from the room.

Making it to the bathroom in time, she bent over the toilet and after choking and gagging, she was able to throw-up – and for the first time in months felt relief. Exhausted, she flushed the toilet, then sipped water from the sink faucet and rinsed her mouth.

When Lauren returned to the living room Mary watched her, concerned but also questioning.

Lauren sunk back onto the couch.

"I am carrying Ben's baby."

There was silence in the room.

Then Mary spoke, her voice barely above a whisper. "God… God has sent us this child. His miracle, His providence, His divine wisdom; and we learn of it on the day that we learn about our Ben. God is speaking to us."

But Lauren didn't feel part of a miracle. Instead, she rushed back to the bathroom and once again retched into the toilet. Then temporarily relieved, she returned to the living room.

Not appearing worried about Lauren's trips to the bathroom, Mary asked, "You feel this don't you? This is God's will: Ben will live on."

God's will! Lauren thought how Mary was reacting as if her pregnancy was some sort of Immaculate Conception; it was far from it. She started to remember her night on the beach with Ben – but felt a darkness beyond pain, and knew it was a place where she couldn't go.

This is when Joe started to get up from the couch, bringing her back to the present. After several attempts he stood up and got his footing, then started toward the liquor cabinet. With a slurred accent he protested as Mary put her arm around his waist.

Her voice was soft, "'Tis the worst day of our lives, and we're having to get through it."

Lauren was touched, as she watched Mary kiss his cheek and steer him from the room.

Within ten minutes she returned. "He'll be suffering from whisky in the morning. But the pain from drink is less than the thoughts he's trying to block." She crossed herself, "Oh dear God, help us all."

This was a side of Mary that Lauren hadn't known. But she thought how Joe, Ben, and Jon must have seen it over the years. And Lauren also thought how it must be wonderful to have a faith as certain as hers.

The two of them sat late into the night, talking, crying, and sometimes falling into their own thoughts. Lauren was trying to understand the impossible: Ben was dead.

She envied Mary's faith. It helped her. And then Lauren thought how in an important way Mary was right.

"It's true, Mary. I love Ben and this baby is part of him – and now is part of our lives."

Within the week Lauren left the University of Portland and moved in with Mary and Joe. They insisted. This was good as Lauren wanted them to be part of the baby's life. Besides, she had no other place to go.

Her grandfather had reenlisted in the Navy as a Chief Petty Officer. His role was opening recruiting stations across the country. Before leaving, he and Lauren moved from his rented house and sold the furnishing. Part of that money was put into an account for Lauren. It was a small amount, but her grandfather said her future would be fine as she would be marrying Ben.

Lauren left a forwarding address at her school dorm and was surprised when she didn't hear from him. But as months went by, and she felt her baby growing she changed. The memories of being pulled from her mother's arms grew recurrent. Not only did she remember her own screams, but she began to understand the devastation her mother had to have suffered. Her grandfather's actions had been final and cruel.

During her pregnancy, Lauren also thought about the day she had gone to see Claire Karriden and was thankful that the doctor had enforced her rules. They had ended up making a huge difference in her life.

Sandra Martin was born in December of 1942. Within minutes of her birth Lauren lay holding her, with Mary and Joe standing beside the hospital bed.

"She's beautiful – Ben's, your, our little girl," Mary said, in spite of the fact that Sandi's face was ruddy and her head slightly elongated from her ten-hour struggle to be born.

"Yes, she's beautiful," Lauren said, and kissed Sandi's forehead.

Chapter Four

Sitting in the backyard, staring at the elm with its age-twisted limbs, Lauren could almost hear the whoops and laughter of Ben and Jon.

"Your daddy loved that old tree," she murmured into Sandi's soft dark curls. "He spent hours throwing balls through those little spaces."

Sandi looked up at Lauren and stretched her tiny fingers in the air.

"You trying to touch my words?" Lauren kissed her. "My beautiful little girl."

The back door opened, and Mary came to sit with them. "What a lovely day. We better enjoy; it will rain tomorrow."

"I know. Besides, today is special."

Mary nodded. "Sandi is three months."

Lauren didn't add that it had been one year since they learned of Ben's death. Mary didn't have to be reminded.

Eight months later.

"Ma-ma-Ma-ma-Ma-ma," Sandi pulled herself up, and was holding onto the edge of her crib.

"Coming," Mary yelled from the kitchen.

"I'm on my way," Lauren yelled at the same time.

Reaching Sandi's doorway, Lauren stood back and waved for Mary to enter first. "The princess has beckoned."

"And here we are, like stooges," Mary laughed.

Sandi leaned against the rail, stretching her arms toward them.

"We should call you Miss Mussolini, you little dictator," Mary said, while lifting her high in the air. Sandi squealed and then wiggled to be put down.

"So, you want to walk, do you? Let's give it a try."

Mary held Sandi's hand as she took wobbly steps toward Lauren. Then Sandi stiffened as Lauren lifted her.

"No, you don't. It's time for breakfast – yum rice and banana," Lauren said, ignoring her protest and carrying her into the kitchen.

Mary followed, and sat drinking coffee while Lauren helped Sandi, who was learning to use a spoon.

"I guess this is as quiet a moment we'll get," Mary said. "Joe and I talked about you yesterday as we walked to church. You're young and smart. We think it's time you get out more, and on with your life. And we want to do something to help make that happen."

"Do something! You take care of Sandi fulltime, while sharing everything with us."

Lauren waved her free hand, pointing to the clutter in the room. The counter was filled with baby food, bottles, bowls, terry towels, and bibs, while musical toys, cloth books, measuring spoons and plastic dishes were scattered across a blanket on the floor.

"This is more than something – way more. And you say 'get on' with my life. My life is full; as full as it can be... I mean...without..."

"I know, Lauren... without Ben." Mary lowered her voice, "We each feel that way."

Sandi broke the mood by squealing, wanting down from the highchair.

"Okay, okay! It's play time." Lauren wiped Sandi's face, and after lifting her to the floor she ran some hot water over a bottle of milk and gave it to her. This was becoming their routine. Instead of heading for the toys, Sandi turned on her back and drank from her bottle.

Before clearing the highchair tray, Lauren turned to Mary, "Did we actually think we could have a real conversation?"

Mary didn't smile. "She may have kept us from going where it's too difficult to go." She sighed, "Now, back to our talk. Joe and I were saying how you've been part of our lives for so long. How old were you when you started coming home from school with Ben? Fourth grade? You were so bright and pretty, with your red hair and great big smile. You, Ben, and Jon – you three filled this house with excitement."

Lauren looked at Sandi who, satiated, closed her eyes. "Just like this one does."

"Well not exactly," Mary laughed. "In her case 'turmoil' is a better word." Then she said, "Joe and I want you to go back to nursing school. It's important that you continue. Ben would want it. And we'll help. We want to pay your tuition, in the same way we would have helped Ben through college."

"Mary, there's no way I would let you do that. You do so much already. Besides, I don't want to go to school – not now." Lauren rushed on, "But it's really a coincidence you brought this up, because I've been doing a lot of thinking. I have hesitated to say anything, but there is something I want to do. I'd like to go to work – contribute to costs around here. As I said, you do so much for Sandi and me, and I do nothing to help."

Mary started to protest, but Lauren stopped her, "You know it's true. But let me finish – the difficult part, and the reason I'm hesitating, is that I'm asking a lot of you. Until I make enough to hire a sitter, you will be watching her. But I'll make certain that I find a job that will allow me to be here during some of her busiest hours." Lauren corrected herself, "Which of course is just about every minute she's not sleeping. So, take your time to think about this."

"I don't need more time," Mary said. "I think it would be the best thing that could happen to Sandi, what with the two of us jumping to attention each time she whimpers." Her expression changed; "Seriously, Lauren, you know how I feel. Sandi is the first one I think of in the morning. I look forward to any excuse to go to her – to hold her."

Mary paused and then smiled. "Besides, think of the poor baby-sitter. Whereas, I can think of no job I could love more than taking care of Miss Mussolini."

Lauren answered an ad at a first-class family restaurant, Henry Thiele's, and within days she was hired as their hostess.

Thiele's was located at the end of Vista Drive, the road that led up to Portland Heights – home to the city's wealthy. Because of Thiele's location, good menu, and "old Portland" reputation, it was frequented by the wealthy and well known – philanthropists, politicians, businessmen, artists, entertainers – people who were often in the news.

On Lauren's first day at work she seated Dr. Claire Karriden and Portland's Chief of Police. The restaurant's owner, Mrs. Thiele, told Lauren that the doctor was a special customer, and that she preferred to be called by her first name. As the week passed Lauren saw that "Claire" lunched often, with either the Chief or her grown daughter, Jane.

For several months neither Lauren nor Claire indicated that they had met before, and Lauren appreciated the discretion. Then on a Sunday morning this changed. Lauren directed her to a table and as she turned to leave Claire stopped her and said, "Miss Martin, I'd like to talk to you."

Lauren was surprised and looked at her with concern.

Claire eyed the empty tables surrounding them. "No one's within earshot, and if they were, so what? You're a hostess at my favorite restaurant. Besides, it's not about what you might be thinking."

Lauren hesitated, and then said, "I assumed you recognize me."

"Yes, but then you do stand out."

It was true. Lauren's fashionable short skirts revealed the curve of her long legs, and her red hair was in rich contrast to the dark dresses she chose for work. Her sense of style attracted notice from well-heeled Heights customers.

Claire continued, "Besides, I never forget clients. Especially you; I remember that you were attending nursing school. I was surprised when I saw you here."

"Nursing school – you remember that? Why? No, don't answer. I have to get back. Customers are waiting."

"Miss Martin, before you leave please take this." Claire offered her a card.

"No thanks," Lauren muttered as she turned and headed toward the front desk.

It was Sunday Brunch and within a short time the foyer filled with diners. Lauren had no time to think about Claire. But, as she hurried to the desk to pull out a stack of menus, Claire was waiting.

"If nothing else, I'm persistent. Please take this; it's my home phone number. Call." Claire handed her the card. "I promise that there is no reason to worry."

Watching Claire leave, tall and assured, Lauren thought of the morning she had waited in her clinic, suspicious of its illusory warmth. She remembered how Claire turned all illusion around. No nonsense, she laid out the facts, and then gave Lauren time to make her decision. Now there was no cause to be rude to her. Lauren tucked the card in her pocket.

Later, after Sandi was asleep and the house was quiet, Lauren lay in bed wide awake. Dr. Karriden had referred to her training at nursing school. Why? Was she thinking of offering her a job at the clinic? Lauren thought of Mary. To her abortion was murder. It was against the canons of her Church, and laws of State.

Then Lauren thought of how Ben would react to her working at an abortion clinic. For certain, the Catholic Church would not influence his opinion. His leaving it had been final when he learned what had happened after Hitler invaded Poland in 1939.

Poland fell and Hitler established his New Order, which was a systematic plan to abuse and eliminate those he called undesirables – mainly Jews and Slavs. The Catholic Church didn't speak-out against this. Worse, Ben learned that many Catholics joined both the Third Reich and the SS. During this same year, Ben learned that Pope Pacellie had a friendly relationship with Hitler; even sending the papal ambassador, Archbishop Orsengio, to open a gala reception for Hitler's fiftieth birthday.

In 1939 Ben was sixteen, and he stopped attending mass. Mary was shocked and angry – first demanding, and then pleading. But she learned that he was as strong about his convictions as she had always been about hers. Ben told her that he would never return to church.

After months of his refusal to attend, Mary relented. "All right Ben. But you'll learn that our Church is ultimately good, with a profound depth that reaches way beyond temporary politics. You will come back to it."

Lauren remembered the expression on Ben's face as he answered, "Temporary politics! Thousands of Jews have been taken from their homes, put on trains, and there are rumors they've been imprisoned. No Mom, I won't come back to the church."

Lauren felt a familiar ache as she thought how he wouldn't come back to the Church, to her – to anything. And she remembered their only weekend together. Ben had matured, but at the same time he appeared less sure of his role in the war. Instead, he had talked about his foreboding. She wondered if he had felt it when he boarded the USS George F Elliot.

The ship had been destroyed by fire. Lauren had not allowed herself to think of how he died. It was too terrible to fathom. She never asked Mary or Joe to show her the telegraph they had received. But the newspaper reported that when the fire raged beyond control the men were ordered to abandon ship. Knowing Ben, Lauren was certain that he wouldn't leave until he helped everyone off.

He would be twenty now – two months younger than she. She thought how the atrocities he had hated were still happening in Europe. But now many Americans were losing their lives trying to stop them. Protecting herself, she avoided reading the list of deaths in the paper.

Instead, she often she closed her eyes and visualized Ben as he was. Loving him was a part of her, and in an important way it was how she kept him alive. More than anything she focused on how lucky she was to have been with him. He was amazing, and the most beautiful part of her life.

Now tonight, thinking of him brought tears. Lauren rubbed them away. They did no good. What helped was Sandi. She looked at her, sleeping with her arms spread loosely above her head. Nothing in her young life could cause a bad dream.

Lauren sighed, thinking how that would change – one way or the other. And it would change fast if she took a job in Dr. Karriden's clinic. Mary's response would be beyond anger.

But then Lauren thought how she didn't agree with Mary, and Ben wouldn't either. In fact, he would approve of her working with Dr. Karriden. Lauren remembered the test that Ben had come-up with for judging people. She was surprised that she hadn't thought of it until now. It was tough, but those who passed it were Ben's most admired people.

It was an answer to one question: "Would this person put his or her own life in jeopardy by protecting those who were being singled out and persecuted by the Nazi Party?"

Lauren knew how Ben would judge Dr. Karriden.

Besides firsthand experience, Lauren had learned a lot about the doctor as she watched her at Henry Thiele's. Both the staff and owner, Mrs. Thiele, respected her, making certain her table was waiting when she arrived for lunch. Also, it appeared that customers went out of their way to stop and talk to her. So much so, that Lauren had wondered how many of these well healed patrons of Thiele's had been to see the doctor over the many years she had practiced.

Importantly, Dr. Karriden had her own code of ethics, and Lauren had learned this firsthand. She refused to do abortions after the third month of pregnancy. And, at the same time, she wouldn't perform surgery during the first trimester if she had cause to believe the mother was ambivalent. In Lauren's situation, the doctor's

concerns were based on both of these rules. She assumed Lauren
had been uncertain as she had waited until the edge of three months.
And the doctor made it clear she wouldn't do the surgery until the
following day.

With certainty, Dr. Karriden would pass Ben's test. She helped
people at the risk of going to prison.

And on a personal basis, Lauren was thankful the doctor had stuck
by her rules.

But then Lauren stopped and thought how none of this mattered!
There was no way that she could consider a job at an abortion clinic.
Not with Mary's attitude.

Tired, she laid back, wanting to sleep. But she couldn't. The fact
was that she disagreed with Mary, and so would Ben.

And there was something else… shallow, but real: The money. Dr.
Karriden's profession was lucrative.

She decided to phone her – find out what the call was about.

Lauren woke to music: Bing Crosby's White Cliffs of Dover. She
looked across the room and saw that Sandi was already up. After
slipping on her robe, Lauren headed for the kitchen. "There'll be
love and laughter and joy ever after; Tomorrow, when the world is
free."

As Lauren opened the door, Mary snapped off the radio and
mumbled, "Free to what? Forget? Turn from losses and croon about
'joy ever-after'"

Lauren shook her head agreeing, while watching Sandi. She was
lying on the playpen mattress, eyes closed, with her bottle hanging
from her mouth. Lauren reached down for her, but Sandi opened
an eye and started a weak protest, before falling back to sleep.

Lauren picked up the bottle and then answered Mary. "I know… I know." Seeing the pain on Mary's face, Lauren thought of the added stress it would cause her if she was offered a job at Claire Karriden's clinic.

Then Lauren thought about the day she had gone to the doctor for help. She had based her decision on her own needs and beliefs and hadn't told Mary. She thought about Ben; there was no question that he would agree with her if she chose to work at the clinic. She knew him: he would want Sandi to grow-up appreciating people like Claire.

But it would be impossible to talk to Mary about calling Dr. Karriden. Lauren felt a shiver:

Chapter Five

Driving her 1941 Lincoln Continental, Claire wound up Vista to Fairmont Boulevard, one of the most beautiful and wealthiest districts in Portland. Only ten minutes from the world Lauren knew, they reached what to her seemed the pinnacle of Portland Heights. Claire pulled into the driveway of her Victorian style mansion.

"This is your home?"

Claire nodded, "A long way from the cozy little house in Pendleton, where I grew up."

As they walked through a mahogany front door and into the living room, Lauren felt dwarfed by everything, including Claire.

Reading her, Claire smiled. "This is part of my reward – and I enjoy it. Come on in and sit down." She pointed to a burgundy velvet couch. "I've brought you here for a purpose. But first, would you rather have Claret, Chardonnay, or maybe some English tea."

"I'll go with the tea."

Before leaving for the kitchen, Claire pointed to the large window. "From where you're sitting you can see my clinic."

Lauren saw much more than the clinic. Claire had a balcony that ran the full width of the room, and beyond this was an amazing view of the city.

"See it?" Claire pointed to the Broadway Building.

Lauren had never seen Portland from a distance. Everything was miniaturized: the people, buildings, tree-lined streets, parks, cars, streetcars. The city's downtown limits were defined by the Willamette River. She saw a barge, loaded with what looked like stacked tinker toys, being tugged underneath the Hawthorne Bridge – which she crossed every morning.

If Claire wanted to impress her, it was working.

Within minutes Claire returned with a silver tray, and poured tea into delicate gold trimmed cups. Lauren was glad a butler wasn't serving.

"This view is amazing. It's so perfect."

"You're right," Claire said. "From a distance it's difficult to see flaws."

Then she walked to a Roman brick wall. "What I love most about this room is over here." Claire was referring to oil portraits above the fireplace. "My family: This is Jane, my daughter, when she was four. You've seen me with her at Thiele's. It's hard to think she's the same person as this little girl."

Lauren didn't comment, but Claire was right. There was nothing sweet looking about Jane now. Her makeup was too thick, hair too black, clothes too tight, and she wore stiletto heels to a casual lunch.

Claire touched a large photograph, "And here are my mother and father in front of our family house. Homey, right? Well it really was; but I didn't appreciate it then." Next, she looked at portrait of two pretty blond girls. "And these are my gorgeous granddaughters."

She came back to the couch and picked up a plate of cookies from the coffee table. "Try them. They're from the Bohemian Bakery – a few blocks from Thiele's."

Lauren took a bite, "Delicious; Thiele's has competition."

Claire nodded and then said, "Now we have to talk. I remember the day you came to the office; you had an awful attitude – the kind I would have had in your situation. You made your feelings clear. I admire that.

"You have mettle – a good combination of spirit and intellect. At the same time, you're concerned about others. I've watched you at Thiele's: you take care of people, sometimes helping them from their wheelchairs into booths, or rushing food to obstreperous kids. But I especially love when you don't show deference to pushy clients, especially those who impatiently tap their feet when waiting in line.

"I've never asked anyone other than Carol, my secretary, to work at my clinic. But we are overwhelmed. For obvious reasons I can't advertise in a newspaper, but I need help. And, as I remember, you were attending nursing school. I need a surgical assistant."

Lauren was surprised, and took time for Claire's offer to sink in.

"I thought you might want to talk about a job helping Carol and I was prepared – I should say I am prepared – to say I can't. But now," Lauren took a breath, "well I'm taken back. You are offering me a chance to work directly with you. I'm flattered.

"It would have been hard to refuse anyway. Not because of all this," Lauren looked around the room. "But because of what you do – the women you help." She paused, "I know about that first-hand."

She took a heavy breath. "I can't. I'm sorry, but my situation at home makes it impossible to accept your offer." She heard her words; they sounded stiff – practiced.

"I'm disappointed," Claire said. "There aren't many I'd ask. But I understand. Had to give it a try – and I'll keep the offer open. As I said, I've watched you for over two months, and I'm a good judge of people. I've had to be, to survive. You're special, and I feel you will do extraordinary things with your life." Claire smiled, "I just wanted to give you a chance to start doing them.

"With that said, let me tell you in defense of my profession that regardless of their beliefs, women come to me from every walk of life. And I believe that what I do is right, or I wouldn't be doing it."

When the meeting was over and they were getting into the car, Lauren asked Claire to drop her off at Thiele's.

"I can drive you home, but I'm assuming you'd rather I don't." Claire sounded weary, "It speaks to the reasons why you can't accept my offer. And there's no offense taken; my feelings don't get hurt that easily. Believe me, if they did I wouldn't be in the profession I'm in.

Instead of apologizing, Lauren said, "You're right about driving me home. If Mary, my baby's grandmother, knew where I've been today she'd throw a conniption fit."

"I understand; believe me." Claire shook her head. "And I'm not saying you aren't right about your concern. You are! To do the work that Carol and I do, you have to live with a special set of rules and values. In some ways my profession is selfish – there are enormous consequences and risks that affect others in my family."

Lauren thought for a minute and then said, "I knew when I came to see you today that you'd be offering me some position at the clinic. And I've been ambivalent ever since you gave me your phone number. You've just described the reasons why I've told myself I can't. But I wouldn't have come if there weren't strong reasons for wanting to. I know personally how you help women.

"And quite honestly, working as a waitress isn't my goal in life. Someday I want to do something that makes a real difference. Even if I finish nursing school, I'd like to limit my work to helping women." Lauren looked at Claire with admiration. "And you're offering me a chance to do that now."

Claire backed the car out of the driveway, and drove down Vista, toward Thiele's.

Halfway down the hill, Lauren said, "I've changed my mind; I'd appreciate a ride home."

Within several days of talking to Claire, Lauren phoned and accepted the job.

As she rode the bus home from her last workday at Thiele's, Lauren knew she couldn't put off telling Mary and Joe. She had tried for the past two weeks but hadn't found the right words. There were none; imagining Mary's reaction caused her stomach to do flips.

Determined, Lauren walked home and hurried up the steps, knowing what needed to be said. Then before she reached the door Mary opened it, holding Sandi.

"Mummy, Mummy, Mum…" Sandi stretched her arms toward Lauren.

"Hi to you, too," Lauren said, carrying her into the house. "Did you and Grandma have a good day?"

Sandi wriggled to get down; then grabbed Lauren's skirt and pulled her to the toy box. She picked-up a stuffed doll that had blue button eyes and bright red lips, embroidered with the same yarn as its hair.

Lauren stooped and smacked the doll with a noisy kiss. Sandi giggled while pulling the doll away and then pushing it back for a repeat kiss. After several times, Lauren stood, picked-up Sandi and the doll, and gave them each an exaggerated kiss.

Again, Sandi laughed, but Lauren felt a chill and pulled her close, mumbling into her hair, "I love you and promise not to hurt you – ever."

Frightened by the supposition of her words, Lauren wanted to continue holding her, but Sandi pulled from her, waved the doll in the air, stretched her arm straight and dropped it. As expected, Lauren dipped down and swept it up. "Poor baby. You dropped her."

Giggling harder, Sandi threw it again.

"Oh oh. Baby bumped her head. Time to give her a rest," Lauren said.

But Sandi stretched her arm toward the doll and screamed – her face turning red.

"Nope, not this time." Lauren said, and then mumbled while pulling Sandi closer, "But keep this stubborn will and you'll be just fine."

Later, after Sandi was tucked in, Lauren went to the front-room. It was time to tell Mary and Joe.

Mary looked up as she entered, "We received a letter from Jon today. I waited till Sandi was asleep to read it to you."

Mary's tone was dark as she read.

Dear Mom, Dad, and Lauren,

Thanks for the box of "everything Irish," including the pictures of you and Dad. I had to fight for a piece of soda cake before my tent mates finished it off. You can expect lots of visitors when we return home – I've told them about your Irish stew.

"These guys are the best buddies I've ever had; and yet I know so little about them – except that we're all similar in an American way. Whether from Iowa, Tennessee, or Oregon we 'get' the same jokes, love the same pin-ups, and have the same goal – to get back home to you-all. Wish I had some idea when that would be, but everything is a secret around here and we're not even told where we'll be headed tomorrow – We just hope that it won't be someplace worse than the hell hole we're in today.

Mary paused and said, "His words have stuck with me since it arrived this morning – haunting."

Yeah, I wish I knew when we'll be coming home. It can't be any too soon. You were right Mom. I should of finished high school before thinking about enlisting. I'm the youngest in our battalion, but since I lied about my age no one knows it.

Thanks for the pics of Sandi and Lauren. The guys around here want to use Lauren as their pin-up girl – and I can see why.

Miss you, Dad, Lauren, Sandi, and, of course, Ben.

Love, Jon

Mary cried, and Lauren put her arm around her shoulder. She wished there was something she could say that would help; especially to Joe. He looked fragile and worn, his pain beyond tears.

After minutes, Mary wiped her eyes. "Oh, Dear God – please God…"

Yes, Lauren thought, please God. They sat silent.

Then Mary stood, squared her shoulders, and said, "I made a peach pie today, and will dish it up." She headed toward the kitchen.

Lauren had no more thoughts about sharing her news that night. It would have to wait.

Lauren tossed during the night, not able to sleep. She couldn't tell Mary. There was no way. She thought of calling Claire – tell her that she couldn't accept the job. But she had made the choice: had quit Thiele's and was to go to the clinic on Monday.

And the truth was she was excited about it, even though she feared

Mary's reaction. She understood where Mary would be coming from, and that she would probably be unforgiving. But Lauren knew that she had to make important decisions based on her own beliefs.

And she knew this decision was right. She understood what women faced when they had 'illegitimate' babies; and she was certain that Claire's clinic was busier than any doctor's office in town. Ironically, one reason the clinic operated in the open was the needs of police officers and others connected with the law. Many of these men had wives, daughters, and girlfriends who had been to it.

Lauren told herself again that this was a chance to do something that was needed.

When morning lit the room, Lauren slipped into her robe and tiptoed into the hall, not wanting to wake Sandi.

Mary was already in the kitchen, making coffee. She was wearing her tattered robe: a Christmas gift from Ben years earlier.

Her voice was barely above a whisper, "You're up early."

Lauren shut the kitchen door. "I couldn't sleep. Something's on my mind, and I've been afraid to tell you."

"Oh – oh, I've been watching you lately… what's happening?" Mary squinted. "You've … You're not thinking of-of leaving us. Taking Sandi…"

"Mary, do you think I'm nuts? You and Joe have given us the best home anyone could ask for. Sandi's spoiled, and I want her to continue to be. Besides," Lauren shook her head, "I'm afraid no one but us would appreciate how loveable she is."

Hesitating, she added, "I just hope you'll keep us here after I tell you what's happening."

Mary looked relieved. "If you're not leaving, there isn't anything that you can't tell us. So out with it."

Lauren felt heat rise to her face. "I'll be going to a new job on Monday."

"Oh, that's it. For heaven's sake, I thought maybe you had met someone the way you're acting." Sorrow hadn't taken the edge off of Mary's humor. She raised her eyebrows. "So where is it you're going to work? Perhaps you'll be dancing at that men's theater, The Star, on Third Avenue."

"No, though that would be easier for you to accept than what I'm about to tell you."

"Oh Lauren, what on earth is it that you can't tell? Sounds important... Can't be serving at a stage door canteen; it's got to be something more secretive, like the OSS."

Mary was turning this into Irish theater, and Lauren stood. "I think I'll get dressed."

"Wait – I apologize. I just can't imagine what it is that you can't share. If you'd rather, I'll drop the subject. But if it's a new job, I'll need some means of contacting you – like a phone number. Now sit down and tell me. Nothing could be as bad as you're making it."

"I'm afraid that to you it will be, Mary." Lauren took a deep breath. "Believe me; I'd rather not have to tell you. But you're right, for Sandi's sake I have no choice. I'm going to work in the office of Dr. Claire Karriden."

Mary squinted; confused. Then her mouth dropped open – dumbfounded. "Claire Karriden? The abortionist?

"Yes."

Mary started – "I…"

Lauren had never known her to be without words. But she also felt at a loss; nothing she could say would modify the effect of what she had just told her, short of not taking the job.

Breaking the silence, Sandi cried and both Mary and Lauren stood.

"I'll get her," Lauren said, rushing from the room.

Lauren picked Sandi up and kissed her, smelling the sweet scent of lavender talc. Holding her close, she worried about her decision.

But she was committed.

She whispered to Sandi, "Claire Karriden helps people and I want to work with her – someday I want you to appreciate people like her." Kissing her again, she added, "And sweetheart, your dad would agree with me."

Sandi started to wiggle, wanting to play.

"Okay," Lauren said as she laid her back down and changed her diaper." And you know one thing big-time, I'll always watch out for you."

Chapter Six

Lauren arrived a little before eight, assuming she'd be early. But when Carol answered the door, it was clear that the clinic had been open for a while. A woman was sitting on the couch, her head bent into her hands. The same couch Lauren had sat on.

"Welcome." Carol spoke softly, acknowledging they weren't alone. "Doctor's busy right now, but I'll take you back to where we can hang your coat."

As Lauren followed her across the room, she remembered how irritating Carol's smile had been. But everything had bothered her on that morning, whereas today she appreciated the warm greeting.

At the door to the hallway Carol turned to the woman, who looked up, worried.

"It won't be long," Carol said. "Dr. Karriden is almost done and will be meeting with you in a short while."

When she and Lauren were in the hall Carol lowered her voice, "She's waiting for her daughter."

Lauren didn't say anything, but she imagined the anxiety the mother was feeling, and thought how Carol dealt with this kind of stress fulltime.

They walked past the surgery room and to the end of the hallway. Carol opened the door.

"This is our room; it's off limits to anyone but us – you are part of 'us' now."

There was a coffee pot, two electric burners, refrigerator, and a table with chairs. Carol pointed to a coat-stand, and then poured Lauren a cup of coffee.

"We hoped to have time to sit with you this morning, but that seldom happens around here. Everyone coming here is in a state of urgency. You'll see what I mean; this is probably going to be the quietest time you'll have this morning.

"So, even though I'd like to sit for a while and cover some of what goes on around here, I'm afraid you'll have on the job training. And by the time today's over, you'll know a lot more than you may want to know."

Before Lauren could respond, Claire entered, wearing her surgical gown. She looked at Carol, "Would you help Margaret into the recovery room, and then meet with her mother? I want to take a few minutes with Lauren."

"Sure." Carol smiled. "I was just telling Lauren what she'll soon learn: there's not much time to sit." As Carol walked from the room, she added, "We'll talk later, Lauren. As I said, we need you."

Claire shook her head, "We sure do."

Then, sitting across from Lauren, she said, "Carol just left to help a girl who's been here before. I'm sure you saw her mother in the office. She's the one I'm really worried about. Poor woman has five kids, no husband, and couldn't handle another baby. We won't charge today; there's no way this family could pay. And it would be disastrous to bring another child into that home.

"Carol will be as soothing as possible, considering the state of things. The girl is seventeen – the oldest child. She helps with all the others, while her mother earns money cleaning houses.

"We'll pay for a taxi to take them home, and they'll leave with sterile wipes, pads, and a bag of canned foods. We keep these supplies in the recovery room, which I hope to turn into another surgery room. But you and I will talk about that later."

Lauren wondered what she was inferring but didn't respond.

"I have about fifteen minutes before my next appointment, and hopefully I can cover a bit of what you'll be doing during the next weeks. I don't want to overwhelm you." Claire chuckled, "So stop me before you quit and head home."

Lauren recognized Claire's laugh from Thiele's: it was deep and somehow lacked humor – instead it had an ironic edge.

"Having been here before, you'll remember how you felt; that will be invaluable when you're assisting me. Now, as you look around I'll explain some of what I do. First, we'll go to the surgery room. By this time Carol has taken Margaret across the hall to recover."

They stood, and Lauren placed her half-filled cup in the sink.

"In this room a lot of coffee goes cold," Claire said as she held the door open, and then directed Lauren to the surgery room.

The first thing Lauren saw was the operating table. It hit her that she would have been on it, with her feet pushing against the stirrups. But on that day she hadn't allowed herself to think of that.

Claire touched her arm. "I know what you're feeling. And those feelings are one of the reasons I chose you. Coming here, sitting in the office waiting for surgery, you understand the desperation that other patients feel."

"However, you stood out from most. You spoke your mind. You're smart, articulate, and, on that morning, you demonstrated a terrible attitude." Claire smiled, "It proved your grit. You need that in my profession.

"Now, there's lots I want to show you – things you need to know, each important.

"First," Claire said as she opened a drawer, "sanitized surgical gloves are in here. You'll need to wear them when assisting me." She put on a pair and handed another to Lauren.

"This here," Claire pointed to an aluminum pan, "is filled with a mixture of water and several cyanide tablets. The instruments in it were first scoured and steamed clean. Believe me, they are germ free. Sanitation is as important as skill. I don't want patients leaving here with an infection."

Claire had Lauren use tongs to lift the tools from the solution, and then lay them in order of their use on a stand next to the bed.

"Some of these I've designed, and each is of the highest quality," Claire said. "You'll watch as I use them today."

Lauren looked at her with surprise, but Claire didn't appear to notice. Instead she pointed to a bedpan in the middle of the surgery table. "I have designed pad and sheets to fit around that." She pulled a white pad from a cabinet and pointed to the circle in its middle that was edged with elastic

Lauren helped her take off the used linens, and then the pan that was filled with what appeared to be blood and sudsy water. Claire poured the water down the sink, while pointing to a large garbage container for the dirty sheets.

"Drop them into that and put your gloves in the container next to it. You'll need a clean pair to help me make the bed."

Claire put the new pan on the bed, and then she showed Lauren how the sheets fit around it.

"Quite honestly, your job description includes just about everything we do in the clinic." Claire took a deep breath. "And importantly, I've got another role for you. You will be surprised by how many adolescent girls we see here. And as you can imagine, their pregnancies are usually connected to ugly situations – often criminal. I always feel a responsibility beyond surgery. But as you will soon learn, I never have enough time to give the extra counseling and care that these girls need."

"You know where I'm heading; I'd like you to talk with them. They're not only frightened about surgery, but so many are victims of abuse – and are afraid to talk about it. As I've said before, I've watched you – and know how you relate to people." Claire smiled. "And importantly, you're tough and not afraid to speak out for what you believe. I know that first hand." She raised an eyebrow, "And that toughness is part of why I wanted you here."

Besides, you're young. The girls will relate to you. And I want to know their situations – if we don't help stop what's happening to them, I'm afraid no one will. You may think you're aware of the dark side of our city, but most of us aren't until we face some of its consequences… and believe me, you'll face them when you work here. But when they involve children, I act. I have connections with professionals: good counselors and police officers.

"Taking time – talking to them matters. So, Lauren, you see that I want you to start handling critical work right away. As I said when I asked you to join us, you have the right qualities to handle this job – and I hope you'll have the energy, as you'll be busy."

Claire looked at her watch, "Now, we have to see our patient, and I'd like you to sit in on the consultation."

Lauren was beginning to worry about all she was taking on. But hearing Claire's latest request, she smiled. "I learned about your consultations – believe me. The one we had is etched in my head."

Claire returned the smile. "I'm sure of that, but you'll be surprised. Each consult is as different as the patients I see. And, as you learned, I don't always do surgery; not just for reasons you remember. Sometimes it's due to health issues, in which case I refer them to doctors I respect.

The new patient, Violet, was twenty -nine years old and pregnant with her fourth child. Her husband left when he learned, telling her he couldn't handle more kids and wanted out. With no support, Violet found a job at Janzen's Knitting Mill. Bu soon learned there was rule: Women are not allowed to work beyond four months of pregnancy.

Claire and Lauren walked with Violet to the surgery room and stepped into the hall while she changed into a hospital gown.

"Now," Claire said, "you're going to watch an abortion." Claire didn't give Lauren time to comment, as she continued explaining, "One of my greatest concerns is pain control. I use several methods to help with both pain and relaxation. Fifteen minutes before surgery, and with the patients' consent, I administer a vapor form of Cannabis. I don't use it on teens under eighteen. For them, and others who prefer it, I do acupuncture, which I learned at Naturopathic School.

"About cannabis, I'm assuming you know it's legal for medical uses. But since abortion is not legal, I purchase the drug from a gynecologist who sends patients to me."

Violet opened the door, dressed in the gown and looking nervous.

"You're going to be fine," Claire assured. "And before starting, I'll help you relax."

Violet sat on the edge of the table, as Claire had her breathe Cannabis vapors. In five minutes, Lauren could see the drug's effect – Violet appeared more relaxed, while still alert.

Claire asked her to lie with her head on the pillow and feet in the stirrups. And within fifteen minutes it was clear the cannabis was doing its job.

Without instructions from Claire, Lauren walked to Violet's side of the table and took her hand, telling her to squeeze when she felt the need.

But Claire interrupted, "I want you over here to observe the surgery. You need to witness what's being done. Violet will do fine; I've practiced for many years and learned to minimize pain."

Claire spoke to Violet, "I have methods of soothing-open the area leading to the uterus. You shouldn't feel much more than pressure during most of the procedure. By the time you do feel pain it will be over in minutes."

Violet nodded, but Lauren could see that she wasn't totally relaxed.

Lauren stood next to Claire, wondering why she was observing instead of holding Violet's hand. She was becoming concerned about role expectations and thought how she and Claire needed to talk.

As Claire worked, she explained every part of the procedure. Under bright globe lighting she gently kneaded the vaginal opening until it became wide enough to place a speculum – which held it open. Then gently, with her right hand she fastened a tool, called a tenaculum, onto the lower lip of the cervix. This allowed her to take a curette into the uterus.

Before Claire did the abortion, she showed Lauren the curette she would use. "I designed this in several sizes. You won't be able to see, but it slips easily into the uterus. After using these curettes many times, I'm good at choosing the correct size."

Lauren couldn't see what was being done, but Claire explained, "Experience has made it easy for me to find the grouping of fetal cells."

Claire was silent, as if concentrating as she probed with the curette. And Violet started to moan."

"Sorry, Love. I'm examining your uterine wall." While searching for the cells, she continued talking. And Violet moaned when Claire examined the uterine wall with the curette. I'm fast and promise this part will take less than a minute. Count to thirty slowly and you'll see that the pain is gone."

Claire continued explaining to Lauren as she probed. "I know the importance of being fast; and I am, because I know what I'm looking for. As I move this curette along the uterine lining, it is smooth. But I'll find a bit of roughness." Within seconds she said, "Here it is."

After another fifteen seconds, she brought the curette out and showed Lauren the small gestational sac, the size of a very small grape, and filled with minute cells. She set it on a tray, and then used another curette to search for cells that could have been left.

Lauren watched Violet's expression – it was stoic. Lauren thought how desperation sometimes allowed for pain.

Just to be certain there wasn't another sac, or cells left behind, Claire did a third search of the uterus. Claire showed Lauren the curette. "As you see, there are no more cells. And I'm glad to say there's very little blood. The area is clean"

Claire instructed Violet to breathe deep and relax. "We're almost done. I'll wash and sanitize carefully, and then you'll rest before getting dressed. Your surgery has been successful."

After she had thoroughly cleansed the surgical area, Claire showed Lauren the cells that had been contained in the gestational sac. "These are what are found at two and a half months. As you know, I will not operate beyond three months.

"However, many women request abortions after this time. And when I believe that someone is facing life-threatening problems, I call one of the doctors I trust, and make arrangements for her to be seen right away."

Lauren was impressed. In less than ten minutes, Claire had removed the fetal cells, and then done the final cauterizing, sanitizing, and removal of equipment. The whole process, from the time Violet sat on the table, had taken less than half of an hour.

Claire took off her mask and said, "You'll heal well."

Lauren learned that patients left the clinic with minimal bleeding and pain, and minuscule chance of having problems from the procedure.

Claire guarded privacy of patients and was careful about the cleaning women she hired. She never allowed anyone in the surgical room other than patients, herself, Carol, and now Lauren.

Lauren followed Claire's rules. After stripping and remaking the surgical bed, she put all used towels and linens into a container for laundry service. She cleaned surfaces with alcohol wipes, sterilized instruments, spread them on a tray in order of their use, and then made certain pain medications were ready.

Besides all of this and working with the young patients, Claire asked Lauren to observe five more abortions during her first three days at the clinic. But more than observing, Claire asked her to pass instruments, and explained the use of each.

Then on her fourth day, Lauren became concerned. Until this time she had been assisting, but Claire asked for more than passing instruments. She wanted Lauren to step close enough to actually see her clamp the speculum into place.

Lauren asked why, and Claire answered, "I want you to learn."

"Why?" Lauren asked again and didn't move close enough to observe.

Claire continued the surgery without requesting more assistance.

After cleansing and removing instruments she had her patient sit until she felt strong enough to walk. Then she helped her from table and had her stand on her own before walking with her to the recovery room.

Claire returned when Lauren was preparing instruments for steaming, and said, "Perhaps I was too presumptuous."

Lauren looked concerned. "Things are moving fast, and I'm not certain about your expectations for me. I've only been here four days and they've been so busy we haven't had time to talk."

Claire nodded, "I know. This week has been too full. I wish I could say that's unusual.

"As I've said before, I'm good at sizing-up people. You're smart, capable... Claire stopped, shook her head, and started over, "You're right, we need time to talk. And as things never let up around here, we better take it now. I'll go to the office and tell my new patient that I'm running behind. Knowing what it's like for most women who come here, she'll choose to wait instead of returning on another day.

"So I'll meet you for a cup of coffee in minutes." Claire looked around and added, "After we talk, you, Carol, and I will finish getting this area ready for our next patient."

As Lauren prepared coffee, she thought how she was about to make a big decision. Everything was happening too fast. But she understood why. All patients were desperate to be helped and Claire's reputation for excellence was well known – and there was no one to share the load. On Lauren's first day Claire had explained why she never recommended other abortionists: "I know my skill, not theirs."

Claire came in, shaking her head. "It's still morning and another prospective patient just arrived."

Lauren handed her a cup of coffee, poured one for herself and sat across the table.

Claire sipped as she sank back into the chair. "The days roll into each other, one always as busy as the other."

"I'm sorry, Lauren, but I knew you would speak-up when you had concerns. The truth is, I've had big plans for you before you started this week." Claire stretched her neck, looking tired. "I should have leveled with you up-front, but I couldn't until I knew more. And of course, now I do: you're competent, catch-on fast, and are sure of yourself."

Lauren didn't respond, wanting to hear where Claire was going.

"I want to keep you here in whichever role you decide to take. I know I'm right about your helping with adolescent patients. When you helped me interview Terry, who's only thirteen, she looked at you as she talked. You said little, but I watched – she felt your concern.

"Then, when you held her hand during surgery, it was clear that she wanted you there – and it was such a help to me. When patients are that young, unless Carol can come in I end up doing surgery while trying to provide the comfort they need. This takes much more time than working with adults – that makes surgery longer and therefore harder on the girls.

"After surgery you walked back to the recovery room with Terry and stayed for a half-hour – even though I had plenty else planned for you." Claire smiled, "It's always been clear that you set your own priorities. That's good."

"Now, about today, you're smart and understood what I'm aiming for. I believe you have the ability to do surgery, and it's obvious that I need another surgeon here. But we definitely needed to talk, and I was being way too presumptuous. Going from assisting, to actually doing part of the procedure is a huge step, and I apologize for putting you in that position without our talking.

"But let me tell you, I would never ask anyone to help do surgery if I didn't trust their competency, as well as know their courage. If you decide to join me in that capacity, it's a huge step. It's one thing to work in the clinic, but quite another to actually do abortions which are against the law. That risk can't be ignored."

Claire shook her head. "We each know these risks. And I certainly have learned that attitudes toward me definitely changed when I became an abortionist. And once you are, the label is there. Life isn't the same." She sighed, "So I shouldn't have rushed you today. You have options. Go home tonight and think about them. Make your decision." Claire chuckled, "And tell me by Monday. I don't want to sound desperate, but I need help"

Lauren thought how this wouldn't be easy – not just because of Mary's reactions. Much more important, it could affect Sandi. She shook her head no, and said, "It would affect much more than my own life."

Claire nodded, "Yes." Then she added, "But remember, Laruen, you know firsthand the desperation women feel, and why they take chances while knowing the law. Besides, I have to add that there are rewards from doing surgery that makes all the problems worthwhile, and I'm not referring to money. The truth is, I like knowing I'm helping women during one of the most difficult times in their lives. I also believe that all babies have a right to come into this world wanted and loved."

Lauren shook her head yes. "Of course, I agree, or I wouldn't be here. And Claire, I have watched you, and know I'm lucky to be working here. Your work is excellent; patients go home in good shape. You're a talented surgeon. And Claire, if you were in this profession for money, you wouldn't spend the time you do – talking, seeking reasons, helping with decisions, and comforting. After all, I remember the time you took with me and the difference it made in my life.

"But about today, I hadn't considered doing surgery, even when you had me stand next to you and assist. Then when you asked me to watch you put the speculum in place, I wasn't prepared. It's a huge leap from all else I've been doing, and I haven't been here a full week. I haven't had time to sort out my thoughts."

As if thinking out loud Lauren added, "It wouldn't make a huge difference to Mary. As far as she knows, I'm already assisting with abortions. She never asks; she never talks about anything anymore, other than what's necessary because of Sandi."

Claire sighed, "Mary represents the world out there. But Lauren this is your decision." Claire got up and rinsed her coffee cup. "And now, I need to get back to my patient. I think you already know and will find a way to make it happen. But, I could be wrong."

She left the room and Lauren sat for a moment longer and shook her head no. This while thinking how Claire was right. Lauren knew her own capability and wanted to do surgery.

On the following morning Lauren came to work ready to learn. She had decided that it wasn't necessary to say anything to Mary.

So, on the Friday of Lauren's first week, Claire slowed down and taught Lauren every step of each abortion.

Lauren knew her own ability; but she also understood what could go wrong. She followed directions meticulously, while worrying about adding pain or extra time to each surgery.

By the end of the day, Lauren felt a sense of accomplishment. She recognized her own ability, and knew she was capable of doing surgery on her own when it was necessary.

Their first patient on Monday morning was Darla. She was thirty-six and had five children ranging from age two to eighteen. Lauren walked her to the surgery room, gave her a hospital gown, and left while she changed into it. When Lauren returned to the room, Darla was lying on the table, her feet in the stirrups – she had been here before.

Within seconds Claire entered and put on a hospital jacket and gloves. Then she spoke to Lauren with her usual calm. "Today you will do surgeries. I'll be here during each and will hand you instruments as you request them. I've talked to Darla; she knows that you're competent and ready."

Lauren thought how she had to be: Darla depended on her.

After putting on her facemask, Lauren adjusted the globe light, and within seconds gave her first order. "The speculum."

Claire handed her the instrument, then stood watching as Lauren put it in place.

"Now, the tenaculum," Lauren said, sounding confident.

Next, Claire handed her the small curette, and then spoke to Darla. "You'll feel this, so squeeze and count to forty. It will be over quick."

As Lauren started to remove the gestational sac, Darla cried, "Ouch, stop!"

Lauren stopped, but before Claire could speak she said, "I know this hurts, but I'll need you to hold really still and I promise to be fast. Count from ten down to one – slow enough for me to finish this most important part."

Lauren removed the sac. then carefully pulled out the curette, and asked Claire to hand her another one.

After passing it to her, Claire inspected the curette Lauren had used. "You got most of it on the first sweep. Good."

Lauren spoke to Darla. "I'm going to make certain all cells are gone."

She used several other curettes, and the last was totally clear of cells. "You did really well, and the pain should be relieved. Now I'm going to make certain that everything is sanitized so you'll be safe when you leave here."

After using a sterilizing solution on the area, Claire handed Lauren the small hose. Lauren rinsed with warm sudsy liquid, and then finished with clear water. It flowed into the pan beneath Darla.

Within fifteen minutes the total procedure was complete.

When Darla left the clinic, Lauren confided to Claire, "I was too absorbed in getting it done right to be nervous. But afterwards I felt my heart pounding, I also marveled at what I had just done, and on my own." She quickly added, "Of course I knew you were right there every minute – the most talented assistant in the world."

Claire smiled, "And now you've got a new role at this clinic. That surgery was done well, as I knew it would be."

With Lauren doing abortions, Claire had more time to interview patients. She even got out for more lunches at Thiele's.

But not for long as the war was bringing more women to the clinic, plus its reputation for safe abortions was growing. As the clinic became busier than ever, Claire decided to turn the recovery room into another surgery room.

No matter how busy, Lauren asked Carol to schedule extra time for her young patients. They were the most heartbreaking part of her days, but also the most gratifying during the times that she helped beyond the abortion. This sometimes involved contacting social agencies that Claire had learned to trust.

Lauren had begun to assume that Claire was unflappable. But she was visibly upset when she learned about Priscilla, who had come to the clinic ten years earlier. Her mother, Katy, had been sixteen. And Carol had read stories to Priscilla while Katy had an abortion.

Claire filled Lauren in. "Now Priscilla just turned twelve and wasn't aware of her pregnancy, until yesterday when I examined her. She doesn't understand what an abortion is.

"Her mother, Katy, brought her to us when she learned what was happening. She knew that Priscilla had one period about three months ago. When she didn't have another, Katy assumed it was part of puberty. But when other signs started, she worried. And then became suspicious, before learning.

"Priscilla has been raped repeatedly, and it's been by her mother's pimp. Yes! Katy calls him 'the arranger.' He's been arranging all right! He'd take Katy to men, then come back and hit on little – and I mean little – Priscilla, who weighs under a hundred pounds.

"Katy learned when one of her customers drove her home and she discovered her pimp all over Priscilla. Now she's over three months pregnant, and I'll break my rule and do surgery. I'm not going to put her through the stress of going someplace else." Claire took a deep breath. "As you will learn, there are exceptions to rules and Priscilla is one of them."

Lauren understood that the world of pimps and prostitutes was very real in Portland, but until working at the clinic she hadn't felt its impact.

"What are we going to do? The bastard has to be stopped."

"I'll notify a detective; one who Chief trusts. The pimp will be taken off the streets," Claire shook her head, frustrated, "but he'll be replaced by others who will seek-out Katy. She's big on their list – makes good money for them. It takes something overwhelming to get girls like her off the street."

More than anger, Lauren felt horrified. "You would think what happened to Priscilla would do that!"

"Right," Claire looked worn-down. "I'll notify a counselor who I trust – one who police often use with juveniles. I want her to work with both Katy and Priscilla. And if Katy steps back onto the streets, Priscilla will be taken from her and placed in foster care. That's ugly. But not even close to as ugly as what's been happening."

From the beginning of her work at the clinic, Lauren saw that Claire practiced with amazing dexterity, had a studied knowledge of female anatomy, and confidence in her own ability. She also witnessed Claire's genuine concern about each patient. And as Lauren learned on her first day at the clinic, Claire never refused a patient for lack of money. Carol had set up a sliding scale that started at zero.

However, Lauren noted that most people came prepared to pay the asking price. With an average of nine patients a day, she calculated that the clinic easily brought in over ten thousand dollars a week.

The war had facilitated America's rise from the depression. But at Claire's office it was happening at exponential speed, and Lauren had never anticipated the kind of money she was being paid. Claire had given her an advance of seven hundred dollars for her first month's work: five times what she had been making at Thiele's.

Chapter Seven

The wind roared; tree limbs slammed against the house, and rain hit with a crackle like pellets. Lauren had heard on the radio that the storm would be damaging. But it was early Saturday morning and she sat at the table sipping coffee, appreciating the refuge of the warm, dry kitchen.

Mary came in a few minutes later and looked surprised. "Oh! I didn't hear you in here." Her expression turned cold. She poured coffee and started to leave.

"Mary, don't go. Sit down, let's talk. I miss hearing about your day – and all the little things that Sandi does. I know how she keeps you hopping and..."

Mary interrupted, "No Lauren, you know nothing of our days."

"What? What are you saying?" Without waiting for an answer, Lauren decided it was time to be direct. "This has to end; we have to talk. I'm not comfortable with what's happening."

"Not comfortable!" Mary mocked. "I can imagine you're not comfortable. Your comfort is the last thing I'm worried about. And I don't know what we could possibly say that wouldn't make our situation worse. I have decided to hold my tongue, knowing how strong minded you can be."

"'I' can be? Look Mary, if you don't want to talk we won't. But I have no intention of continuing to live the way it's been around here this past month. It's awful for me, and not good for Sandi. Our relationship is growing worse each day and it will affect her if it hasn't already."

Lauren stopped and hesitated, then said what she had been thinking. "Sandi loves you; I don't want to have to take her from here. But I will if things continue as they've become."

The words seemed to hit Mary physically; she looked shocked. "You wouldn't do that! Take her from her home – you wouldn't."

"Yes. I would. Sandi is my little girl and I don't want her growing up in a house filled with anger."

She stopped. Mary looked pathetic – something Lauren had never seen. No matter what hit, Mary seemed to stubbornly hold herself together.

"This has been harder than you could understand," Mary said. "You arrive home and ask about our day! Well, here it is. We go to church. Yes – Sandi and I. I pray for forgiveness – for you, and for myself, because by not saying more – not doing more to stop you – it's as if I condone what you do.

"You don't know how difficult it is for me: you're working at that place." She set her coffee on the table. "I've been talking with Father Cory."

Lauren interrupted, "With Sandi listening, you've been talking to Father Cory!"

Mary put sugar in her coffee and stirred, watching it dissolve, then continued as if she hadn't heard Lauren. "And… Father Cory told me to talk to you. Explain how I feel. But I couldn't. You obviously… I mean, it's clear that you don't believe what I know to be true." She faced Lauren. "Abortion is an act of murder. If you could see that, you wouldn't be at that clinic."

"Murder! You've got to be…" Lauren looked at her with disbelief. "You took Sandi with you to this priest and talked about me! My sins! Just what did you say to him?" She glared; then threw her hand out, stopping her. "Don't tell me. I don't want to hear more. I need to stop and try to breathe. I don't make empty threats, and believe me – I will not accept what you're doing."

Her pause was short – she was too upset to stop. "I want to make this very clear, Mary. You are never to talk to a priest or anyone else in front of Sandi, about what you consider to be my sins. It's amazing that you can't see the harm that this could cause her."

"Harm?" Strength returned to Mary's voice. "Where are you coming from? Do you live on another planet? What do you think is going to happen to Sandi if you continue at that clinic? You have to be aware that abortion is against the laws of both Church and State? Do you have any idea how your working at that clinic is going to influence attitudes toward Sandi? Think what she is being threatened with. Wait until neighbors get wind of it. Wait till she is old enough to hear their talk. And don't think it won't happen. Nothing as evil as what happens in that clinic goes unnoticed. Everyone I know is aware of Claire Karriden – and wouldn't allow her near their homes, let alone their children."

"Mary it's impossible to argue with you. I never have talked about your faith, though I don't agree with some of its premises. But now it is definitely not what I want for Sandi. It's my hope that when she's old enough to be aware of the attitudes you describe, she'll have learned that they're wrong.

"Believe me; I wouldn't spend a day in the clinic if I didn't know what Dr. Karriden does. She makes a huge difference in the lives of so many women, and importantly young girls – some as young as twelve. The doctor saves them from the gossip of neighbors like the ones you just described. And think of the babies who would be born into a world that shames unwed mothers, and where there is no money or family for their care. Just think if I had given birth to our Sandi, without you and Joe here, loving and caring for her."

As she referred to their help, Lauren looked at Mary's expression, and thought how it was like talking to the wind.

"Mary, we'll never agree about some things. But one thing we both want is the best for Sandi, and I've been lucky up until these past months. As I've said before, life would have been difficult – near impossible – without you and Joe. That's what it's like for unwed mothers."

Lauren walked to the counter, threw out the cold coffee and filled her cup. Sitting back down, she said, "If we stay, things have to change. I don't want to live the way it's been this past month, and I'm not quitting my job. I'm proud of what I do at the clinic. But I know how most people feel; especially those at your church. So for your sake and therefore Sandi's, I'll make a deal. I'll do all I can to separate my work from our lives here."

She thought, then added, "I'll change my name at work. I'll do it on Monday morning."

"Lauren you don't understand where I'm coming from. Not talking about it, changing your name, those things might help for a while because Sandi is so young. But regardless of what we say or who you call yourself, you'll still be working at that place – and people will know.

"But more than that, it's your soul that concerns me. Yes I talk to Father Cory, because I ask him to pray for your soul." She paused, "It is at risk."

The words stood alone for a second. Then Mary heaved a heavy breath – resigned. "But it would be awful if you and Sandi left."

Lauren read the expression on her face. "Mary, I feel for you – I know how deeply you hold your beliefs. I am asking you to respect that mine are different."

She waited, but Mary didn't respond.

"We're not ever going to agree about this." Lauren spoke as she stood. "With that said, we do agree about one big thing. Sandi is a happy girl and I want her to remain so."

Mary still said nothing.

Leaving the room, Lauren felt discouraged. She went to Sandi, who was still sleeping – unaware that her world could soon change.

She whispered, "You are a happy girl, and I want you to stay this way."

The tension in the house was palpable as the morning continued. Escaping, Lauren placed Sandi in her stroller and walked to Laurelhurst Park, which was six blocks away.

She sat in a swing, holding Sandi while pumping in rhythm with the other children. Sandi loved the excitement, and waved her tiny hand in the air. Lauren whispered into her hair, "This is what I want for you – days in the park, laughing."

And she thought how it was Mary and Joe who provided this luxury. She hugged Sandi, "What have I done, Little One?" Even as she said it, she knew that what she wanted for Sandi was right, and added, "You would like Claire, or more important, you should."

It was then that two young women walked past the swings – chatting, enjoying the day – no fear on their faces. Lauren stopped pushing the swing and watched them stroll away.

This drew immediate protest from Sandi, "More!"

"Okay, okay." Lauren pushed the swing as she mumbled, "But look, Sandi. The women I see have no one else to turn to."

Sandi stuck her legs out as if pumping. "More."

Lauren pushed hard enough for the swing to soar. Then spoke clearly, "Okay, Little One, what about this: Mommy isn't going to quit. You're going to accept my world. I'll make certain of that."

Sandi, caught up in the excitement, waved her hands wildly. And Lauren pushed harder.

In the rush of Sandi's excitement – and happiness, it occurred to Lauren that she was now able to buy a swing for their backyard.

At the clinic on Monday morning Lauren Martin became Anne Thompson.

The war affected everyone's life. But Lauren, Claire, and Carol saw a side of this effect that many didn't see. Husbands, fiancés, boyfriends, and strangers came home on furloughs, aware they would be returning to battle. And many of the women they left behind came to the clinic, afraid and in need. They were busier than ever.

Lauren did as many abortions during the day as Claire – who often stayed late into night. But Lauren stuck to her five o'clock rule, even though the demand grew and every woman felt her situation was urgent. Above all else, Lauren knew the importance of being home evenings with Sandi.

She wished Mary could listen to the women who came to the clinic. Rape, incest, passion, shame – these words took on a sharp reality. The women were from every walk of life: wealthy, poor, religious, liberal, conservative, educated, uneducated, students, teachers, prostitutes. Each had one thing in common: they were desperate.

And there were children. As Lauren learned with Priscilla, some patients had barely started menses. She wondered how Mary would react if she saw these young girls – some eleven or twelve years old. Lauren wished that Mary knew the effort that she and Claire took to comfort, while relieving them from facing motherhood.

Chapter Eight

During this time Lauren got to know Claire's daughter, Jane. She often waited in the back room for Claire, before they left together for lunch.

Lauren figured Jane wanted the attention she drew. Claire didn't smoke at the clinic, but Jane usually lit a cigarette as soon as she arrived. Smoking was a statement. She would take the cigarette from a gold case, tap it, and then place it into a long diamond studded filter. With deliberate flair, she held it while displaying the underside of her thin wrist, long red fingernails, and slender hand. After a deep drag, Jane released smoke into the air as if it smelled of lilacs.

And Lauren thought how her jewelry and clothes took real planning. She managed to create a look that was both expensive and in bad taste. Her hands glittered with gold rings, some with large diamonds. And she wore her skirts too short and tops too tight.

She sat drinking coffee, in the private room at the end of the hall. And when Lauren ran in for short breaks the two of them talked. Lauren had never known anyone like her. She was brassy, tough, and funny; while sensitive – especially to the emotional and physical pain of others, including women who came to the clinic. For those who couldn't pay, she brought cloth bags filled with fruit, bread and pastries, ground coffee-beans, plus a one-size terry cloth robe.

As weeks went by and they became friends, Lauren realized that Jane's style wasn't for effect. In fact, she loved the flash of diamonds, stiletto shoes, long cigarette holders – they were natural to her. She had grown up in Claire's world – setting her own rules and being proud of them. Jane thrived on being independent of most convention.

There were no limits to what Jane would say. As they grew to know each other, she talked about her two ex-husbands and her boyfriends, and confided that she had been on her mother's table more than once. But she made it clear: that was past-tense after the birth of her first daughter.

"I have two perfect girls. And now no one touches me without a condom, and believe me I take care of myself immediately afterwards. No more abortions. For one thing, Mom has limits; and has made that clear. But more than that, I love my girls, and want them to have everything that I can give them – other than another sister or brother."

Lauren appreciated her honesty, and so much more. She thought how Ben would like her. She met his standard for judging people: she would hide families from Nazis, putting herself at risk.

Jane was defiant and appeared to be tougher than nails. And she got that toughness from growing up feeling the effects of Claire's notoriety. Jane watched out for the underdog – people who couldn't fight back for themselves. It was natural for her to reach out to women at the clinic, especially those who were unmarried with little means of support.

Lauren grew to value the time she spent talking with Jane. And when Jane asked her to join them for lunch, she wanted to – but couldn't. Not spreading work beyond five, there was no time to leave during the day.

Lauren was explaining this, when Claire entered the room.

"Easy to remedy that," Claire said. "Why don't you come to Thiele's with us after work? Change your Friday schedule, and join us. As you may have noticed, I don't usually work late into Friday night. That's because it's our evening out."

Lauren started, "I can't…"

Claire stopped her, "I bet you could if we leave early. At least let's try. On the next Friday that your schedule is free, tell Carol not to book anyone after two-thirty. That way you'll be able to leave by four. Then I'll drive, and you'll have time for at least a drink. I'll even give you a ride home. How's that for service?"

"Sounds good – I mean too good. I wouldn't let you leave Thiele's just to drive me home." Lauren smiled, "And with my new job I can afford a cab.

"But very honestly, even if I left early, I'd head straight home. Mary takes care of Sandi for long hours. And unfortunately, there are other reasons. Mary is a devout Catholic – I mean devout! She knows where I'm working. Do I need to say more?"

Jane looked at Lauren with disbelief. "She's running your life. Of course you can come. My girls have a babysitter they love. I'll drive, and we can pick Sandi up and bring her to my house." Reading Lauren's reaction, she added, "Don't worry; I'll park down the street. Don't want to throw Grandma into a Hail Mary tizzy."

Lauren shook her head; "Believe me, she would do much more than Hail Marys."

"So how do you survive in that house?"

"Sandi is my girl, therefore Mary needs me – and I don't want to push a fragile situation to the edge. Mary recognizes this and also the irony. She hates this place and me for working here, but knows it provides enough money for me to take Sandi and live elsewhere. Mary also knows that what keeps me with her and Joe is that Sandi loves them. In truth, I appreciate the good life they give her, even though I've had concerns lately.

"So, there you have it. I'll miss out on the fun Friday nights, but need to be with Sandi."

Claire nodded. "Understand, even though we'd like to have you join us. So, if it works out that you can come once in a while, we'll do all we can to help."

Jane shook her head. "Mom's more understanding than I. You need to get out, and we want you to join us. Besides, you worked at Thiele's. They know you there, and would love to have you come in. Just try it – come with us and we'll get you home. Mary doesn't need to know."

Lauren nodded and smiled, "I'm a push-over. I'll think about it."

Several weeks later, as Claire and Jane left the office, Lauren looked at her schedule. It was booked solid for two weeks. She marked time off on the first Friday afternoon that she was available.

She, Claire, and Jane walked into the bar and sat at a table near the front. Jan, the skinny energetic barmaid, greeted them with a Martini for Jane and red wine for Claire.

She looked at Lauren, "Welcome back to Thiele's; you've come of age. What'll you have?"

"Red wine or Irish toddy – the limits of my experience."

"French Cabernet, 1940," Jan said as she hurried back to the bar.

The room was filling, and just about everyone greeted Claire and Jane. When the police chief arrived, he walked to their table.

Claire stood, gave him a hug, and then said, "Anne, meet Chief Richards."

Anne! Lauren shot Claire a look, but before she could say anything the chief stretched out his hand.

"I guess we haven't met, but I remember you from here. And Claire has given you high praise."

Lauren alerted further; he knew too much. Reluctant, she shook his hand.

"It's Lauren – my name."

His smile was too smooth. "I apologize, Lauren."

She had seen him at Thiele's with Claire. Then, as now, he was in civilian clothes: Harris Tweed sport coat and creased trousers. 'Chief' was a good title; he looked like someone who took charge. Maybe in his early sixties, his hair was thick and white, and he was medium height. There was strength in his square jaw, shoulders and the grasp of his handshake. Nothing about him appeared soft.

He sat next to Claire, and Lauren took note as he turned and said hello to Jane. He didn't smile, and Jane didn't reply. Instead she took the last sip of her martini.

The barmaid returned with Lauren's wine, a Manhattan for the chief, and another martini for Jane.

The room was filling quickly. Everyone seemed to know each other, and as Lauren had noted during the time she had worked there, Claire was treated like a celebrity.

But to her surprise, Lauren was also receiving greetings – from people she had never met. Lauren smiled back, until someone stopped at the table and called her Anne. She didn't answer, and decided to leave after finishing her glass of wine.

With the background noise she strained to hear the chief, who was talking about Broadway Boys – a gang of "truant" teenagers who met downtown. Lauren bent forward and he raised his voice, "smoking, drinking, sneaking into movies, shop-lifting, and sniffing out girls. Good old Judge McNair has taken it upon himself to send them to the recruiting office instead of jail."

"You've got to be kidding," Lauren said. "Does this judge read the names listed everyday on the front page of The Oregonian?" She didn't need to add: killed in action.

The chief's expression was measured cool. "You've got a point. But have you gone to any recruiting station and seen the lines from eight to five every day? Or better yet, go out to McClaren's School for Boys; see how rehabilitating you think that would be."

"At least they're alive," Lauren said, thinking how this was a man who should know about war. Then it occurred to her that he had probably served in the last one. And Claire liked him – described him as tough and fair.

She backed off, "You're right though, about the lines at the recruiting offices. The war has to be fought – but not by under-aged boys."

She looked at her watch, wanting to call a cab and go home to Sandi.

The chief smiled. "Truce. Your point is well taken."

Before Lauren could reply, Jane grabbed their attention. She stood, and watched a swarthy, somehow frightening man enter the bar from the dining section. He looked at her, gave no acknowledgment, then turned and walked toward a group of men at the back of the room.

Jane headed toward him, a martini in one hand and cigarette in the other. Her black dress was accented by a single gold-strand necklace. Its simplicity contrasted with the black seams of her net stockings and gold colored three-inch heels.

It seemed to Lauren that everyone in the room was caught in the seductiveness of her movements. And Lauren wanted to go to her – stop her. But instead she watched as Jane approached him. His back toward her; he had joined the others at the table. She touched him, and he turned toward her – not smiling.

Lauren was holding her breath and let it out – telling herself to relax. Jane could take care of herself.

The man pulled out a chair, and Jane shook her head, no. Then he stood and motioned for her to sit. Lauren felt Jane's reluctance. But, she put her empty glass on the table and slid into the chair. The other men seemed friendly, appearing to introduce themselves. And one motioned for another round of drinks.

Lauren quit watching; hoping that others in the room would do the same. And when everything seemed to have settled to normal she looked at her watch. It was time to leave. She missed Sandi, and wanted to get away from this scene and strangers who called her Anne.

As she turned to grab her jacket from the chair, she saw Claire, who was watching Jane. It was clear that she was worried. Lauren decided to stick around a little longer and make sure Jane was all right.

She was glad she did. After about fifteen minutes, Jane stood and spoke so everyone could hear, "Take your money and shove it!" She sprinkled bills over his head, and then walked toward the door.

Lauren grabbed her jacket and met Jane at the door. They walked out together.

"What happened?"

"Don't even ask. He's not worth talking about. I'm glad I'm out of there, just wish I had poured his goddamned drink over his head. But just as well; I made my point."

She stopped and looked at Lauren, "Thanks."

"For what?"

"For leaving with me." Jane seemed younger, vulnerable. "Nobody

has ever openly been there for me – I mean, nobody but my mother."
She stopped, and then repeated, "Thanks. Doing that… it means
a lot to me."

"Jane – why wouldn't I be there for you? You're my friend."

Jane looked touched. "That's nice. This crazy evening is turning out
to be special."

She raised her brow as if in wonder, then shook her head, "Now
let's get out of this lot. Do you have more time; I'd like to buy you
some dinner."

"By the time we got to a place, I'd have to leave to go home, but
can we take a rain-check on that."

Jane smiled, "You have turned a bad night into one of my best."
She put her arm through Lauren's. "Rain-check it is. Now let me
drive you home. Promise, I won't drive close enough for Grandmother
Mary to see me."

"Thanks, Jane. And yes, I want you to drive up to the house."

Chapter Nine

As Jane turned the corner, Lauren saw flashing lights.

"That's my house!"

Jane pulled to the curb and parked a slight way from the ambulance.

"I'm going to stay right here till I know what's going on."

Lauren thanked her as she hopped from the car, and ran into the house.

Mary was standing in the doorway of their bedroom – hers and Joe's. "Thank God you're here. I couldn't leave Sandi, and they're going to move him."

Lauren hurried toward her; then saw Joe. He was gray and limp, and had an oxygen mask over his mouth. The medics were lifting him onto a gurney.

"Joe..." Lauren started to ask but didn't; it was clear what was happening. Putting her arm around Mary, the two of them stood back as medics guided the gurney through the hall.

As the medic reached the front door he turned to face Mary, "Ma'am, you can ride with us to the hospital."

Mary ran and got her coat, and then motioned to Sandi's room. "She slept through this."

Lauren followed as far as the porch and watched. Before stepping into the ambulance, Mary turned toward her and called, "We'll be at Providence Hospital."

Seconds later the noise of sirens filled the neighborhood.

"We'll be at Providence," Lauren repeated. She had an overwhelming fear that Joe wouldn't make it, though it was only four blocks away.

She hurried to Sandi and started to lift her. Sandi puckered, not ready to wake from her nap. "It's okay, sweetheart. We have to move fast. You're going with Mommy."

Sandi stiffened, protesting; but Lauren held her closer. "We're going to see Grandma."

She stopped crying and looked toward the door. "Grandma?"

"Not yet, Sweetheart; she had to leave. We'll see her in a little while."

Within minutes Lauren was carrying Sandi and her stroller to Jane's car. And without asking, Jane drove to Providence Hospital's emergency door.

"Can I drive Sandi to my house? My girls will love her, and it will be easier for you – as well as for her."

"Thanks, Jane. I hope Joe will be able…," Lauren stopped. "I know Mary will want her here.

Jane hopped from the car, pulled out the stroller and opened it. "Okay," she said. "I'm going home. I'll be here in an instance if I can help in any way."

Lauren gave her a quick hug and then fastened Sandi in the stroller. By the time Jane drove away, Lauren and Sandi were walking toward the intake desk.

Lauren's heart sank when she saw that the secretary was waiting for them, looking sympathetic.

"I have bad news for you."

Reading her face, Lauren shook her head no.

"I'm sorry. Your mother-in-law was with him in the ambulance when he died."

With Sandi in her stroller, Lauren walked to a small chapel. On its door was a wooden cross with an ivory carving of slender hands in prayer. Entering, Lauren was caught by an oil painting of Jesus; his soulful eyes seeming to focus on Mary who sat with her head bent.

Mary looked up. "The doctor called it a massive coronary. He was unconscious when it happened and felt no pain."

Lauren pushed the stroller toward Mary and sat. Touching her hand, she thought how Mary had been with Joe for all of her adult life; nothing could have prepared her for this.

Mary straightened her shoulders and spoke in a voice that was muffled by tears. "His heart gave out from the sadness. I could see it after Ben was killed; but I did nothing." She shook her head, as if to rid herself of thoughts. "Too filled with my own pain; he had nothing to hold onto. Not me. Not anything."

"Mary, that isn't true. You were always there for Joe; and he knew it."

Mary stopped crying and seemed to study Lauren's face before answering. "You may be right, I don't know. But I do know that I can't change what happened to us after Ben died." She sat straight. "I'll have to live with it."

Along with all else, Lauren thought, but let it go. She asked, "What can I do, Mary? I want to help."

Mary looked at Sandi, who had fallen back to sleep. "Thank God for our little girl. We'll make it. I'll call Father Cory in the morning. He'll help us. I am so tired. Father will tell us what to do."

"Yes," Lauren said, "Father Cory – in the morning."

Lauren took off work for the next two weeks.

The sense of Joe filled every room. Lauren entered the living room expecting him to be by his radio. She would start to set the table for three, then would stop and feel the loss. She wondered how it felt for Mary, lying in bed – the empty sheet next to her.

And Sandi? How could they tell her that he was gone? She didn't understand forever.

"She'll grow up and never know who Grandpa Joe was," Mary said. "But he is part of her; he has made a difference in her life. And thank God she doesn't know he's not coming back."

Lauren thought how Joe's death intensified feelings about Ben. But she and Mary avoided talking about him.

However, they did talk about Jon. Mary hadn't heard from him for weeks before Joe died. She phoned the Red Cross, as they handled emergency calls to servicemen.

"We hope you can get the message to him right away. We need him home for his father's funeral. He's our only living son." Mary collapsed into tears as she said this, and Lauren finished the call.

Within three days they got a telegraph from Jon:

"Mum, my sadness about Dad is beyond words. Want to be with you and can't. There are only two ways that anyone goes home from here. Give love to Lauren and hug Sandi. Wish I were there; Love you and Dad always, Jon.

"Only two ways – Oh God…" Mary stopped, and Lauren knew from her expression that her words were not a prayer; they were an admonishment! It was the first time that Lauren heard Mary question God.

Sometimes Lauren felt as if the house had absorbed the laughter, tears, love, anger – all the emotions that had filled its rooms over the years and could never be felt by a stranger. Especially now, when ordinary things had taken on special significance: tables, chairs, beds, old clothes, cooking-tools. Each had become part of its story, tinting memories and enhancing pain. The house allowed no escape from either.

Mary talked of how Jon had pulled himself up to lean against the couch at nine months; at age eight he whooped like an Indian as Ben chased him from room to room; he was twelve when he carried an injured bird from the street and placed it on a pillow. Scenes, half forgotten, were now haunting. Mary would turn her head and squeeze her eyes shut. But Lauren knew she couldn't rid herself of pain – and fear.

Chapter Ten

When Lauren was at work she was consumed by the demands of the moment. But now, during her two weeks at home, she had little time to think about the clinic.

Mary came into the living room as Lauren was picking up toys.

"Sit for a while," Mary said.

Lauren did, concerned that this was going to be about the clinic.

Mary took one of her deep breaths which Lauren saw as attempts to refuel. "When you and Sandi were out today, Joe's boss came by and let me know the state of things. After working at that mill for over twenty years, Joe will receive little insurance. The company carried a policy of four hundred dollars. Other than that, he had no retirement. His coworkers chipped in and came up with enough to pay the costs of his funeral and a month's salary. None of them have much and I appreciate what they did."

Mary emphasized her words, "But now I need to make some changes."

"Some changes?" Lauren asked.

"Yes. I've been thinking that it's time to look for a position; perhaps at Kaiser Shipyards. I'll work the night shift so I'll be home while you're gone. And we could be a little more frugal with utilities, clothes, even food."

"Is this what you want, Mary – to work at the shipyards?"

"We don't usually have the luxury to do just as we want, Lauren. Working at the lumber mill wasn't part of Joe's dream. But he did, and we lived well enough." Mary corrected herself, "We lived very well."

"Besides a lot of women are working there. It would be an interesting experience."

"Could be, but" Lauren repeated, "it's important that you do what you really want." She smiled, nodding toward Sandi's room, "I can understand how you'd like to be out of the house – talk to real people once in a while."

"You know that's not so. Besides, no one but you and I would understand just how much she needs spoiling." Mary didn't smile. "Facts are, I don't want her to be with anyone besides us. We'll just have to coordinate our hours. That is, if they'll take me at the shipyards. I've never worked outside of home."

Lauren was careful and thought before speaking. "Of course, they'll take you. But you're right about Sandi. Having a stranger take care of her would be hard. I hope you know how much I appreciate your being home with her." She paused and took a heavy breath, knowing she was about to ignite a firestorm. "Mary let me suggest something."

"Don't! Don't say it, Lauren. Let's be clear: There is no way that I would live off of the money you make."

"You're right about being clear, and I don't want to circle the truth. You and I know our differences; we've certainly made them clear. But there's much at stake, so please listen."

Mary shook her head no, but Lauren rushed on, "First, I'll be continuing at the clinic, whatever else happens. Not just because I know what I do helps others, but there's another reason – an important one, especially now. I make good money and…"

Mary stopped her, "Don't say it! Our security should not come at the price of our souls."

"Oh Mary, here we go. We've been through this before, and I hate to get into it now. But this is too important; we're going to have to talk. Would you just try to understand that my beliefs are as valid to me as yours are to you! I know what I do is right!"

As Mary started to protest, Lauren spoke over her. "Listen just a moment. I am earning over two thousand dollars a month, with the promise of more. I can provide enough for us to pay monthly bills, all debts, and put money away for Sandi's future. Think of it; she would be…"

Mary's expression stopped her. "Two thousand dollars! You have been making two thousand dollars a month!" She shook her head, disgusted. "You have been bought and want us to share the riches of your sins."

"Mary! Stop! Do you know how you sound? Come down from the pulpit. A lot of people don't agree with your righteous definition of sin. You know I don't! I save women from the horror of people who sin in ways you don't see; this includes some pious folk in esteemed positions. Some who use women, while calling them whores. These same folk label children as illegitimate – like there's such a thing as an illegitimate child".

"Let me make it clear; I help women whether they pay or not." Lauren didn't pause, "And there's something you don't know. I – myself – went to Claire Karriden for help."

She saw the shock on Mary's face.

"Yes, Mary. And I would have had an abortion if not for Ben's death." The words bounced back at Lauren. She softened her voice, adding, "And because you and Joe were there for me.

"Do you know what it would have been like – giving birth and then caring for Sandi without your help? I would have faced the lonely world of single mothers and their bastard babies.

"Yes, that's what they're called. Think what could have happened to our little girl."

She waited, but Mary didn't reply. Finally, Lauren sank into her chair – tired. She hadn't intended to argue with Mary; not now, so close to Joe's death.

After minutes of silence Lauren sighed. "Do what you want. Go to work if that's what you choose to do. Whether you do or not I will continue at the clinic. And I want to provide more – a lot more – for Sandi's needs."

Mary still didn't speak, but her expression changed. The arch of her eyebrows, her pursed lips – they were gone. Lauren was ready for stubbornness, anger, arrogance, but not submissiveness.

"Mary – you're wearing me down. I'm about to offer a compromise. Something I've thought about, but…" Lauren hesitated, then said, "I'll make a deal with you; after a year I will quit."

Watching Mary, who shook her head no, Lauren wanted to take back her words.

"A year? That's a long time. Lauren, I know how you feel, and I'll try to leave my beliefs out of this argument. I understand that you are able to help us financially. But think of the real price. Do you want the stigma of what you are doing, which is illegal and against Christian ethics, to be put on Sandi?"

Lauren said, "We have talked about this before, and I've made every effort to separate my work from our home. I have changed my name at work and I …"

Mary interrupted, "Lauren, do you think God doesn't know who you are? What you do?"

Lauren took a breath, exasperated. "Mary, the God I believe in doesn't judge in the same way as yours. But regardless of how we define God, we agree on our need to watch out for Sandi. Let me work for another year. We'll save enough money so that neither of us will have to leave her the following year. Unless you really want to go to work, please don't. It would make an enormous change in Sandi's life."

Mary didn't answer. She sat staring at her hands.

"Just one year," Lauren said, thinking how one year would be the right time to quit.

Mary said nothing.

Lauren put eight hundred dollars a month into an account in Mary's name, and told her to use it freely. At first it wasn't touched. But after several months, when the money from Joe's co-workers ran out, Mary began to write checks. Neither she nor Lauren mentioned it, but Lauren was pleased.

After the withdrawals began, Lauren noted a remarkable change. Mary quit talking about Father Cory, the parish, and church. Then, when she stopped attending weekend mass, Lauren became concerned. Religion was integral to Mary; she wouldn't just walk away from it.

Lauren watched, looking for problems. One thing was certain: Mary's days were totally filled with Sandi, who was reaching, grabbing, squeezing, tasting, or dropping everything she was tall enough to touch. Smart, stubborn, funny, and totally adored, Sandi was a handful.

Mary's response was easy: "She's Irish, with fire, spunk, and determination; she'll go a long way – this one."

Neighborhood moms, years younger than Mary, started visiting, and Lauren heard children in the background when she phoned home during the day. Where Sandi was concerned, Mary was upbeat.

However, there was nothing upbeat about Mary after Sandi went to sleep at night. Lauren did dishes while Mary picked up Sandi's mess. When Mary finished, rather than sitting and talking, she went to bed. Even when Lauren woke late at night, she saw light shining through the crack of her door.

The exception to Mary's routine was when Jon's letters arrived. After weeks of waiting, ten or so were delivered in a bundle.

Those evenings were different. As Lauren stepped in from work, she could read Mary's face – the sadness. But it wasn't until after Sandi was in bed that Mary would take the letters from the top of the refrigerator and hand them to Lauren.

"These are from Jon, written to both of us."

Then, back to routine, Mary went to her room. Lauren wanted to reach out to her, but Mary didn't give her a chance.

The letters touched deep. Jon talked about buddies with affectionate ridicule, but never mentioned the conditions in Tunisia. He didn't need to. The newspaper was enough, with its daily report of battles and Oregonians killed in action.

Lauren wished she and Mary could share pain, anger – anything. But they didn't. Mary's withdrawal was alarming. Especially with her disconnect from the parish. Months had passed since she started using the 'tainted' money, and as far as Lauren could tell, she hadn't returned to church.

Lauren watched, but didn't comment. Knowing Mary, she believed that she would eventually speak her mind. But too much time passed without a word, and Lauren decided to say something.

Mary was headed for her bedroom, when Lauren stopped her. "Don't leave. Take a seat, I want to talk."

"Oh oh. Something I need to sit for?"

Lauren laughed, "Yep. I want you to sit here for a while. I miss talking with you."

Mary remained standing, "Can this wait till tomorrow?"

"No it can't. But if you prefer to stand, do. Just listen, okay?" Lauren rushed her words. "I miss getting out, going to movies, shopping – just being free, and I know you must miss it too."

Mary frowned and stood waiting.

"I want some time for us, just the two of us – to do things together. And, before you say anything, let me tell you there's a girl who lives right down the street. I've seen her with the neighbor's kids; apparently babysitting. If she's as nice as she appears, I'm going to ask her if she can stay with Sandi on Sunday afternoons. I'd like us to see a movie, shop, have dinner – get out for a while."

Looking tired, Mary sat, rubbed her forehead, and then said, "I'd like that."

Lauren released the breath she had been holding and smiled. "Done deal. We go this Sunday – wherever you decide."

On the following Sunday they went to a movie: Girl Crazy with Judy Garland and Mickey Rooney. Afterwards they shopped at Portland's biggest department store, Meier and Franks, and then took a bus uptown to Thiele's for dinner.

Before eating they shared a carafe of red-wine and talked. Mary didn't just lead up to her greatest concern, she jumped in. "Jon never mentions the battles, but you and I know what's happening. I want him home."

"Oh Mary, so do I. He writes about buddies, food that tastes like dog-treats, two-hundred-degree weather, no girls – but never about the war. And we know why."

Mary's eyes clouded. "Too well."

They each sat for seconds, not speaking, and then Mary said, "I spend so much time feeling angry, and sometimes feel it's turning me brittle. Like, one more thing and I'll crumble."

Lauren waited; concerned, but not certain of where she was going.

"We both feel the pain. Look what we're living like, Lauren – differences too deep to touch. But that aside; we need to share, especially about Jon. I'm afraid every time the postman comes to the door."

Lauren shook her head. "Oh, God, it's terrible. I can tell the days when you receive the letters. I hear it in your voice; but I haven't known what to say."

Mary nodded, "That's been my fault, Lauren. You know my fears about Jon, and we need to share. But as you know, there are other reasons why we can't; some I try to resolve, but that's not easy. My faith has always guided me, but now I don't know how to deal with it. I'm tired of being angry – frightened – I'm terribly lost."

Lauren reached across the table and covered Mary's hand with hers. And Mary didn't pull away.

Their relationship grew more open at home; Mary was trying to reach out. And Sandi was keeping her so busy that Lauren felt Mary didn't have much time to deal with where money came from.

Lauren looked forward to their next weekend. Talking was the only way they could work through their feelings. And she felt she had to ask a serious question.

They went shopping, and then to Henry's. As before, Lauren waited until they finished dinner, and sat drinking wine.

Lauren was direct. "You don't attend mass anymore. Why?"

Mary looked at her, and then took time finishing the wine.

"I've had a falling out with Father Cory. When I tried to explain that what you do is out of my control, he admonished me. I felt both guilt and anger. He gave me no help. It was then that I decided to accept your money. And since then…" Mary fingered her empty glass. "I haven't been able to talk to him.

"But it's worse than that. I was already having problems. I haven't expressed my feelings to anyone till now. It's difficult – frightening – to put them into words."

Her voice was close to a whisper. "For the first time in my life I question my church. I have struggled, trying to understand why…, Mary hesitated, "why God allows the suffering: Ben's, then Joe's, whose pain killed him, and now Jon. I'm afraid to pray, as if my prayers are – well – they seem to have worked against me. And worse, against them: Ben, Joe, and…" Mary shuddered. "It's a terrible thought. And for the first time in my life I'm afraid to pray. I'm afraid of God.

"You see, Lauren, all my life I've had no doubts. And now, it's not just the questioning and fear. Oh God help me – it's my anger. I'm angry at God. If He's not personally punishing me, then I wonder if He's complicit. Does He allow, or worse, condone what man does – the killing, the torture, pain and suffering?

"I prayed." She paused, "but now I no longer pray. It's been terrible."

Mary didn't look at Lauren. "Perhaps my view of Him has been too simplistic, too narrow." She paused. "I feel lost. I've always been so certain. And now I'm afraid, and not . . ." Her sentence dangled, unfinished.

Lauren searched for words that could help her. They all felt shallow.

Then, after minutes, Mary surprised Lauren.

Her expression changed, and she pulled herself straight, looked directly at Lauren and said, "When you said you wanted to talk you got more than you expected. But Lauren, with all that I have said it's important to know one thing that I'm certain about: Our little girl, Sandi, she saves me. With all the ugliness in the world, I want happiness for her. I want her to see its beauty. And it is strange – as I watch her I feel happy in spite of all else. It's as if I can erase things – I mean those fears. Sandi is proof that no matter what, God still provides Good. He takes so much from us, but then He gives. Our Sandi is so perfect."

Mary shook her head. "So, there you have it – my confusion, and my breach with…"

She couldn't finish the sentence, and Lauren nodded, "I understand."

"But," Mary's expression was intense, "I've got to be clear. In-spite of the turmoil of my soul, I don't condone things that I know are wrong. I believe that abortion is a terrible sin; but I recognize that like many other things, I will live with it."

Months passed and Lauren hoped that Mary wasn't thinking of the promise she had made to leave the clinic. It wasn't a good time to quit. Instead, she was looking for the right time to approach Mary about a greater commitment: A larger home. One with the luxury of a room for Sandi, a private yard with a garden and a view, a garage for her new car – and so much more.

She approached the subject at Thiele's over a Sunday dinner. "Mary, I need to talk to you about something."

"Hmm; should I worry? What?"

With a weak smile, Lauren launched in, "Okay; here I go. I've been thinking about our moving into another house. I love our home, but it would be nice for Sandi to have her own room and a large backyard with a playhouse and swings for friends; one in an open area where dogs can run free."

Eyebrows arched, lips pursed – Lauren recognized Mary's expression. She hurried on, "Mary. I know you've been in your home for so many years, and what it means to you. I love it to."

Watching her, Lauren equivocated, "As I said, I've just been thinking about it. Why don't you give it a thought? We've got lots of time. But as Sandi gets older it would be nice."

Mary expression softened. "Now I'm going to surprise you. I've been thinking of the same thing, but for different reasons. That house – our home – has too many memories. Every time I walk into my room I think of Joe, and my heart aches, and Ben…" She took a heavy breath. "I fight thinking too much – I have to for Sandi."

Lauren was surprised and touched. Mary had been thinking of moving, but her reasons were deeper.

"But," Mary said, "I wouldn't move at this time; I'm concerned about Jon. It's his home, and he needs to come back to it. The decision will be his."

Lauren shook her head, agreeing. Her own fears had grown increasingly worse. They hadn't heard from Jon for over a month.

"I agree, Mary; nothing will be done until Jon returns home and he will decide. And let me add; I don't want us to sell the house. I couldn't imagine someone else living in it. I always want it in our family. After Jon comes home, if we all decide to move, we will hire gardeners, care-takers – whatever's necessary to keep it up."

Lauren smiled, "Or who knows, maybe Jon will want to take it over. I mean have a place without us two hovering over him."

Mary didn't laugh; Lauren recognized the expression on her face.

"I hope so, Lauren. I pray that he comes home."

Chapter Eleven

At five the next morning the phone rang. Both Lauren and Mary ran to answer.

Mary grabbed the receiver, "Yes."

Her expression changed – Lauren had seen it before. She stood frozen as Mary picked up a pen and wrote: Brook Army Hospital – San Antonio. Tears smudged the ink.

"Oh God, why..." Mary begged into the receiver, "Don't let him... Don't... We're on our way."

Hanging up, she mouthed Jon's name, then cleared her throat. "He's unconscious. We need to leave now."

Lauren looked at the paper: Brook Hospital was a burn center. "You're right, I'll run and..."

Mary wasn't listening. Wiping away tears, she picked up the phone and dialed.

"Operator, would you connect me to TWA?."

Of course, Lauren thought, we need reservations! Seeing the terror on Mary's face, Lauren reached for the phone. "Let me take care of this. Sit down. You need to…"

"Sit? I'm going to pack. We need to get to that hospital now."

An agent at TWA told Lauren there were no seats available. Lauren pleaded, but was told that there were hundreds like her across the country, each with a serious emergency."

Worried, Lauren picked up the phone again and asked the operator to connect her to Southern Pacific Railroad.

An hour later she, Sandi, and Mary boarded a crowded train.

It stopped at numerous posts, towns, and cities – taking sixty long hours. Lauren saw it as trekking toward another catastrophe. She feared the worst had already happened, but they had no way of contacting the hospital during the two-and-a-half day ride.

Sandi was two, and excited. She teased, running back and forth in the aisle – taunting Lauren into chasing her, and getting constant attention from young recruits heading to training camps.

"Thank God for these guys," Lauren said to Mary. "Rather than disturbed, they're laughing – and Sandi's eating it up."

Mary agreed and then said, "They're also watching you, Lauren – though you don't seem to notice. Always, from the time you used to come home from school with Ben, you've stood out: so smart and beautiful. I chose you for him way back then. Not that it would have mattered. Ben always chose for himself.

"He'd be so proud of you. I know Ben." Mary sighed, "He'd probably support your career – though I've tried not to think so.

"I would get angry over his attitudes toward church; but I can't recall one unkind act from him – toward me or anyone else." Mary paused and then said, "This is the first time that I've put that together. Hmm, another revelation; they seem to happen often lately.

Lauren felt sad. Nothing in life could have prepared Mary for all she had been through – and what they were heading for now.

Mary continued as if reading her. "You know, beyond everything I'm still afraid to pray. My prayers have been answered with cruelty, as if God were punishing me in unmerciful ways. Why?"

She faced Lauren. "You're fortunate. You keep God at a distance. He can never let you down."

Sandi was sound asleep in Lauren's arms as they entered the room.

There were six patients: each swathed in bandages, each silent. Lauren caught the eyes of one. She knew he wasn't Jon; but his eyes spoke to her. There was nothing she could do. He was pleading for more than was possible.

Several nurses bustled from bed to bed, checking and measuring, recording, adjusting sheets and clips – and offering gentle smiles and words that couldn't be acknowledged.

A nurse approached Lauren and Mary and asked, "Mrs. Sullivan?"

"Yes," Mary answered, "and this is Jon's sister-in-law." Her voice quivered, barely above a whisper, "Which…Where is Jon?"

A crazy question – but Lauren understood. How could she know? How could other mothers and wives know? Limbs in white gauze, heads too – only two with faces – and they were patched and taped.

Mary tried to explain. "I mean…" Tears filled her eyes, "Please, take me to my son."

The nurse nodded. "I'm sorry, Mrs. Sullivan. You weren't prepared; how could anyone be?" She looked worn-out. "Jon is in bed 295."

Lauren avoided looking at the other men as she and Mary scanned bed numbers and came to 295. Except for his mouth and nose, Jon's face was wrapped. Blankets were pulled up to his neck, which was also dressed in gauze, but one arm lay exposed – plugged with needles and tubes.

When the doctor had talked to Mary he had told her that Jon had been badly wounded, but the nurse was right, she wasn't prepared for this.

"Oh, Jon – Jonny – it's me. I'm here and will stay." Tears clouded

Mary's words as she bent and kissed his hand.

They stayed as the sun dimmed outside his window, and evening became night. Mary's tears dried as lights in the room were turned off. The quiet was uncanny, strangely peaceful – spiritual. She rested her head against his hand, needing to feel the touch of his skin.

With Sandi sleeping on her lap, Lauren sat far enough away to let Mary be alone with Jon.

Daylight was showing through the closed drapes when the nurse spoke. "I'm sorry, Mrs. Sullivan, but we are going to have to ask you and your family to step into the waiting room."

Without waiting for her to leave, the nurse switched on his light and measured the urine in the bag attached to his bed. She excused herself as she reached past Mary to continue her routine, reinforcing that the family needed to leave. As Mary walked away, the nurse was checking the breathing apparatus that kept Jon alive.

Lauren didn't look at Mary until they closed the door behind them. And when she did, she thought how, through everything, she had never seen anyone's face as contorted with pain.

"God – my God – could not exist. He would not let this happen. And if He does not exist, what kind of horrible force had damned Jon and these young men to this place beyond Purgatory."

Jon was awarded the Medal of Honor posthumously. He was the bombardier on a B 17 that was shot down. Heading back into the burning plane, he pulled three crew members to safety before he was engulfed by flames.

When Mary was told that she and her family would be flown to

Arlington National Cemetery, where he would receive full military honors for valor above and beyond the call of duty, she answered that she had not wanted either of her boys to join the military, let alone become heroes.

But she did attend, honoring Jon. He had chosen to serve.

She, Lauren and Sandi stood on a gray and rainy day at Arlington, listening to Taps and watching as 'Jonathon B. Sullivan' was laid to rest.

Mary didn't join in the prayers offered by the Catholic priest.

Several months after their trip to Arlington, Mary told Lauren that it was time to move.

"It's best for Sandi, as memories stop me all day long."

Lauren understood. She also felt it – a pain that was smothering. But she was able to step from it when she left in the morning. For Mary there was little escape.

By this time Lauren was earning more money than she had dreamed possible. It was within her means to buy a large house she had been admiring, just up the road from Claire. The neighborhood was home to Portland's wealthiest citizens: the same condescending people who Lauren had seated at Thiele's, and sometimes arrived at the clinic in desperate need.

A Cape Cod, built in the twenties by one of Portland's lumber families, it had a magnificent view of city lights and sat on an acre of land – mostly gated.

When she signed the mortgage papers it was clear that she would have to work for several more years. She and Mary didn't talk about this. They never discussed her money or what it provided, nor anything else connected with Lauren's workdays.

Chapter Twelve

Three Years Later

Claire almost bumped into Lauren as they each stepped from surgical rooms into the hall.

"Hi Stranger."

Lauren nodded. "It feels that way. Wish we could take a break, sit and catch up – have one of our long lunches."

"I know how busy you are, and I didn't have time for even a cracker today." Claire looked at her watch. "It's already three. And by the way it's Friday. Please stop by my house; it's the only way we'll get to talk."

"This evening I will. Feel like getting out – I need to. It's been quite a week: eight patients were under sixteen."

"I've had a few, too." Claire kept her voice low, "Maybe they ought to start checking ID's at drive-ins, especially when Duel in the Sun's playing."

Instead of Thiele's, Claire had started having Friday gatherings at her house. She handpicked her guests. Except for Chief Richards, most were outspoken liberals. They included artists, lawyers, and professors. Lauren viewed most with skepticism, suspecting they used Claire and her hospitality. It was their risqué adventure: a night out with Portland's darker side.

Jokes and stories were often political – involving names that Lauren knew. Opinions were argued and bantered about, but she seldom gave hers. She didn't want to attract attention – though she always got more than her share. Men made overtures, but no one interested her enough to share a phone-number. She always left early and alone.

And this evening, she thought of leaving as soon as she entered the room. The usual group was there, and she never felt comfortable. But Claire was expecting her, so she walked in, said a few hellos and then made her way to the porch. It was spring; Portland was in full bloom with the sweet scent of lilacs filling the air. Lauren stood, enjoying the fresh air.

It had rained earlier in the day, and the chairs were covered, so after minutes Lauren walked over and started to pull one out.

"Let me get that for you."

She looked up, surprised. "Where'd you come from?"

"Inside – watching you."

"Hmm; I hadn't noticed."

He smiled. "That's because you're used to being watched."

Too smooth, she thought, but it didn't fit his appearance. He had rugged good looks: unruly sand-colored hair, and an outdoorish tan. Dressed in a blue denim shirt and khaki pants, he looked as if he had just stepped from a sailboat.

As he pulled the chair from its cover, she said, "Should I feel frightened or flattered?"

"Both."

He's quick, she thought, noticing the blue of his eyes.

Then, before Lauren answered, Claire stepped onto the deck. "Here you are. I was going to introduce you around. Seems you two have already met."

"Not really." He looked at Lauren, "Dan Carter. And you are?"

When Lauren didn't answer, Claire said, "You might as well tell him, Anne. He's going to find out anyway. Dan's a reporter for Esquire." She looked at Lauren. "Don't worry, I'll tell you more – later."

Claire put her arm through his and steered him through the door.

He looked back at Lauren and she caught his shrug as Claire talked. "I came looking for you, because I want you to meet one of my other guests. He'll give you his impressions of how Portland ticks and its undercurrent of…" Her voice faded as they left the deck.

Lauren didn't sit; instead she walked inside and left without goodbyes. On her way home, she was more worried than annoyed.

But beyond this she felt something else – something she hadn't felt for a long time.

She shook her head, reprimanding, "Are you nuts!"

Lauren phoned Claire the next morning. "What was that about with the reporter; and why shouldn't I be concerned?"

"Because I'm not. He's on our side and will not put us in jeopardy."

"Claire, forgive me, but isn't that a little naive? He's a reporter! They thrive on offbeat stories, regardless of who gets hurt."

"Lauren – Anne – one thing I'm not is naive."

"Would complacent be a better word? For God's sake, Claire, are you beginning to believe in some mythical shield that protects us from the law?"

"Dan doesn't know your real name. And if he did, he wouldn't use it – or 'Anne' for that matter. Trust me on this, Lauren. He's doing an important piece; something that will expose the hypocrisy that you and I face. With guarantees not to identify his sources, he's interviewed women who've received our services, and police and politicians who take risks by looking the other way."

"Who, besides enjoying your generosity, know we're here when they need us. Hope Mr. Carter doesn't decide to make that his next story."

"Come on Lauren, trust me. I chose to help him on this one. He sent me the proposal before I gave him my permission – with a few stipulations. For one, there will be no reference to you or Carol by name.

"Wait and see," Claire continued. "You will like what he says, and it will be read across the country."

"Esquire? Mostly by men."

"And many women. Besides, let's face it, men not women run the police, legislature, courts – you name it. I hate to say this, but if things are going to change for women, it's going to have to be done by men."

"Maybe you're right, Claire. But things haven't changed, and I don't want this Dan Carter blowing my daughter's future."

"Nor I; you know that. I talked to him, filled him in on our rules – the safety precautions we take. He flew in from New York to talk to people I chose and is leaving tomorrow. You will not be approached."

Claire added, "At least with anything to do with the story. He was certainly asking about you. I gave him absolutely nothing – especially after seeing the look on your face when I mentioned Esquire. As far as he knows, you're a stranger who crashed the party."

"Good. I hope you're right."

"Before hanging up let me add that we'll see the story in next month's issue, and you'll learn that I'm right about him. I think you've forgotten; I've got a good sense about those I choose to work with." Claire's voice lightened. "And I read people well. He certainly likes you. Who knows, you might end-up falling in love with the guy when you see where he's coming from."

"You've just leapt from unlikely to ridiculous." Then Lauren added, "But I'll admit he is kind of cute."

"I knew it; I recognized it when I caught you two on the balcony."

"Oh yeah – 'caught.'"

"Yes, caught. See you Monday."

Before leaving town, Dan phoned Claire.

"About Anne Thompson, the young woman I met last night, can you help me? She's apparently not listed in the phone book. I need a number."

"How'd you learn her last name?" Claire asked. "Oh, never mind how, just don't use it in your story. And sorry Dan, I can't give you her number. But if that article is as good as I know it will be – she might make an exception."

"You're brilliant; what an incentive! It will be good. I'll be back and find out from her if she likes it."

On the same morning that Dan called Claire, Lauren walked her six-month lab, Madeline – nicknamed Maddie – on a trail near her home. Created by hundreds of dogs and their wealthy owners, the trail stretched along a span of wooded property with a view that included downtown Portland, the Willamette River, and Mt. Hood.

Lauren had never gotten used to the luxury of this view: seeing the city without clutter, crowds, or commotion. It was as if perfection came from distance, which living on the hill provided.

However, this morning her mind was elsewhere. She was thinking of the reporter and was smiling! Feeling stupid, she walked fast, trying to put him from her mind.

Releasing Maddie from her leash, she yelled, "Go girl."

Maddie raced ahead, only slowing for side-trips, where she sniffed her way through dense weeds. When Lauren was able to rein her in, they were a good mile from home.

As they walked back, Lauren kept smiling.

Three weeks later the story was in print. And Claire stopped Lauren when she walked into the clinic.

"Dan Carter phoned last night. His story hit the magazine stands yesterday and he's flying to Portland. Asked if I was having a Friday night soiree, and I told him it would be in his honor."

Claire handed Lauren a copy of Esquire. "You're going to love this. He makes us sound like warriors.

"And, his reason for flying here so quickly is pretty clear. I assured him that you will be at the celebration."

Lauren had brought a change of clothes to the clinic, and wore a lilac colored sweater, tucked into the waist of a matching skirt. A single pearl on a thin gold chain accented the curve of her breasts, and she had loosened her chignon so that her red hair fell across her shoulders.

When she arrived, the party was in full swing: Champagne was flowing, guests were talking and laughing. And then she saw him and felt a rush of heat hit her face. He was in the middle of the room surrounded by people, some whom she hadn't seen before at Claire's parties. He was telling a story – enjoying his audience. It was his night.

Lauren thought how this was just one of many. She had done some checking; his articles were often in the New York Times along with numerous other papers and magazines.

As she stepped from the foyer into the living room, he stopped talking and walked toward her.

"Miss Thompson at last; I was beginning to wonder if you weren't coming, rendering my trip a waste."

"That's flattering, but I've never seen Claire's living room this full. And you're the one who's filled it."

"The room was empty till now." He grinned, acknowledging the repartee.

Then he looked at her without smiling. "You're beautiful."

Taking hold of her arm, he steered her toward the balcony. But within seconds they were surrounded, and Lauren slipped away. She walked to the balcony and waited.

Lauren would always remember that evening. But she had a beautiful reminder. Dan wrote a note when he returned to New York. She kept it in a red velvet case that held his letters.

"I saw you standing on the balcony at dusk, back-dropped by the sparkle of early city lights – the lavender of the wisteria that trailed the arbor blending with your high color. I knew that I would make you part of my life."

Chapter Thirteen

Lauren and Dan drove to the Hill Villa, a restaurant built in a wooded area overlooking the Willamette River. They sat at a small table, drinking martinis.

"Anne Thompson, I love you."

"Hmm, just like that. You know nothing about me."

"You're beautiful – exquisite." He reached across the table and touched her lips with his fingers. "The most beautiful woman I have seen. And…."

She interrupted, "Don't. It's too soon."

"Too soon? I've been looking for you my whole life."

"That's flattering." She smiled, and then added, "I won't deny you're tempting. And I love the way I feel right now. But there's no rush."

"No rush! Why do you think I wrote the story and got it to the publisher the day I returned to New York? It was you. When I first saw you, standing in the sun on Claire's balcony, I fell in love."

Lauren shook her head no, but then said, "Truth is, you've been on my mind since that evening, before I read your story – which, by the way, is extraordinary."

"As I said, I was motivat…" A large group entered the room, drowning his words. He waved for the waiter. "Let's get out of here."

Walking from the restaurant, he put his arm around her shoulder. At the car, they kissed. Then, interrupting, a boisterous group roared from the restaurant, laughing and shouting goodbyes, heading toward them.

She whispered, "I feel like a teenager standing here." Ignitions started and headlights glared. "Do you think they'll run over us?"

"Not sure I'd notice."

She laughed and pulled away.

As they drove from the lot she lowered the convertible top and switched on the radio. Frank Sinatra, a new crooner, was singing. Lyrics floated in the air. This is a lovely way to spend an evening. Can't think of anyone as lovely as you.

The music, a breeze touching her face, a night filled with stars – Lauren thought how it was too perfect.

They pulled up at the Benson Hotel and he asked her to come in.

"It's tempting." She took a deep breath. "But I can't. It's not real – not yet."

"Jesus Christ, if this isn't real, then reality doesn't exist. I love you, Anne Thompson, and need you and …"

"Anne Thompson," she repeated. "There's so much you don't know. I've got to go home." She turned the ignition back on, and then faced him. "I have a little girl."

Not commenting, he lit a cigarette.

She sat waiting for a response, thinking she was right. The evening had been too perfect.

He crushed his un-smoked cigarette into the ashtray, then reached over and ran his fingers across her cheek. "So the mystery unfolds. When do I get to meet her?"

She took a deep breath. "Thank you. I'm glad you asked. Call me in the light of day. There's pen and paper in the glove box."

She gave him the number. "You can decide tomorrow if you still want to call."

"Decide? There is no deciding. I can't help myself. I'm in love."

"The power of the night; its magic got us."

"The magic is you. What time do you get up? What about breakfast? Lunch? Dinner under the stars? I'm not leaving Portland till…" He paused – giving weight to what he was about to say, "Until you come with me."

She raised both eyebrows. "Can see why you hesitated on that one." Her expression softened. "Right now we need a strong dose of daylight. Everything is too perfect."

"What a skeptic. That wasn't hesitation. I was searching for a way to tell you the inevitable. You will come with me; it's just a matter of when. " He opened his door, "I'll think about you all night – which is going to be a long one." Stepping from the car, he tried again, "Just one drink?"

"Can't."

"Then tomorrow, seven a. m." He looked at his watch. "I'll be awake, ticking off the minutes till then."

Lauren watched him through the rearview mirror as she pulled away. He pointed to his watch and held up seven fingers.

Lauren woke at five. Unable to sleep, she took Maddie for a walk. As happens in Portland, the clear night had turned into a cloudy morning. It would be a wet day. As always, Maddie sniffed her way along the path, identifying dogs that had left their mark before her. Lauren didn't rush, figuring her day would be too busy for another walk.

Returning home, she showered and took time choosing clothes that would take her into evening. Then, thinking how Dan would call in less than an hour, she decided to invite him for breakfast.

By the time Mary came into the kitchen, Lauren had squeezed fresh orange juice and grated potatoes for pancakes. Mary poured herself a cup of coffee and glanced at the headlines of the paper Lauren had brought in.

"You're up early and wasting no time I see."

"Couldn't sleep and thought I might as well get an early start today," Lauren answered, knowing that little slipped past Mary.

"Hmm, so it seems." She looked at the batter Lauren was mixing. "Going to have Queen Elizabeth for breakfast, are we?"

"Oh, this." Lauren didn't want to lie, but wasn't prepared to mention Dan until he phoned.

"Yes this." Mary said. "Perhaps you're remembering that Sandi goes to ballet this morning, and you want to get her off with a nice full stomach."

"Oh no, you're right. It's Saturday!" She looked at the clock; it was almost seven. "Hmm. The pancakes might be a little much before class."

Knowing she wasn't making sense, Lauren took a breath and poured Mary a glass of orange juice. "Did you sleep well?"

"I did, thank you. What a luxury, that bed of mine. I heard you take Maddie out this morning. Instead of getting up I just laid there enjoying the plush warmth – a long way from my home in Dublin." She sipped the orange juice and then added, "Been thinking about my sisters lately. Would love to have them come here, or..."

"That would be wonderful." Lauren spoke without enthusiasm; she was listening for the phone to ring. And it did. It was exactly seven.

Surprising Lauren, Mary rushed to answer. "What a coincidence; my sister's calling earlier than usual."

Lauren followed her, feeling helpless.

"A good day to you," Mary's accent was thick.

But as she listened, her expression changed. "There is no Anne Thompson at this number."

"Here, Mary, it's for me." Lauren ignored her withering look, and took the phone. "Dan?"

"Yes; but it sounds like I've reached Ireland." He chuckled, "This is Anne Thompson. Correct?"

"Not exactly. Hmm – if we meet, I'll tell you."

"If? Ah – the cold light of day. Of course, we'll meet. I'll catch a cab and pick you up for breakfast within the hour."

Her voice lightened, "Let's make that lunch, and I'll pick you up. I've got to take Sandi, my girl, to ballet lessons."

"Sandra – a nice name and a student of ballet. Now, tell me, who is the not-too-friendly woman who answered the phone."

Lauren spoke softly, "That's Mary, Sandi's grandmother. I was going to have you here for breakfast, but it's best we go out. I've got lots to tell you. Why don't I pick you up at 11:30?"

"I'll be waiting in front of the hotel."

Lauren walked back to the kitchen and faced Mary, who had returned to the nook and was writing.

"Mary, you heard me talking on the phone."

Mary didn't look up, "Yes, to the man who calls you Anne Thompson."

"Today he'll learn my real name. I just met him – and…"

Mary looked up. "You met him at your work – and he called here?"

"No, Mary, I didn't meet him at the clinic. I – well – I met him, okay? And he's quite extraordinary. But there's so much he doesn't know about me." Lauren stopped, and shook her head, "I can't tell you much, as I have so much to learn…"

Lauren poured coffee and sat across the table from Mary.

"I don't know where this is going; if it's going anywhere. It's the first time I've even considered seeing someone since… well you know… since Ben."

Mary's expression changed to concern. "But why does he know you by that name?"

"Mary, there's so much you and I don't talk about and I respect that. Just believe me; he's not part of the clinic. But he knows me as Anne. That will change if I plan on seeing him more."

Mary squinted as if studying the situation. "Lauren, I know there's a world that I'm closely connected to but have refused to acknowledge… while… well you know what I'm thinking.

"That aside, I respect you. And," Mary paused, "I have known that this would happen – that you would meet someone. You are still in your twenties. Young. And I needn't tell you to be careful. You have waited. This man must be special, because you are."

Lauren was touched. They had lived together for over seven years, and Mary seldom complimented her.

"Thank you, Mary. I will be careful; you and Sandi are my reasons."

Later in the morning, when Lauren and Sandi returned home from the ballet class, a dozen roses were on the dining room table. She pulled the card from its envelope and read: To Anne – my future. Dan.

Having flown from the steamy heat of New York, Dan hadn't prepared for Portland. His light windbreaker soaked up rain as he stood waiting in front of the hotel. Seeing Lauren, he thumbed for a ride.

She pulled to the curb, then reached across the seat and opened the door.

He poked his head in, "Would a lady offer a fellow American a dime?"

Lauren laughed – on one of their Sundays out, she and Mary had seen Treasure of Sierra Madre.

"Hop in, Bogart."

She pulled into traffic. "What kind of food?"

"Doesn't matter; as long as we're in from the rain, and they offer a good Pinot.

She drove to Thiele's. Mrs. Thiele greeted them, asking Lauren if they wanted her regular table. But Dan suggested the bar, and Lauren chose a booth by a window.

"I suggest the light of day, this morning. It can be quite sobering."

Dan laughed, and ordered a bottle of Pinot Noir. Then, while waiting, he told her about his night.

"I couldn't sleep after you left, so I went to the bar and met a couple of guys who were racing sailboats from Portland to Astoria. Would like to do a story on sailing the Columbia; a great way to combine work with pleasure. Have you sailed?

She shook her head. "No; can't swim."

"We'll remedy that."

"Oh, we will."

"Yes: we. If you don't feel it now, you will." He studied her; then added, "You have to; it's right and it's real."

"Real? Not exactly. You don't know anything about me."

"I know that you're the most beautiful woman I have ever seen and …"

The barmaid approached their table and smiled. "Here, toast the most beautiful woman with this." She winked at Lauren, then filled their glasses and set the bottle on the table.

Dan picked up the glass. "To the most…"

Lauren laughed, "Enough!"

Sipping the wine, it was tempting to relax – let everything happen as it would. But she had come with a purpose.

"Are you ready?"

"For anything."

"Time to introduce myself," she said. "I told you I have a daughter, Sandi – the most important person in my life."

He listened without interrupting.

"It's hard, but here I go: Two lives in-a-nutshell. Her father is Ben. He and I met in grade school."

Holding emotions tight, she spoke without a break. Until the end, when her eyes filled with tears.

"We spent a weekend at the beach before he shipped out; planned on getting married when he returned on leave. He was killed within months – six months before I gave birth to Sandi."

Seeing the concern on Dan's face, she dried her eyes and took a sip of wine. She hadn't intended to share pain.

Changing directions, she asked, "Did you serve?"

"I worked for the Associated Press on the European front: War Correspondent. Last assignment was the Battle of the Bulge. It was bad, but I didn't experience what you did." He reached for her hand.

"I'm sorry. I haven't talked about him for a long time." She stopped, wanting to avoid more tears. "I appreciate your concern."

"Appreciate," he repeated. "I'm not just a sympathetic listener."

She withdrew her hand from his, and sipped wine. "There's more; a lot more. Perhaps we should wait till…"

"You don't have to tell me anything. You've been in my thoughts from the first time I saw you. I know you think I'm half-lunatic and one-hundred percent impulsive, but I've never felt like this about anyone before. There is nothing you could say that would take away what I feel. Even if you told me to go take a leap off the Empire State Building, I couldn't stop. I'm in love, and you, Anne, and…"

She put her hand out, stopping him. "I'm not Anne! That's the name I use at the clinic. From your article I couldn't tell if you knew I work with Claire. I'm an abortionist: One of the people you wrote about. My real name is Lauren Martin. I changed it to protect Sandi from repercussions from my work."

"Those who call me Anne are connected to the clinic. But I'm Lauren to friends and family. I keep it this way, and it hasn't caused any problem yet. But then, I haven't gone out with anyone since Ben died. I live with his mother and Sandi, and we keep our lives quite separate from the clinic.

"So, there it is. What I needed to tell you. And don't say you don't give a hoot, that's too easy and probably not true."

He appeared to be contemplating: then said, "All right."

"All right, what?"

"All right, I won't say I don't give a hoot, whatever that means. You ready for some lunch?"

After they ordered, Lauren said, "So, say something."

"Okay, even if you assume I don't know what I'm talking about. Lauren," he emphasized her name, "I know how I feel and can't be dissuaded. In fact, my repertoire of emotions is expanding. I'm intrigued.

"And about your comment, yes, I knew about Anne Thompson. I had given my word to Claire and didn't refer to you in the story. Now, tell me more. Like how did you get into the abortion business?"

"I had gone to a year of nursing school before Sandi. After she was born I worked here at Thiele's. Claire was a customer, and she asked me to come to see her about a job. There you have it. Except, I should add that I believe in what I do – for all the reasons you stated in the article."

Dan looked at her, studying; then nodded, "You're right. I didn't really know you. Guess you thought you could get rid of me easily, but it has backfired. You're not only beautiful; you're independent, smart, and courageous."

"Hmm," Lauren frowned. "Since you have a stubborn mindset, let me tell you something more. If it doesn't scare you away, then you're the one with courage. I have thought about you way too much since the night of Claire's party. I'm not sure what's happening but you are – well, what can I say – some kind of force to be reckoned with." She hesitated, then added, "Quite simply, I feel happy, but in a nervous way. Maybe it's fear. Fear that you might find a relationship much easier to start than to end."

"There won't be an end."

This time she reached over and touched his lips. "You have been warned."

Their food came, but they ate little. He asked, and she described Sandi. Then he told her about New York City.

"Other than Central Park, little is green, few birds fly, the moon can't be seen, there's lots of noise, fumes, bright lights, and crowds, and people are rude – able to walk past tragedy without stopping. And I love it; every part of it and want to take you there."

They finished the wine and he left money for the bill. "Let's get out of here."

The phone rang at seven. Lauren answered; her voice slightly groggy. "It's me."

"You escaped," he said.

"It was harder than you can imagine. I almost woke you, but you looked so peaceful."

"I was dreaming that I was with the love of my life. Come back."

"Why don't you come over here? I'll make the potato pancakes I started – back when? My God, it was only yesterday."

"I'll call a cab," he said. What time?"

"Give me a couple of hours to get Sandi and Mary up. You still have the directions?"

"Memorized."

Dan gave the driver her address and looked out the window. The rain had stopped and steam rose from scoured streets, evaporating into the clearing sky. The route was the same as to Claire's house; past Vista with its lush lawns and tree-lined sidewalks, and uphill to Fairmont, which wound past mansions.

The driver pulled up to a white picket fence.

"This is the address, Sir." He addressed him with more deference than when he had picked him up.

Dan stepped out and reached for his wallet.

"Five dollars, Sir."

"Ouch!" That wasn't what the meter indicated, but Dan handed it to him, figuring it was the price paid when visiting the top of the world.

He opened the gate and walked into an English garden, with its mélange of color. Patches of flowers spread between lush shrubs and blossoming shade trees; roses, sweet peas, and veronica climbed an arbor. Cushioned benches had been placed in shaded nooks. And hummingbirds zipped in and out of their wooden home as he approached the front porch.

If this was the correct address, Lauren resided in a four thousand square-foot Cape Cod – white with beige trim, surrounded by a private park. It occurred to him that he hadn't mentioned the lucrative side of abortion in his story.

He rang the bell and heard barking – then Lauren, "It's all right, girl."

The bark stopped and she answered the door, looking as radiant as the surroundings. "You're here." She was smiling and reached for his hand. "Come in."

Maddie stood, her head cocked, watching.

"This is Madeline; a member of the family. She seldom sees men at this door."

She turned to Maddie. "It's okay, Girl. This is a very special man."

As if permission had been given, Madeline bounced across the room and picked up a ball.

Lauren shook her head, "Later, Girl." Then she squeezed Dan's hand, "Come to the kitchen and meet Sandi."

"Wait." He looked back at the luxurious yard, "This is a long way from New York – even from Portland Oregon. Where am I?"

"I told you I keep my life separate. You, Dan Carter, have been invited to our – my, Mary, and Sandi's – retreat. Come on in."

She led him to the kitchen. Sandi was on a stool mixing a batter of muffins, and had smudges of blueberries on her lips. She turned, and then looked puzzled: her mother was holding a man's hand – a stranger.

He caught the look and asked Lauren, "So this is the chef, now where is the daughter I came to meet?"

"Chef Sandra, meet Dan."

Sandi giggled and the tension was gone.

Lauren poured coffee as he sat at the table in the nook – with its background of city, river, and mountain.

"Nice," he said, with an exaggerated squint, "A view of the world."

He watched Lauren put on an apron and pull eggs and milk from the refrigerator.

Within minutes Mary came into the room. In spite of her losses, Mary had weathered well. Her skin was fair, with few wrinkles and there was no gray in her dark brown hair. As often, she quickly proved her quick wit.

Sandi asked, "Grandma, guess what we're having for breakfast?"

"Company," Mary answered.

Sandi put her stained hand on her hip. "Guess what we're really having for breakfast."

Mary walked over and looked into the bowl. "Looks like Blue Bird Pudding to me."

Then, turning toward Dan, she smiled, "As you just heard, I'm Sandi's grandmother, Mary Sullivan."

She picked up the coffee pot and poured a cup for herself, then walked over and added to his. "It's a lovely day after yesterday's rain. I'm going to drink this outside. Would you join me?"

Dan followed her onto the deck, which ran the length of the house. A telescope was fastened to the railing but seemed superfluous on a clear day. He could see for miles.

Lauren watched Mary use her charm on Dan, with Maddie lying next to them, and Sandi dishing spoonfuls of batter into the muffin pan. It was the first time Lauren understood how it felt to have her heart dance.

Chapter Fourteen

"Careful" was one of the words that described Dan and Lauren's relationship that year.

Lauren would not stay overnight because of Sandi, so they spent late afternoons or evenings at hotels where Dan stayed. She called their meetings "trysts," enjoying the idea of being secreted away – just the two of them.

During time away from him she could feel his touch, and more than once would head toward the phone before it rang – Dan calling to say he loved her. Whenever possible he would fly to Portland on weekends. But when work kept him away, he phoned at least twice a day.

As the months passed, Lauren grew to appreciate everything about him. He was bright, articulate, talented, and funny – qualities she loved; the same qualities that placed him in demand as a journalist.

Sometimes when he stepped from the plane he looked tired, and she wished he could come home with her. He could sit on the patio, take walks with Maddie, grab a beer from the fridge, and linger at the table over Sunday's paper after sleeping late – next to her. She began to consider buying another home, just for them. The time was right; the country was prospering; and Lauren was rich.

The lifestyle her money provided would be difficult to walk away from; which she intended to do before Sandi was much older. Knowing this, she started making investments – especially in real-estate. Portland was growing and housing was limited.

Thinking of Dan's love of sailing she checked out property on Sauvie Island, off of the Columbia River. It was a short ferry ride to highways that went directly to downtown Portland. And a bridge was already being planned, so before long the island would be much more accessible.

Lauren bought a large acreage of land with a quarter mile of river beachfront. Then, with Maddie padding along, she plotted where everything would be: their home, garden, path to the beach, and dock for the boat Dan would buy.

Dan had been away for a month – the longest time they had been separated – doing a story on Senator Joseph McCarthy. His phone calls to Lauren were full of anger over the direction America appeared to be heading. Freedom of speech was seriously threatened. Dan and other critics were being labeled Communist sympathizers.

On the afternoon of his arrival, Lauren waited impatiently at the Portland airport. He was among the first off the plane and she studied him as he walked toward the entrance. He looked tired – too solemn. For a fleeting moment she was frightened: afraid that things would change.

But when he saw her, he smiled. Almost running, she met him.

"Love of my life, I've missed you." It was his usual greeting, but she felt a difference. And as they walked toward the car, he told her he could only stay for the weekend.

She felt his intensity as they made love. Afterwards, whispering that he couldn't get enough of her, he pulled her back. Later as they lay close, she wished she could hold onto time.

It was dark when they went downstairs for dinner. The Heathman had the dignity of a grand historical hotel: elegant with burgundy upholstered furniture, dark hardwood floors, and worn but rich oriental rugs.

Starting with a bottle of Pinot Noir, she offered the toast, "To afternoons just like today."

They sipped from the wine, and then she decided it was time to tell him about Sauvie Island. "There's something special that I've been waiting to share."

His expression surprised her, and she shook her head. "No, Dan. If it were what you're thinking, I'm not quite certain how I'd tell you. But from the look on your face, I'd know to do it with care."

He chuckled and reached for her hand. "What can I say? The truth is, Lauren, I would be happy. No, ecstatic is a better word. You're the only one I want as the mother of my child."

Weaving her fingers through his, she sat quietly before saying, "What I have to tell you has somewhat shrunk in importance. I have bought us a piece of land on Sauvie Island, on the Columbia. I believe it's perfect for us, and you'll be pleased. It's so we'll have our own place when you're in town."

He looked at her, troubled, and she stopped.

"What?"

He shook his head. "I had lots to tell you also – and to ask."

The waiter interrupted; taking an inordinate amount of time serving.

"First, before all," Dan continued, "I want us to marry. It's time. I want to be with you for the rest of my life, and I want to be with Sandi. No more leaving at night. Another home? Yes; but in New York. I want you there when I return from assignments."

"Wait." She held up her hand. "I'm still registering the word 'marry.' My God, Dan, I love you. And maybe that's… Have you really thought about this?"

"No. I just propose when I see beautiful women, and you are the most beautiful I've ever seen. What the hell do you think? Of course, I've thought about it. I've thought about it from the first time I met you."

She didn't answer. There was more to say, but not now.

Instead, as they ate she shifted gear and told him a Sandi story.

"During share-time Sandi told the class 'my best friend, Dan, doesn't like bad men who want to hurt Communists.' Mrs. Grady, her teacher, said Sandi actually pronounced it correctly. But when one of the kids asked what a Communist was, Sandi said – 'it's someone who has parties.'"

Dan smiled, "That class is getting an interesting education."

"Yeah, Mrs. Grady felt it was best to just let her definition be. She wasn't quite ready to teach Communist Manifesto to third graders."

After dinner they moved to the bar, where a jazz quartet was doing its rendition of World War II ballads. The music, wine, his hand touching hers – she said, "Dan, I want nothing more than to marry you."

"That sounds as if it's going to be followed with a 'however'."

"My God, Dan, do you have any idea how much I love you – everything about you. I'm scared, because somewhere in the back of my mind I'm afraid that feeling this happy can't last forever. Of course, I'll marry you; and everyday I'll hope that what we have never changes one tiny bit."

"It will," he said. "It will just keep getting better. You and Sandi will come to New York. It's my headquarters; I need to be there and want you with me."

"New York," Lauren repeated, thinking of Sandi – moving her from home and school. And there was Claire…

Dan was watching her, waiting; but she skirted an answer. "For now I want you to see Sauvie Island. It's a beautiful spot, and one that will be for us – our get-away – even if we live in New York."

"If," he shook his head. "We will live in New York. Selfishly, I want you there when I come home from assignments. But this Island sounds nice. I'd like to see it."

"You will tomorrow, after our day with Sandi, but before dark. I want to start creating our path down to the river."

His expression surprised her; something was wrong.

"Sounds good, but I catch the plane out of here tomorrow at ten a.m."

"That soon?"

"I should have told you sooner. On Thursday I fly to Pusan, on the southern tip of Korea. In a nutshell, this is where General MacArthur's troops are holding on in an effort to save the South from occupation by the North. Monday, after inoculations, I'll start receiving briefings from the military."

"Oh, my God!" She looked at him, stunned. "What if I said don't go?"

"I wouldn't. You come first and always will. But it's an exciting assignment. It's a job I'm qualified for." He paused, "And should do."

She shook her head no, and then said, "Of course you'll go. How long will you be gone?"

"Don't worry about me; I'll come back to you. I'll be protected by U.S. Marines – they don't come tougher than that. Time there? At least six weeks, but with you here, I won't spend a minute longer than needed."

Before leaving for Korea, Dan's piece on Senator Joseph McCarthy hit the stands. He wrote of McCarthy gaining his senate seat through inflated claims about his WWII record. And now he was gaining his power through claims that were faulty.

Dan's last paragraph read: "In a country where Communists are being described as conspirators, defectors, and traitors we should not forget that Socialism and Communism are political parties, based on belief; and that our Constitution guarantees each of us the right to believe as we choose."

Within several months of the article, Lauren wrote Dan:

"I know you are aware that Senator McCarthy just gave a speech naming 205 supposed Communist in the State Department, and some commentators have said that he's started a political storm. The effects of this seem to have brought out every conservative in the country. And they aren't just after Communists. They're after everyone they don't approve of. That, of course, includes abortionists."

As Lauren parked in front of Claire's house, she thought how there were no other cars, even though it was Friday evening: A statement of how their world was changing.

Claire met her at the door and they walked past the front room and into the kitchen.

"Look at this place, it's deserted." Claire said, as she poured two glasses of wine. "As you know, over the years I quit needing to invite anyone. Those I wanted at my parties just showed-up. When they stopped coming, I phoned a few, and got excuses of other engagements, sick relatives. You know! And Chief – he hasn't been around either. I could expect it of most, but not him."

This confirmed Lauren's long-time feelings. The whole bunch of them had been using Claire; enjoying the excitement of evenings at an infamous abortionist's home. Now, with everybody under scrutiny, their 'friendship' with Claire wasn't worth the risk.

Claire lit a cigarette and took a deep drag – letting it out slowly.

"Go ahead and say what you're thinking, Lauren. The so-called friends were a goddamn bunch of cockroaches who no longer recognize me when we pass on the street." She crushed out the cigarette, "But one thing has been made clear: they're not coming here is a symptom of the times – and a huge warning to us."

Lauren nodded. "I agree and have felt it big-time at the clinic. There's a shroud of secrecy that is so much greater than in the past. I'm worry about Sandi."

"I know the feeling. Poor Jane's already been through tough times; she doesn't need more. And the grandkids..." She didn't finish the sentence.

"Your grandkids, my Sandi. . . we're both thinking the same thing." Lauren didn't hesitate –"It's time to get out."

Claire didn't answer, and it was difficult to read her, but Lauren continued, "Heaven knows we have enough money to take care of us for the rest of our lives."

"Lauren, you know as well as I, that's it's not just money. Every one of those women needs us, especially the young ones – the girls. If we close our doors, who will they go to? You know what it's like to turn anyone down."

"Yes, but I also know that my daughter comes first. I always said I would quit at the time I felt my work threatened her." Lauren felt a chill, "I'm afraid... so afraid... that the time is already passed."

Claire's voice was weak, "Perhaps it has."

Lauren was nervous about every knock on the clinic door. She wanted to quit totally, but the demand was constant. She stopped accepting more than five patients a day, and they were young girls whose lives would be devastated by pregnancy. Many of them couldn't pay, but that had never deterred her or Claire.

Claire was having less success in limiting patients. Since the early 1930's she had been dedicated to helping women, and she had a hard time turning them away. As Lauren cut back, Claire's days grew longer.

They were riding on luck, as their clinic remained untouched though other "vice" in Portland, especially gambling, was under siege. Lauren heard about other abortionists being arrested throughout the country. Screening of patients became more important. She, Claire, and Carol feared being set-up for a raid.

Chapter Fifteen

"I'm going to do it again," Claire announced to Carol and Lauren. "Next week, after a small ceremony, Bill and I are taking off for my ranch."

Lauren felt dumbstruck. She hadn't paid much attention to Bill – figuring he was Claire's way of getting over Chief.

"Claire, tell me you're kidding."

"Don't look so shocked. It's only my fourth – and it just might work." Her voice went flat, and she shook her head. "Oh well, I usually enjoy the honeymoon."

Lauren understood Claire: flip lines covered a lot of worry. Feeling a flood of love, she gave her a hug and said, "I'll order a cake and champagne for the ceremony."

The week Claire honeymooned, Lauren was busier than usual. She was still with a patient at six p.m. when Carol stepped into the surgery room saying that Mary had just phoned.

Lauren was frightened. Mary had never called before. She had gone back to attending mass. But she didn't talk about it – or about Lauren's clinic.

"I'll get the phone. But I need you to stay with Doris; she needs to rest for at least thirty minutes."

Carol walked over and rubbed the girl's forehead. "Of course. She'll be fine."

Lauren stripped off her glove and hurried to the phone.

Mary was succinct, "We need you here right away."

"What's happening? Tell me."

"You have to be here. It's something that can't be handled over the phone."

Lauren hung up and told Carol she had to leave.

"Go! Our girl is doing fine. Her friend will be picking her up within the next hour and – well, you know the procedure. I'll make certain she gets to the car safely. Don't worry."

Lauren was out of the clinic and home within twenty minutes.

They sat on the couch. Sandi, her eyes red and swollen, scrunched against Mary.

"What?" Lauren asked, while sitting next to Sandi.

"Some kids at school were teasing her today – about you," Mary said.

"What!" Lauren felt her heart drop, as she reached to pull Sandi to her.

Sandi stiffened; her voice was muffled by tears, "They said bad things. They're mean and liars. Especially Jamie, I hate her."

Again, Lauren reached for her, and this time Sandi relented.

Angry, Mary watched; then stood and left the room, shaking her head.

"Jamie said you kill babies." Sandi looked up to read Lauren, looking for shock and anger – for denial.

Lauren felt both shock and anger as she searched for words. "Sandi, you're right, those are mean things to say. And Jamie's wrong."

Sandi stopped crying and moved away from Lauren – wide-eyed.

"She told Nancy that you take babies out of mothers' stomachs and you throw them away."

"Sandi: that is wrong! So wrong."

Lauren's mind raced – there was little she could say that Sandi would understand.

"Sandi, listen to me carefully. Nancy said a horrible and untrue thing. You know that I would never do such a thing. I help people. Someday, when you're a little older we'll talk; but for now, you must trust me when I say I would never hurt a baby."

"Will you call Jamie's mother? She's told Jamie you put them in the garbage." Sandi's lip quivered, "She hates you."

"I'll take care of things, Sandi." Lauren knew this was inadequate. In fact, she was overwhelmed. No answer could be good enough to satisfy Sandi – she was too young.

"How? It's not just Jamie. Other kids said things, and Gail told me her mother doesn't like you and won't let me come to her house again – even for her birthday party."

Lauren told herself to breathe, as she lifted Sandi's chin and met her eyes. "Sandi, listen carefully. When anyone hurts you, she hurts me. And as I said, what those girls and their mothers are saying is wrong. I spend my days helping people; never hurting them."

Sandi looked so small and young.

"How?" she asked, and then backed from Lauren – challenging, needing the right answer.

Lauren decided to be as open as possible. If that didn't work – she'd have to help Sandi be strong; not easy, when you're only eight.

Lauren enunciated each word. "Honey you must believe me. I would never hurt a living breathing baby – never. What Jamie's mother said is not true; it simply isn't." She pulled Sandi close, "Please, Sweetheart, trust me on this."

Hugging her, she searched for more to say. But nothing came to her. Sandi was too young to understand. Lauren thought how she needed time to think – to find the best way to help her. But for now, she needed to get her through the night – and past the pain she was suffering.

"Sandi, let's try to do something different. Let's have a special evening. We both need it. Whatever you want to do, we'll do. We could go to the Carnival Restaurant and buy a double-chocolate malt and burger?"

"I don't really want to go. What if someone I know is there?"

"If they are, you say hello and so will I. They're wrong, Sandi – and not worth one tiny tear of yours. But if you don't want to go, that's all right. I'll make you the biggest and best milkshake you've ever tasted, right here. Come on and help me."

They got through the evening: cooking, eating, even half-heartedly playing a game of monopoly – pretending a dark cloud wasn't hovering over them. It was after eleven when Sandi climbed into bed.

As Lauren started to leave her room, Sandi asked, "Do I have to go to school tomorrow?"

"No Sweetheart. But we'll see how you feel in the morning, okay?" Lauren walked back to her bed and kissed her again; knowing it wouldn't be an easy night.

Then she walked to the kitchen where Mary was waiting.

"Of the tragedies in my life this stands out as one of the worst," Mary said. Then added, her eyes flashing, "And you were warned."

"Mary, don't! I ache for Sandi. But the tragedy lies in the narrow attitudes of…"

"Narrow attitudes!" Mary erupted. "What world do you live in? I find this incredible. You don't see that this whole thing is a tragedy that was waiting to happen! And you were well aware of it."

Lauren's voice rose above hers "Stop!" She took a deep breath. "What good is arguing going to do now, except make things worse. I know what you believe, and I…" Lauren felt tears rising, and held them back. "Oh Mary, I don't want to get into this with you. We each know how we believe, and this is not the time to deal with it."

Lauren slumped into a chair, exhausted. But she continued talking – feeling her way through what needed to be said. "Sandi is hurting, and the important thing now is to figure a way to help her get through this – help her gain defenses." Lauren continued, as if to herself. "I don't want her to grow up thinking anything those girls said was right. And I don't want her to believe I – and importantly she has done anything to merit their behavior."

Mary started to speak, and Lauren put her hand out. "Don't, Mary." Lauren sighed, "The irony is that I was getting ready to quit the practice. It was time. The country is changing, and I was quitting in spite of the need that's always…"

"Lauren you've said enough; now let me talk. As you just said, you know how I feel about abortion, and you obviously don't care. But I'm glad you're finally quitting that place – for whatever reasons. Just sorry it wasn't sooner.

"And you're right; this isn't the time to discuss that. Harm has been done, and you can't rationalize that it hasn't.

"Now listen to me; I'm going to suggest something and hope you will hear me out. And remember that this is only suggested as a temporary arrangement – something to take Sandi away from all this."

Before Lauren could protest, Mary rushed on. "As you know I've been exchanging letters with two of my sisters in Ireland. They continually ask me to visit. Perhaps this is the time to go, and I mean with Sandi. She could meet her Irish cousins, while you take care of what needs to be done over here. Then we'll return. At that time, we should consider options for Sandi; perhaps moving out of the area."

Lauren knew there was merit in what Mary was saying but shook her head. "No. I have never been away from Sandi, and Ireland is out of the question. It's too far." She rubbed her eyes. "You know something; I don't want to talk anymore tonight. Quite honestly, I'm too tired to think straight."

But Lauren didn't sleep. Instead she went over every part of the evening. And then she thought about Mary's suggestion. Perhaps her answer had been too quick. It was almost summer – this could be a vacation; one Sandi needed right now.

In the morning she told Mary that her plan had merit.

They talked until Sandi woke, and by the time she came downstairs it had been decided. Lauren would buy roundtrip air tickets to New York, then, as no transatlantic planes flew out of New York to Ireland, she would make reservations for Sandi and Mary to sail. She would also transfer money into Mary's checking for her to set-up a temporary account in Dublin. Most important, within weeks of their arrival, Lauren would join them. Perhaps Dan would come along, and they would all take a trip through Ireland.

"And Mary, when we return to Portland, I will leave the clinic." She didn't add that she was hoping Claire would agree to closing it. "We can sell our house; we'll talk about that.

"Dan hopes we'll join him in New York. And I mean 'we.' You'll have a house close to us; one Sandi can walk to. I have the money to always provide for you."

Mary gave her a sharp look. "We – including Sandi – are paying a high price for that money."

Lauren winced, but this time she said nothing.

"Am I going with Grandma so I won't have to see Jamie and her friends? I don't want to go unless you're with us. I'll go to school here; I don't care what they say."

Lauren wrapped her arms around Sandi. "And I don't like that you're leaving without me, but I'll be there within weeks. Meanwhile you'll get to meet Grandma's sisters, your great aunts and their grandchildren, your cousins. You'll get to see where Grandma was born and the house where she grew-up. It'll be a fun trip for you – a vacation. Then, when we come back things will be different, I promise."

"They will?" Sandi's eyes were trusting. "Are you going to call their mothers?"

Lauren hugged her. "Don't worry; I'll take care of things."

After being in Korea for over a month, Dan returned to New York to finish a piece about the possibility of withdrawing all forces below the 38th parallel. A focal point of massive attacks, he knew that one strong push from the North would derail plans of armistice, outdating his story.

After Lauren's phone call about Sandi, he worked through the night. In the morning he delivered the piece to his editor, and then boarded the first plane to Portland.

Ten hours later Lauren stood watching as he walked across the tarmac. And Sandi ran to meet him as he entered the airport.

He caught her in his arms. "You drive here alone today?"

"Yes. Mom said she was too busy."

"Too busy, huh. Well she'll be sorry. Those who come to meet me get presents."

Sandi beamed. "Where? Let's see."

He put her down, pulled a small package from his jacket pocket and handed it to her as Lauren walked up.

"Ah ha, you weren't being exactly truthful," he chided, then reached for Lauren's hand.

Sandi ripped off the wrappings of the package, and opened a white satin box.A delicate ballerina appeared, twirling to the music of Swan Lake. She was an inch tall and crafted in ivory with exquisite detail. Sandi's eyes glowed.

He looked at Lauren, "I've missed you – both of you."

"I am so thankful you are here. Come home, we need you with us."

On the following Tuesday, Lauren and Dan watched as Pan Am took off, flying Mary and Sandi to New York, where they would board the Queen Mary for a five-day cruise to England, before ferrying to Dublin.

"I can't believe this is happening. I wanted to yell 'no – you're not going.'"

"I know." Dan was solemn.

Lauren studied his face. Since arriving home he had been cool to Mary but said nothing.

"What is it, Dan?" He didn't answer, but she knew. "You're right. I shouldn't have let her go. The decision was made too fast, and it's the most important one I've ever had to make."

He put his arm around her and they walked to the car.

Arriving home, they entered by way of the kitchen. Sandi's stool at the counter loomed large. Lauren felt an ominous sense of loss.

"Since deciding she could go, I've tried to believe it's the best thing for her. Besides I've got it planned. No cruise for us. We'll board the new flight from Gander and go straight to Belfast – making it to Dublin within days of their arrival."

Dan didn't speak but looked troubled.

"I read what you're thinking. But Dan, I will be with her within weeks." Emphasizing will, made her words less positive. She repeated, "I mean I really will be there."

This sounded worse. Trying to shrug away the ominous feeling, she walked over and kissed Dan on his cheek.

"Thank God you're here with me. By the way have I ever thanked you for how wonderful you are with Sandi?"

"Thanked me! It's clear you don't understand how I feel about her."

Maddie interrupted with two barks, her usual call to be let in. Dan opened the patio door and was greeted by a jig of wiggles and jumps.

Lauren smiled at the scene. "I certainly have a good idea, and again thank you – for being you."

Later he sat at the table, watching Lauren move about the kitchen. She had tied her red hair into a ponytail and strands had fallen free. An early summer had added a few light freckles to the high color of her complexion, and her short skirt accented the length and curve of her legs. He thought how she didn't fit any mold but her own; there was no one like her.

She poured coffee and set out a plate of fruits and rolls, then sat across from him.

"There's so much I need to do in a short time. I want to leave now – bring her back."

She felt a shiver. "My God, everything has changed."

"Not everything." He said. "One thing hasn't – no two – three, as-a-matter-of-fact."

"Three?"

"Yes. First, you are the smartest and most beautiful woman I have ever known. Second, I love you. And third I want us to get married."

"Do you know what you'd be taking on right now?"

"Is this another stall tactic?"

"Stall? It's fear; afraid you'll take a realistic look at what I'm facing in the next few months – and adios."

"Realistic? Lauren, I know what you're facing; I want you and Sandi with me in New York. And I want to marry you, now."

"And I know how lucky I am. After we get Sandi, you name the date."

"No. Now, before we go to Ireland. I want us to be a family when we go. I want the two of you to come live with me. I'll find a larger place in Manhattan – one near Central Park, where you and Sandi can run Maddie. You'll love New York, and New York will love you."

"New York's a million miles from my life, but it's more than that." She hesitated. "Everything is changing; not just my world, but yours – I really mean ours. I haven't said anything, but before last week and all that's happened, I started worrying about us. When you're gone, I know that your life is totally different from mine. I, along with millions of others, read your work: Korea – war – world politics. I'm always proud of you, but there's a part of me that shrinks, intimidated – frightened about where I fit."

"Frightened? You? I'm the one who should be afraid. Each time I arrive and see you at the airport, radiant and beautiful – all eyes on you, I ask myself what I've ever done to deserve you. No one, nothing – no person, award, money could mean as much to me. You're perfect and the love of my life."

"See? That's it! You say these things that worry me. No one else has ever called me perfect, and it's only a matter of time till you see the real me." She broke into a smile and walked to him. "You're right – we better marry soon, before that happens."

She kissed him. "Are we nuts?"

"Yes. Let's marry now while we're nuts. I want you as part of my life – forever. We'll never settle into routine; you know that. I'm never certain where my next assignment will take me. Selfishly, I want to have you waiting when I come home."

"A nice thought; I've had practice and know what it's like each time you arrive. But this would be different. I have always been independent. Housewife?" She made a face. "Normally I couldn't imagine myself in that role. However and quite honestly, it's a good plan for now. I want to be home for Sandi – at least for a few years. The idea of becoming both full-time mother and wife is rather appealing. Yes, I would like that."

"It's settled. We'll marry right away. Then you and I will get Sandi; bring her here – just long enough for the three of you, that includes Maddie, to prepare for the move to New York.

"I begged time off after you phoned about Sandi, even though things have been insane over there. An armistice isn't even going to make it to the table. The North isn't about to stop its push into the South, and UN forces aren't going to give-up until they do.

"No one ever accused me of being a nice guy. I'll have to leave right away after flying back from Ireland. I don't have much of a choice. I committed to the story when I first went over. And they need me. My Korean has picked up. I know when I'm being cussed at."

She didn't smile. "You like the challenge, and I wouldn't want you to change. Not to say that I don't hate it when you're that far away and in the middle of a war.

"But about New York, I'm concerned. That will take some planning. I know I need to leave the clinic right away, but I worry about Claire. I've just taken six days off, and she's taken my patients. I'm in the process of quitting, but it will take a little time. When I return tomorrow, girls – too young and desperate – will be waiting.

"I will quit, and I mean soon – by the time Sandi returns home." Lauren stretched her neck, trying to relieve tension. "Claire and I have talked about closing the office before. Now with Sandi at risk, decisions have to be made quickly. I'll talk to Claire tomorrow. It's not going to be easy, I can't just walk away."

Dan shook his head. "I think you can and should – and so should Claire. Things are changing across America. Politicians are winning with promises to clean up the cities; especially here in Portland with your mayor, Dorothy McCullough Lee. Portlanders may be jeering 'Do-Good Dottie,' but she's grabbing positive headlines across the country. It's just a matter of time till abortion gets hit. In short, it's time for you to get out – now."

"I know you're right and I will as quickly as possible. But I have to think of Claire. She's been like family and is my best friend. Besides, I owe her. This house – everything I own – is because of her. She trusted me, included me in her world. Now we need to work this out together."

"Lauren, it isn't instinct that tells me you have to get out of there – it's reality. You don't have the luxury of waiting."

"Tomorrow, Claire and I will talk. She's ready to close." Lauren looked worried, "But I haven't even told her that I need to be on the plane for Ireland within weeks."

That evening they ate dinner in, and talked about plans for a 'quick' wedding in Reno – flying out on Saturday morning and returning late Tuesday. Lauren thought how she couldn't ask Claire to take on more, and would have Carol reschedule patients to evening hours.

"A short honeymoon, but we'll spread it over the years." Dan said, then walked to the closet and pulled a silver box from the pocket of his suit jacket.

"Remember at the airport when I told Sandi I had two presents. This one is yours."

It was a ring – an emerald with a diamond on each side. The inscription inside the platinum band read, Love of My Life.

Saturday morning, after dropping Maddie off at Claire's, they flew to Reno, rented a car, and drove to Carson City for a license. From there they drove to Lake Tahoe and were married by a Justice of Peace.

Chapter Sixteen

The phone was ringing as they entered the house, even though it was late Tuesday night. Lauren ran to answer. It was Dan's office at the New York Times.

Listening and reading his expression, she knew that more plans were changing.

He put the receiver back and turned to her. "Well Mrs. Carter, our honeymoon is going to have to be continued in New York. I have to leave right away and want you to come with me." He put his hand out to stop her, "But I know you can't yet. I also know I should be here, but."

"Oh God, Dan, don't tell me you'll be leaving for Korea."

He pulled her to him. "I'm going to try putting if off…" More words left dangling – this time because Maddie whined, poking her paw against Dan's leg.

"Okay, girl." He walked back to the kitchen and poured dried food into her bowl.

Lauren followed, and they sat at the dinette.

"Tell me what's happening," she said.

"First-of-all, Mrs Carter, I love you and will change plans if you ask. The Communists have refused to acknowledge Korea's 38th parallel as a demarcation line, ending hope for a ceasefire. For now, I can work from the office, receiving enough information by phone and wire… thus my trip to New York."

He paused, wanting to emphasize his words, "But one of my priorities is to start an adoption process. I want us, you, Sandi, and me, to be a real family. I'll need to find a good attorney to handle it."

Lauren looked at him with wonder. "With all that's happening in your life right now, you think of us. I love you, Dan… And thank you."

"Thank me? Lauren, you and Sandi are my life. And when we go to Ireland, we'll be family."

That night Lauren couldn't sleep. Sitting at the kitchen dinette, she wrote a note to Dan – to give to him later in their marriage.

Dan,

I will never be able to look back at our wedding without its being intertwined with the days before and after. I wonder if pleasure and pain gain intensity by one eclipsing the other – and if most happiness is remembered with a tinge of bittersweet.

Love you always, Lauren.

Dan left for the airport at five o'clock the following morning.

Two hours later Lauren drove to the clinic. There was so much to be done; but most difficult would be telling Claire. She hoped she could catch her before patients.

But as Lauren stepped from the elevator she saw blotches of dried blood on the wood floors that became a large stain by the clinic door. She rushed into the office.

Claire was sitting at the desk, her face pale.

"What?" Lauren asked.

"I came in early this morning thinking I'd get some bookwork done." She nodded toward the door. "You see where the girl was when I approached. She was bent over in pain."

Carol came out of the back room carrying a pail of scrub water. She gave Lauren a sinking look.

"There was no choice but to phone an ambulance immediately," Claire said. "I had examined her on Friday, she was eight weeks along. Young – thirteen, told us her name was Barbara Smith. She was with a woman who claimed to be her mother. Carol gave her general instructions and made an appointment for this morning.

"Unfortunately, she attempted to do the job herself. The woman, the one who came with her last Friday, dropped her off this morning – hemorrhaging and in shock.

Claire looked worn out. "I just got back from the hospital. The woman who claimed to be her mother is a thirty-five-year-old kitchen aide at St. Theresa's Home. And I learned that the girl, Barbara Smith, is actually Geraldine Francini. She has lived at St. Theresa's since her parents abandoned her at age three.

"She was a very sick young lady this morning. By the time I left the hospital, she was all right – and will survive. But my God, I'm left with more than a few problems." She hesitated and then added, "I wish Chief was still around."

"Hmm," Lauren sighed, "I don't think Chief would have much clout with Mayor Dorothy. What about the emergency staff? Anyone we know?"

"Busy and professional; it seems they didn't know who I was. Unfortunately, I had never met the young intern on duty and have no idea of where he stands on abortion or if he knows who I am – and how professional our clinic is. It was clear that Geraldine had either tried to self-abort or had help, and he may think that I caused those injuries. He finished the abortion, cleaned her up, and now there will be an investigation."

"I'm worried," Lauren said. "Things have changed. We need to close. Become invisible." As she said it, Lauren knew it couldn't be done that easily.

And Claire looked at the appointment book. "Wishful thought. Today ten women are scheduled. I'm sorry, Lauren. I know the problems you're having at home. You don't need this. But unfortunately, when something like this happens it threatens us both. And I fear it's not going to just go away. That young doctor was a lot friendlier to Sister – who was angry when she came to the hospital – than he was to me."

Claire is right, Lauren thought; it could affect her whole life – Sandi, Dan, everything. She wanted out before that happened. But watching Claire, she knew that wasn't an option today.

Claire picked up the phone. "I'm going to call O'Riley, one of Chief's old buddies – a sergeant who has skated so far."

Lauren listened. Claire's conversation was brief. Before hanging-up she thanked him and added, "I know things have changed. But appreciate your concern."

Then, setting the phone in its cradle, Claire rubbed her eyes. "He said he'd get back to me if he hears anything; but let's not hold our breath. Chief would have known everything coming-down as it happened. I don't think O'Riley would tell me even if he knows."

Claire looked at the clock and sighed. "Is it only ten after eight? I feel as if the day should be ending."

Later in the morning, Lauren poured coffee for Carol, and asked if she had a minute to talk.

"I'll make it – let's ignore the phone for a while."

"I've got to tell you something that's going to make the day even worse. I won't be able to see patients next week."

Lauren read her exasperation. "I'm sorry, Carol. It's a bad time to put this on you. I'll do the calling and will work evenings and through the weekend – Monday if necessary."

Carol looked apologetic. "No, Lauren, I'm just tired. Of course, I'll call them. After this morning it wouldn't be a bad idea to cancel Claire's also."

"You're right." Lauren took a sip of coffee – hesitating before adding, "I won't be accepting new patients."

Carol nodded, "I don't blame you."

Lauren read the sadness in her eyes – an acknowledgement that their lives were never going to be the same. She felt the gravity of the moment, but simply said, "Thanks, Carol."

The next morning Lauren came in early and caught Claire when she arrived.

"We need to schedule a time when we can sit down and talk."

Claire nodded, "How's tomorrow for dinner?"

"Good. My last patient is scheduled for seven."

"I saw that you were staying late. Is this part of what we'll be talking about?" Claire asked.

"Yes. I meant to talk to you yesterday, but it wasn't the day to do it. And today, looking at schedules, our shadows will barely cross. We don't have time to say hello anymore."

"True and it worries me. These rooms are always full. Too full," Claire said.

Lauren thought how her own needs right now, with over-scheduling and late hours, were placing the clinic in greater jeopardy. But then she wondered if, in fact, they were already being tagged – even before the Geraldine Francini situation. Raids were happening weekly across the country. And their clinic had hardly been secret; they did more abortions than all other abortionists on the west coast.

Chapter Seventeen

Receiving the hospital report, connecting Claire with Geraldine Francini's botched abortion, was all it took. The police arrived at the clinic two days later at ten o'clock.

Lauren heard Carol yell, "What the…" And then there were voices – angry and bullying. "Don't touch anything…Hands in the air… Search Warrant…Sit… Hands up…just doing our job…"

Above the chaos Carol yelled, sending a warning to the back rooms. "Was it necessary to bring the press with you?"

Lauren, her heart pulsing through her head, tried to finish her surgery, knowing she only had minutes – or less. Shouts were coming from the hallway.

Then she heard Claire, "Stop! You're not coming in here."

"Ah, Dr. Karriden… You are wrong."

Lauren cringed, and pushed the double lock on her door.

Alice, her thirteen-year-old patient, was crying. "What's happening? Who's out there?"

There was no time to explain. The surgery was almost complete, but she couldn't risk infection. She rinsed Alice's uterus with an antiseptic solution and removed the tenaculum. Then, as she cauterized, she heard voices – close.

Grabbing penicillin, she had Alice take it as the police pounded on the door.

Alice sobbed, "I want to go home."

Lauren put her arm around her and helped her up. "I know, Honey "The surgery is done. Now you're going to have to be brave." Lauren knew she was asking too much. "I'll help all I can, but..."

She was interrupted by the pounding on her door.

Alice looked terrified. "What's happening?"

"The police are here," Lauren was blunt. "And you've got to get dressed." She handed her a belt with a large sanitary pad, "You'll need this first."

Lauren grabbed her clothes from the small closet and put them on the bed.

"There's no time. You need to be quick. I'll step into the hall and stall them while you dress."

Someone tried to open the locked door as Lauren put her arm around Alice, helped her off the bed, and then mouthed, "Dress!"

The doorknob rattled.

"Hold on," Lauren shouted.

"Open the door or we'll break it."

There was no choice: Lauren opened it a crack, peeked out, and was hit by flashing lights. She glared into the cameras. "Get those goddamned lights out of my eyes." Slipping into the hall, she closed the door and stood guard. "What is this? A Gestapo raid? With the number of police in this hallway, the whole precinct must be here – along with the press corps."

The officer, who had to be the one who had pounded on her door, looked as if he had just reeled in a seventy-five-pound salmon.

"Anne Thompson?"

Lauren put her hand above her eyes, squinting. "Call off the cameras, so I can see who I'm talking to."

"Talk later; for now, stand aside and let us in that room."

"I can't do that. As you should know this is a medical office and I was in the process of an exam as you broke in. The girl in there needs time to get dressed."

"Exam, huh? Just move!" He reached for the doorknob.

Lauren put her hand out. "Wait!" I told you there is someone in there, dressing. You can't just walk in on her. Let me go back in first."

"Can't do that," the officer said. "But we'll let you walk before us. So open that door. Now!"

Lauren refused to move, and he started to reach past her – to an officer carrying handcuffs. There was no choice. She opened the door and stepped in.

Alice stood, looking trapped – her face wet with tears. She was dressed, but her blouse was unbuttoned. Knowing she was too young and timid to face this posse of uniformed men and flashing cameras, Lauren grabbed a towel from a shelf and threw it to her.

"Quick. Cover your face."

Then Lauren stood in front of her as if she could hold everyone back. But within seconds the room was crowded, and she and Alice were surrounded. Putting her arm around her shoulder, pulling her close, Lauren tried to move forward; but was stopped. Flashing bulbs, mikes pushing at them, and an impenetrable wall of uniforms – it was suffocating.

"Step back! Let us breathe!" Lauren shouted, "Look at you. What in God's name is happening? This young girl isn't a criminal. Step back; give her room."

Lauren squinted into the lights. "Who's in charge here? Help us…"

Then she saw him – a sergeant. He gave an order, "Move Back."

Without waiting, he raised his voice, "Now! And I mean out of this room, the hall, and the office."

Everyone stood back, giving him room.

Approaching Lauren, he continued his orders, "Joe and Dick stay. You two," he pointed to other officers, "take care of the situation in the office. Everyone else, out!"

A few photographers moved closer and the sergeant barked, "Joe, confiscate those cameras."

The sergeant watched as the area cleared. When a few reporters remained near the hallway door, he frowned. "Do you have problems with my order? Let me be clear. Anyone remaining in this hall or the front office in three minutes will be arrested for interfering in an arrest. Now move!"

Lauren was amazed. Within seconds the hall was vacated and quiet. She loosened her hold on Alice and addressed the sergeant, "Whatever else you do today I thank you for that."

The sergeant frowned. "You won't be thanking me for long. You, Miss Thompson, are under arrest."

Under arrest! Lauren felt a queasy fullness in her throat and swallowed hard. Before she could speak, Alice leaned into her, wanting protection.

"Sergeant," Lauren pleaded, "what about her? She's so young."

"You're something else. What about her? Who put her in this mess?" His expression was a mixture of anger and concern. "How old is she? Twelve?"

He turned, "Rob, you take care of this young lady. Drive her to Victim's Medical. Make certain that Nurse Hodges sees her. Stay with her until that happens."

Rob wrinkled his face, pleading, "Sarge…"

"Just do it!"

The policeman stepped toward Alice as Lauren interrupted. "Wait. Let me talk to her."

She bent and spoke softly, "It will be okay. I know Nurse Hodges; she'll help you, and then see that you get home safely."

Toughness gone, the policeman placed his hand on Alice's shoulder. "Don't make this hard on yourself. Come on." His eyes were sympathetic. "You'll see it won't be all that bad."

Lauren ached as she watched Alice, who had let the towel fall to the floor. Her steps were hesitant and her shoulders bent, as she wiped at tears."

The sergeant shook his head. "You people. Look what you cause. She's just a child." Without waiting for a comment from Lauren, he turned to another policeman. "Cuff her."

The sergeant left the hall, and the other officer took over.

"Miss Thompson, put out your hands."

"Do you have to do this? It's clear I can't run away."

"Just following orders. Don't give me problems; get those hands out."

Lauren looked at the steel cuffs. She would be photographed wearing these as she was taken to the police car. The pictures would be in papers beyond Portland. They would make it to Dublin, just as Mary and Sandi would be arriving.

"Officer, when we leave please call off the cameras. There are people – innocent people – who will be hurt by photos."

"Do I look like I'm Chief of Police? I take orders. Now put out the hands and let me do my job. Make it easier on yourself."

Lauren was cuffed and led through the vacated clinic, and to the elevator.

Then as she stepped into the lobby, it felt as if every photographer in Portland was waiting. She tried to avert her eyes from the flashes by facing the floor. Questions came from everywhere and mikes were pushed within inches of her face. But two officers held her arms, directing her out of the building, through a larger crowd, and into the backseat of a police car.

She actually felt relief; not only was she away from the mob, but Claire was sitting next to her. And, surprising to Lauren, Claire appeared to be in control. Holding her head high, she glared at the crowd that was clamoring to get past the police and to the car.

As they pulled from the curb Claire spoke in a low voice. "Some faces I recognize." She sighed, and then turned to face Lauren. "We'll be out on bail and home tonight. I've phoned Will Jones and he's meeting us."

"Oh great! Just great." It hit Lauren: arraignment would be next, then bail – and she would have to depend on Will Jones. She had never taken him seriously, mostly because of his drunken come-ons at Claire's parties.

"I thought Will Jones was a tax attorney."

"He is. But there's no one else who I can trust right now. As you know the DA is ambitious, smart and, unfortunately, a good Catholic. Will knows him; he was a class behind him at Central Catholic High. Hopefully that will make a difference."

Lauren looked at her with disbelief. "Knowing Will, it might make a difference all right – the wrong kind."

"If you can come up with another name, good; if not, he's who we have right now." Claire's voice was sharp.

Lauren thought how Claire was in the same predicament as she – Jane and the girls probably already knew what was happening. She started to apologize, but Claire stopped her, and motioned toward the driver. He was watching them in his rearview mirror. They remained quiet for the rest of the drive to municipal jail.

It seemed to Lauren that most of Portland was crowded in front of the police station. Cuffed, she couldn't cover her face, so she looked toward the ground and didn't respond to questions. However as she reached the steps this became less necessary as attention was focused on Claire.

Farrell Seigart, a well-known Oregonian columnist, yelled, "Hi Doctor. Tell us, are you guilty as charged?"

Lauren watched Claire, who looked at Seigart with cool contempt.

"Why Mr. Seigart, I'm surprised that you would ask such a question. Certainly you understand about people who live in glass houses."

It was a good moment in a horrible day, and Lauren felt some relief. Claire wasn't acquiescing. Watching her turn and walk with dignity into municipal court, Lauren began to breathe more evenly. Claire, who had been her mentor, was now showing her the importance of fighting back – especially when you are about to be eaten alive.

The police station lobby was quiet when Lauren stepped in. It almost felt safe after what she had been through. But far from safe, she knew it was part of the nightmare this day had become.

She thought of Sandi, seven thousand miles away – and her plans to join her in a week.

Will Jones had arranged for their bail, and within hours Lauren, Claire, and Carol were released with instructions to return for arraignment in five days.

Lauren asked Will Jones to check on her patient, Alice. He phoned Nurse Hodges, who had worked with other young patients from the clinic. Alice was safe; no juvenile charges were made, and the nurse said she would watch out for her. Lauren thought how, in the middle of all else, she was thankful for that.

Reporters weren't permitted in the back parking lot, making it easy for Jane to pick them up.

Carol asked to be driven to her car in a private lot. Then Jane drove Lauren and Claire to her own house, several houses away from theirs.

Later, when it was dark, Claire opted to stay at Jane's, and Lauren started walking the wooded path to her house.

About halfway home Lauren heard Maddie barking, and remembered that she had left her out before leaving for work. Her bark grew closer, and Lauren searched ahead with the flashlight. Maddie was running toward her, and within seconds jumped, wiggled, twirled, and whined as Lauren cried.

"Thank you, Girl. You don't know how much I need you right now."

The news had hit the late afternoon paper, The Journal. Lauren's picture was on the front page – one that would hit papers throughout the country and, on the following day, Ireland.

Lauren appeared to be scolding the police as she guarded her young patient. Beautiful and photogenic, caught in distress, accused of a morals crime, it had sex appeal. There was something both savory and incongruous about Anne Thompson, who looked like a fashion model but was depicted as the queen of vice.

Dan read about the raid minutes after it hit the wires; and he saw Lauren's picture. Within two hours he boarded a plane.

It was a ten-hour flight to Portland, giving him time to finish the piece that he had been working on. Then he thought of how his life was about to change. One thing was clear: he would stay with Lauren; forgoing his next assignment in Korea. This was a first: he had turned down a plum assignment.

In the taxi to her house Dan read The Oregonian's story:

"Will Jones, a high-priced civil attorney is handling Abortionist Case. The two abortionists had no problems making bail, having accumulated great wealth through their alleged crimes…"

Dan cringed. Will Jones was high priced all right – as a tax attorney. Dan knew him from trips to Portland, and suspected he was way out of his league in Criminal Law.

Unable to sleep, Lauren poured drinks from a bottle of Irish whisky that Mary used for hot toddies. After four or five shots she stretched out on the couch.

When Dan arrived in the morning Maddie greeted him with her usual jumps and twirls.

"Missed you too, girl," he bent to pat her; then looked around. "So where is she?"

Maddie rushed ahead, into the living-room.

Lauren mumbled, "Dan?"

"Who else?"

"Thank God you're here."

"Got here as soon as I could catch a plane out." He bent to kiss her but was stopped by the ring of the phone.

"Don't answer," he said.

She jolted up. "It might be Mary or Sandi."

Lauren said hello, listened for seconds and then hung-up. "You're right; I should have let it ring. It was that bastard, Farrell Seigart – you know – the columnist. I thought Claire had gotten rid of him yesterday. He harassed her and she stood up to him – warning him of 'glass houses.' But I should have known the jerk wasn't worried. He'd headline his own mother if it meant a story."

"I wish I had been here." Dan said. "I took the earliest plane I could get, and the whole way here I've been thinking of what needs to be done. First – if Seigart has your number, so do others. Reporters will be camping in your front yard within minutes. We'll go to Sauvie Island. You said it's finished, and if there's ever a time for a hide-away, it's now."

She shook her head. "I can't. Sandi and Mary have this phone number."

"I suspect you had a phone installed in that house. Call them when we get there. We've got to get going."

"Of course. I'll grab some things, fast."

She pulled out her suitcase – the one she had taken to Reno less than a week earlier. Now she was filling it to go hide. She felt the gnawing in her gut that had started during the raid; nothing could ever be the same. She faced going to prison.

They filled the trunk with suitcases, fresh food from the refrigerator, and a large painting of Sandi. Then Maddie hopped into the backseat.

Before leaving Dan turned on lights and the radio, hoping to deceive reporters,

They pulled out of the driveway fifteen minutes before the first cameraman arrived at the front gate. The deception worked. Portland's late afternoon paper, The Journal, reported: Anne Thompson Refuses to Leave House.

They parked the car in the garage, padlocked the gate, and walked into their Sauvie Island getaway. Everything was as Lauren had wanted it for Dan. But she was aware of how different it all seemed now, from a month earlier when she had directed the placement of furniture.

Intended to be a country cottage, it had turned into a four thousand square foot ranch house, plus decks and an attached garage. The north walls were mostly window, with a sweeping view of the Columbia. The den, kitchen, and master bedroom had doors opening onto the deck that stretched the full length of the house. And their bedroom had a fireplace, with a king-sized bed facing the river.

It was built on a raised part of the island, protecting them from floods like the one that covered the beach in 1948. A path wound its way down to the river, where Lauren had planned to build a ramp and dock for Dan's sailboat.

Now, she thought how that would not happen.

She had been worried that the fence around the front area would detract from the feeling of wilderness the house was designed to capture; but now she had the chilling awareness that it had been one of her best choices. No one could drive onto their property without a key.

Dan stood at the living-room window, looking at the trail to the river. "Last night when I thought of our coming here, I didn't know it was to Shangri-La."

"That was my intent." Lauren rubbed her temples, trying to relieve a nudging headache. She looked through the stocked bar and pulled out the Scotch. "I had planned for us: our secluded getaway. But right now, to be honest, I want something to soothe this hangover, and help me through the day." She poured a shot.

Dan walked to the fireplace and took logs from the stack beside the hearth. After arranging and lighting them, he looked up. "Pour me some of that. It's been one hell-of-a twenty-four hours, and I think we can both use it."

Dan woke in early-morning and studied her: red hair spread across the pillow and the curve of her breasts rising under the loosely draped sheet. He bent and kissed her forehead, then got up and walked into the kitchen.

Stepping onto the deck as he let Maddie out, Dan stood in the crisp air admiring the view; then walked back in and put on coffee.

Within minutes she came into the room – pale, her hair uncombed. She had slipped into a silk robe that flowed as she walked, revealing her long legs.

"You're beautiful."

"Ravished is a better description."

"Ravishing."

She opened a cupboard door. "Whatever, we got through our first day here."

"That's what you call 'getting through?'" He reached for her, but she pulled away.

"I need a big strawberry milkshake. Want one?" She put strawberries, milk, and ice cream in a blender. "Got to get my head on straight."

"Ah, well, when you're done, you're done. Yeah, mix me up one." He looked out of the window, "But first, let's take a walk. You're right about this island. I want us to keep this house – no matter where we move."

It was a perfect summer day. The property eased down a fertile slope to a sandy beach on the Columbia. Maddie had the spring of a young pup as she explored the new grounds. Feeling safe in a wilderness, protected from strangers, Lauren and Dan walked holding hands. Then, catching a breeze as they came to the river, they stood, his arm around her shoulders.

"I wish it were two weeks ago and we were here, just as we are. I wish we could have kept everything from happening," she said.

He kept his arm around her, as they moved closer to the river. Slender whitecaps were forming on the water, and the breeze was cooling. He thought how quickly everything changes.

Chapter Eighteen

After eight rings Mary's sister, Margaret, answered the phone and said hello as if it were a question.

"Sorry," Lauren said. "It sounds as if I woke you."

"Since it's the middle of night, your assumption is right."

Rather than anger, Lauren heard a yawn behind her words.

"I'm Sandi's mother and I've tried to reach you for hours, but no one's been home."

"That is also correct. Mary and Sandra just arrived yesterday and have been bombarded by relatives ever since. It was after eleven last night when the last of the cousins left and we dropped in bed." With a drowsy sigh, Margaret added, "But Sandra will want to talk with you and I'll wake her."

Lauren listened, thinking she would hear interaction between Margaret and Sandi – giving some indication that Margaret was more pleasant than she sounded on the phone. But she heard nothing until Sandi answered.

"Mom, I miss you. I wanted to call you before I went to bed, but they said it was too late."

"I miss you too, Darling; and it's never too late for your call. I want to hear everything: your trip over, your aunts, cousins, where you are, plans, every…

Sandi interrupted, "I want to come home and be with you. I don't want to be here."

Lauren swallowed hard; she couldn't go to Sandi or bring her home – not now.

"We'll talk every day," she forced enthusiasm, "until I get there. You tell me everything that you see and do. Enjoy time with Grandma and before you know it you'll be back home."

"But I don't want to stay here. Grandma and I are in the same room, and it's cold in the house, and I miss you. I don't want to be here without you."

Lauren ached. "Sweetheart, you'll be home soon. But for now you need to have fun."

"Mom, I don't care about Jamie or her mother or anyone. I miss you."

Lauren stifled tears. "I promise; we'll be together soon, okay? Try to be strong while I make plans. Is Grandma up? I'd like to talk to her."

"I'll wake her. You'll get her to bring me back?"

"I'd like her to do that, Sweetheart. But you just got there, so try to enjoy everything. We'll be together in a short while." As she said it, Lauren was aware that this couldn't happen – not now.

She waited, worrying about what to say. If Mary didn't know what was happening in Portland, she would soon.

It took minutes for Mary to answer the phone. "What can it be in the middle of the night? What's happening?"

"I'm sorry for the hour, but I miss Sandi, and she sounds homesick. We need to talk about her returning." As she said it, Lauren felt blood rush to her face. It was a lie! Sandi couldn't return to Portland. Not now!

"Oh. I thought something was wrong, glad 'tis not. But it's three in the morning over here." Mary stifled a yawn. "It will take a few days and she'll be acting herself. We'll be meeting cousins her own age in the morning, and they'll get her playing. When you phone the next time, things will be better."

Lauren thought how she sounded more Irish than she had in years.

"I don't know, Mary – she sounds upset, and I'm concerned. I plan on being there as soon as I can get out of the office." Another lie! "In the meantime, I'm worried."

"You're rushing things. We just got here; give her a bit – let her feel some Irish laughter tomorrow with her cousins; she'll come around. Besides, it's a short time until you'll be here."

"Mary, I miss her. And – well – I want to – I will come soon. And Dan talks about our – I mean all of us – going to New York when things free up around here."

"And how are things going? You had a lot to do when we left. Since you're thinking of New York, things must be moving along."

Lauren felt a chill: neither Mary nor Sandi knew about their marriage. But that was minor to all else they didn't know.

"Yes, there's a lot happening," she slipped over the words. "But Mary, I'm worried. Sandi's never been away from me and…"

Mary broke in, "Don't worry anymore, Lauren. Sandi will come around; after all she's of Irish heritage."

Lauren wondered if this was a bit of humor or just plain irrational. Regardless, it was clear that Mary couldn't just hop on a plane and come home. And now, with bail… Lauren pushed thoughts away.

"I am worried, and until I can be with her I want to talk to her daily. Whenever Sandi expresses that she misses me or simply wants to talk, I want her to call home.

"Which reminds me – I have a new phone number. I'm temporarily staying at the place I built on Sauvie Island." She gave Mary the number. "I decided to stay here for a while; it was too difficult being at home without you two there." She recognized that she was digging herself deeper into the lie.

Mary's voice sounded sharp, "I can understand how you feel. It's best to move away from some pains – if it can be done."

Lauren knew Mary and was frightened by her words.

"Mary, please put Sandi back on the phone. I need to talk to her."

"It's terribly late; but then, she's already awake."

As if she had been standing near, Sandi answered within seconds, "When will you come get me, Mom?

"Soon; it won't be long." Lauren stopped short of adding a date.

"Promise?"

"I promise – I'll be there just as soon as I can."

That evening Lauren phoned Will Jones, who had been trying to reach her. He talked about the political atmosphere and how it could affect the case. Then he told her that the D.A. was pushing for a felony against Claire: second-degree manslaughter.

"But you have kept a lower profile," he said. "Until lately, not as many people have heard of Anne Thompson. Of course, that's changed big-time now. Your face isn't easy to forget, and it's been on television and the front page of The Oregonian for three days running. Still, I'm hoping to make a deal – get you off on a lighter charge – even a misdemeanor."

"What do you mean by 'make a deal'?" Lauren asked.

"This is the hard part. I would have to offer the D.A. something. There are a few options. One would work, but I wouldn't suggest nor have any part of it – especially as I represent you both. That would be your testifying against Claire."

Lauren had never liked Will. His come-ons at Claire's parties had been in the form of a tease, when, in fact, they both understood that he was testing. Now he appeared to be testing again, but about something much more serious.

"You're off base and should know it. Claire is much more than a partner to me. And you're correct, Will, she is your client, the one who has retained you over the years, as well as choosing you for this trial."

He cleared his throat. "That's why I would not suggest it. But as your attorney I need to lay out all options, even when I don't approve. And," he added as an excuse, "I know how district attorneys think."

"Hmm." She doubted if he had ever worked with a D.A. "And what are my other options?"

"You're not in a good position for options, Anne. A patient was in your office, which limits your choices. But since you weren't caught in the act of abortion, we could contest the manslaughter charge – argue that you were performing an exam and try to make a deal. It would seem to me that the witness would be pleased to contend she had gone in for a physical."

A picture of Alice flashed into Lauren's mind. "I hope that young girl never has to come into court. And, Will, I told the arresting officer that I was giving an exam, and he scoffed. Thinking it would work on a district attorney is almost laughable."

"Anne, let me explain things. When I bargain with the D.A. it's a process that he expects. I need to give him something – toss an idea at him, and hope that he's looking for an avenue that will be a reasonable out, especially if he has doubts about his case.

"And," Will's sigh was audible, "I shouldn't have to point out that if we could bargain a settlement without going to trial, it could relieve you from more than the risk of jail time. You could be avoiding a much greater invasion by the press. Greater than you can even imagine."

"You're wrong, Will, I can imagine it." She looked at Dan, who motioned for her to hang-up. "Give me a chance to mull this over. I'll get back to you."

"Don't think too long, there's work to be done here. The D.A. will be taking your case to the grand jury on Tuesday and I need to meet with him before then. I'll phone you back today. What's your number?"

"I can't give it to anyone. I'll call you." She put the receiver down, shaking her head in disgust.

Dan smiled. "Why do I have the feeling that you're not too crazy about Will Jones? He certainly admires you. So what did he suggest?"

"The jerk hinted that I could get off by testifying against Claire. You heard my answer to that. Next he suggested a 'receiving an exam' argument – saying it would give the DA a way out."

Lauren shook her head, "If it weren't for Sandi, I'd skip Will Jones and his pleas, and go into the courtroom arguing about the hypocrisy and danger of abortion laws. Tell how our clinic was filled each day with girls, many under 16, who have no place else to turn." Lauren sank onto the couch, "But that's not going to happen."

"And I'd be in court with you," Dan said. "But I agree about Sandi. In today's climate things will get a hell of a lot worse if this isn't handled right – especially with your do-good mayor gaining fame throughout the country."

Dan thought of the Oregonian's picture of Lauren: gorgeous and caught in an illicit business. By now it was on the front page of his paper – The Times and was probably being seen in Dublin. In Ireland the picture would put Anne Thompson in league with the devil.

Lauren watched him and recognized the expression on his face. She waited.

Within minutes he said, "But you have a point. We're being totally defensive; maybe it's time to turn things around. There are a lot of women who know the reality of things. Taking on archaic laws might be the way to go.

"However, with this said, there's one thing to keep in mind while deciding our direction. Where is the D.A. coming from? You and Claire are high profile and drawing attention; he's not going to miss this chance to gain free publicity. But that publicity has to be weighted on his side; he'll want to come out the hero."

Dan rubbed his chin. "And that is going to depend on the direction public opinion goes; I have some skills that might influence that."

The following morning the phone rang at six. Lauren woke with a start and ran to answer. Then hesitated before picking it up.

"Mary?"

There was no lilt in Mary's voice, "You appear to have left out some important things when we talked yesterday."

Lauren didn't respond.

"It was in the paper today: Your picture. I hid it from Sandi, and my sister has no idea who Anne Thompson might be." Her voice grew increasingly agitated. "You didn't tell me, even though you knew that everything had changed. If that picture made it to Dublin, it's been seen across the United States. You have brought shame on all of us, and now what are we to do?"

"Mary, listen. I was quitting."

Mary's voice rose, "Quitting! You should never have started! I will not – cannot – allow my – our – innocent little girl to become more of a victim of what you have done. I'm hoping you will understand this."

"Mary, stop! What are you saying?" Lauren's mind raced: Mary and Sandi were half a world away. "Stop. You can't just…" Tears clouded her words, "Sandi is to come home. Now! She's my girl. Don't get any idea that…"

"Lauren, I have feelings for you. That makes what needs to be done harder. This isn't about you or me; it's what we need to do for Sandi. I want to protect her from what's happening over there. You certainly should understand and agree with that."

"Oh God, Mary, you know that I would protect Sandi with my life." She rushed words. "Listen to me. Nothing could hurt her more than being separated from me. Nothing! And Mary, things will be better quickly and…"

Mary broke-in, "Lauren, you were warned and now look at you. The worst is happening and what are you saying? You want her there. That's certainly not thinking of what's best for Sandi."

"That's just not true. Please Mary, you know it's not true. Sandi wants to be here. I'll protect her."

"You want her there," Mary repeated. "Of course, you do, even though that would be the worst thing for her. And it's not going to happen. We'll have to talk further, at a later time. There is no sense in talking now; I know what I need to do."

"No-o. Don't hang up, Mary. Don't!" The phone buzzed in her ear.

"Please…no…"

Dan stood behind her with his hands on her shoulders. She looked up and read his expression.

"You were right," Lauren cried. "I shouldn't have let her go."

"When you made that decision things were different." He walked to the coffee table, pulled a cigarette from its package and faced her.

"Lauren, from your end of the phone I gathered that Mary thinks she's got some kind of custodial right. Which she doesn't! No more pleading with her. She has no rights! It's time for us to start fighting."

Lauren shook her head, "I'm not certain you understand what Mary can be like – her righteous indignation, her total belief that God is on her side. Of course, my pleading didn't help. But Dan, she has Sandi! And tell me how I'm going to board a plane to go to Ireland now."

Not waiting for an answer, she picked up the phone and asked the operator to place a call to Ireland. Then she sat listening to the rings.

"Fight? I can't talk to her. There's nothing I can do and I'm scared."

After several more attempts to phone, Lauren rubbed her head as if in pain. Then without comment, she walked to the bar and poured a drink.

Dan watched, but said nothing.

She spent the rest of the morning sitting at the bar. Early in the afternoon, unsteady, she made it to the couch and fell onto it.

Dan called Maddie, who ran ahead as they walked down to the

river. He threw a large stick in the water, which she retrieved and placed by his feet, ready to chase again.

There were several sailboats in the distance that appeared to be racing, picking up warm breezes and tacking across the river. He thought of how Lauren had talked about buying a boat, and wondered how many of their dreams would happen.

On such a beautiful day, so far from the horror of war, he was hit by the irony of their pain – his and Lauren's. His profession took him into the heart of tragedy, and he never ceased to be amazed at the strength of those who survived its devastation.

It was time for strength – not for standing back watching their lives deteriorate.

A sour taste filled her mouth as Lauren ran into the bathroom. Chilled, yet perspiring, she slumped to her knees and retched into the bowl.

Finally, she sat on the floor, her arms around her legs, thinking how she didn't have the strength to pull herself up. Long minutes passed before Dan walked in and helped her into bed. She whispered "thanks," before closing her eyes.

It was late afternoon when she woke. Admonishing herself, she looked at the clock. Six p.m. Twelve hours had passed since she talked to Mary! She threw the covers back, and rushed to the phone, and gave the operator the long-distance number. Again, no one answered.

Dan was right; she had to take charge – and fast. But then the truth hit. She couldn't go to Sandi. She wasn't free…

After taking an aspirin and splashing cold water on her face, she walked into the front room. She called Dan's name, but got no response. Looking in the kitchen, everything was neat: bottles had been put away, dishes washed, the coffee pot cleaned – and Dan was gone.

It was then she saw Maddie looking in the deck window. She dressed quickly and went outdoors. If ever there was a time for a brisk walk, it was now. Maddie ran before her to the river. The wind blew in her face as they walked on the beach.

They returned an hour later.

"Where the hell is he?" she said. Maddie, recognizing the "where" cocked her head "Yeah girl, where? Looks like you and I are here alone." Lauren bent down and stroked Maddie's head, "Well it's time to quit feeling sorry for ourselves, right girl?"

She opened the refrigerator and pulled out sandwich makings. "It's also time to eat and shower." Her voice changed, "But then what? Oh, Madeline, then I call Mary again."

Dan drove into the garage within the hour, carrying a typewriter and shopping bag. She looked surprised. "You've returned. I assumed you were on your way back to New York."

He put the typewriter on the table and took plain and carbon paper from his bag.

"You're a woman of little faith. I didn't want to wake you, but I've been busy. Decided it was time that we start being proactive. So I called a friend from the Associated Press, and she gave me the name Robert Farmer, The Oregonian's affiliate to the AP. Then I went to the library and copied my article in Esquire. Armed, I met him for lunch."

He pointed to the table. "These are my tools. I like the kitchen, but if you want to stick me in another room, I'll move."

She squinted at him, wondering, then thought of his comments about the D.A. and public opinion.

He smiled, "Love of my life, you should know by now that I won't just stand by and watch you – us – get lynched. You talked about how you wish you could use the courts to make a statement. Well, you're not in a position to take that risk, but I can do the job through the press. We've both been hit by its power this week. It's time to hit back. I want to get this in the paper before the grand jury convenes."

His expression changed; he looked puzzled, "By the way, do you ever cook?

"Cook? I'm a great cook. What about a tuna sandwich and Campbell's Cream of Tomato, with real cream and rice?"

"Terrific. I suspected that you had culinary talent. Now let me get busy."

She had never watched him work. He became immersed; typing with two fingers – amazingly fast – and didn't slow down until done.

"You're my editor on this one." He handed it to her; then reached for the sandwich she had placed on the table.

When she finished reading, she shook her head in disbelief.

"What the hell does that mean?" He asked.

"It means that I think you're a genius. You have said everything that I wish I could say in that courtroom."

"Good." He took the last bite of sandwich. "I'm taking this to The Oregonian. Robert has talked to the editor by now. The deadline is nine p.m., and I want it in the morning paper."

Chapter Nineteen

The Oregonian, 1950

Watch Out; Something Important is Being Threatened Here in River City

By Daniel Carter

Napoleon had decreed that French foundling hospitals would have turntable devices so that parents could leave unwanted infants without being recognized. Before this, millions of babies had been drowned, smothered or abandoned; which concerned Napoleon, as the practice would leave the French army short of potential recruits. His effort worked, eventually resulting in over 127,000 babies being left through such methods.

Throughout history man has searched for ways to confront societal problems of unwanted pregnancies. In light of current laws, it appears we still haven't found a good solution. Statistics show that nine out of ten premarital pregnancies end in illegal abortions. It has been estimated that during World War Two, 1.3 million illegal abortions were performed annually – a low number due to the intrinsic secrecy of the subject.

Most abortion laws today arose from religious doctrines. Our constitution guarantees our right to freedom of belief. Unfortunately, it is when belief becomes an integral part of politics that we need to be concerned. Few politicians become elected who are not connected to a mainstream Church, and these men and 'recently' women are well aware of the power of the pulpit.

If there were ever laws that beg to be broken it is those dealing with abortion. If the statistics above aren't explanation enough, think of the consequences when women and schoolgirls are forced to go through nine months of pregnancy and then the shame of giving birth of an "illegitimate" child.

For years it has been known that physicians refer women to medically trained abortionists – people who put their own lives at risk to help others. Without these abortionists, who would inherit the risk? We know the serious medical consequences from attempts to end pregnancy by "home" methods.

This is why competent abortionists have more patients than they can handle. They work long hours – sometimes providing help to women who cannot pay. When one of you needs their service, you want to know it is available, confidential, and most of all, safe.

The arrest and future trial of two Portland abortionists is important. We will be testing laws that stretch the reach of our government by taking away a private and personal choice.

Will Jones chuckled as he read the Oregonian, and his wife asked what was so funny.

"It appears that Anne Thompson has a guardian angel who might make my conversation with the D.A. easier today."

On his way to the courthouse he thought about Dan's column and hoped the district attorney had read it. It would help. But Will was nervous; his background hadn't prepared him for this meeting.

It was exactly eight o'clock when he arrived.

The district attorney, Gerry Fields, was an intense small-framed man who was seldom seen in his office without a cigarette. The smoke curled into a fan above his desk.

"Appreciate promptness," he said. "Have a seat while I ask who Daniel Carter is. A friend of yours?"

Will smiled, relieved; Fields had read the column.

"Appears to be. He lives in New York. I met him over a year ago when he was in town writing a piece on abortion for Esquire. He knows what he's talking about."

Smoke mingled with Gerry's words. "That depends on whether you're defending or prosecuting." He crushed the cigarette in a tray of stubs. "So, what's on your mind?"

Will had heard that this D.A. got right to the point. "Want to present some 'what ifs'."

Gerry smiled, "Don't blame you after your friend's comments. But there are a lot of people out there who won't be impressed." He repeated, 'What's on your mind?"

Gerry lit another cigarette as he listened to Will's "receiving an exam" proposal.

Adding the stub to the tray, he answered, "Let's wait and see what the grand jury decides." Then he stood dismissively, "Thank you, Mr," he looked at his appointment book. "Jones."

Claire answered the phone, sounding cautious.

"Claire, it's me."

"Lauren. Thank God. Where are you? I've been trying to reach you for three days. I don't blame you for not answering or if you've flown to Timbuktu, but I've been worried."

"Sorry. Dan and I are at Sauvie Island, and don't plan on leaving till we have to."

"You're smart. Jane asked me to stay with her and the kids, but the press would find me, and she's dealing with enough. Reporters arrive here early and only, at least I hope, take breaks to pee. I've been ordering groceries from Stroheckers, and the delivery kids seem to enjoy the excitement around here. I don't think the neighbors are experiencing the same fun. I can imagine what it was like at their last association meeting.

"But let's get to more important things. I'm glad you phoned. Give Dan a big kiss; that article is terrific."

"That's one of the things I phoned about," Lauren said. "You and Dan are educating me on how to handle things. I appreciated the way you spoke up to the Oregonian's columnist – Siegart."

"What I said didn't mean a thing to him. He called here the next day. Listen to this – he said he'd like to give me a chance to be heard."

Lauren chuckled, "More like give him a chance to fry us, while he gets paid for a scoop. Anyway, Claire, I appreciated your attitude. It was right." Lauren took a deep breath, before continuing. "My mind was on Sandi from the minute they broke into the clinic – of what it would mean if word of this gets to Mary. As, of course, it has.

"Claire, remember the meeting we were going to have? Wish it had happened. Now Mary…"

Lauren stopped. It wasn't fair to unload on Claire. "Sorry. You don't need to hear this, I know you're dealing with enough. How are the girls doing?

"First, Lauren, don't ever feel that way about talking to me. As far as I'm concerned, you're family. And yes, what hurts most is how this affects our kids."

"Thanks, Claire, and you're right. It's because of them that I won't fight the way I would like. Knowing this, we need to talk about what we should be doing – making sure we're on the same page as we start our defense."

"I've been thinking about that since I read Dan's letter," Claire said. "I like his approach. Tell things as they really are. For us that means using what we know – short of naming names.

"That said, would you believe I've been getting calls here at home from women? Their needs haven't changed. And as for those who had appointments, we owe Carol. On the night of our release she went back to the office and picked up the scheduling books in her locked drawer. Thank God the police didn't return till morning."

After hanging up, Lauren placed a call to Mary. Her sister, Margaret, answered and told her that Mary and Sandi had left.

"She said she'll ring you when they get settled."

"Get settled!"

"That's what she said. I'll tell her you called," Margaret answered, then hung-up.

Lauren sat, stunned. "Settled." The word hit and kept hitting.

"Well, it's causing a stir." Dan spread the Editorial Section of The Oregonian onto the kitchen table and then stood behind her.

"Look!" she said, pointing to, "Public Reacts to Abortion Raid."

The page was filled with letters: Has Anyone Tried Abstinence? Abortion Saves Lives. Abortion as Birth Control. Time to Legalize Abortion. Abortion Kills. Misuse of Courts. Man's Power Over Women, Arrest the Fathers.

Dan chuckled, "That last one I didn't cover in either article."

"Not a bad idea," Lauren said, and looked up at him. "You've done it, Dan. You lit the match, and look."

He kissed her forehead. "Now let's hope it does what was intended."

"It is," she said. "It's already giving us a voice. These people who are speaking-out have courage – especially with what's gone on. Listen to this one:

"For the first time in Oregon people are talking about a hidden truth: Many women have needed the help of an abortionist at some time in their lives. I knew of Claire Karriden when I was a teenager. She saved my friend, who was pregnant and threatening suicide.

"Now Mrs. Karriden and her associate Anne Thompson are being treated like criminals. Why? Aborting a fetus that has not yet developed into a conscious, viable human is not manslaughter.

"It is sad that instead of honoring these women, our politicians are grabbing headlines by enforcing an archaic law that has been ignored for as long as I have lived in Portland.

"It's time to change the law."

Letters continued throughout the week. And then Dan got a call from his editor, telling him that his commentary had been picked-up across the country. He drove to a magazine shop and brought various newspapers home to Lauren.

Surprised by what seemed to be a national groundswell of support, she thought of her patients. There had been one constant among them: fear of being exposed. This, as much as the law, dictated the shroud of secrecy that surrounded the clinic. It occurred to her that things might be changing.

But she knew this would never happen in Ireland.

Bart Miller, the Deputy District Attorney, went straight to Gerry Field's office after the Grand Jury decision came in.

"So?" Gerry said, taking a long drag on his cigarette. "How'd it go?"

Bart wiped his forehead as if clearing sweat, "Manslaughter by Abortion."

"Good," Gerry exhaled. "Any interesting discussion – comments problems?"

"Yeah. Not quite to the level of insurgency, but a few jurors got off track. I gave them a little talk, reminding them that their job was to find if evidence merited a trial, not to judge the fairness of the law."

Gerry looked concerned, "Just how much off track?"

"As much as the letters in the paper this past week. I wasn't surprised."

Gerry mumbled as if to himself, "That strong, huh."

"No question, those jurors have been following this."

"Hmm. The public is speaking," Gerry said while crushing out his cigarette. Not wasting time, he picked up the phone and asked his secretary to get hold of Will Jones.

Dan left to take Maddie for an early walk just a few minutes before Lauren heard the news on the radio: She and Claire had been indicted for manslaughter. Then, almost simultaneously, the phone rang. Lauren flinched as she answered.

It was Mary.

"Thank God it's you. I've been so worried. I want to speak to Sandi. I miss her, it's been awful not hearing – not talking to her."

"I know, I know. It's a sad thing, but I'm doing what I must."

Lauren stiffened. "Mary, I don't know what you mean. Sandi is my girl, and I make the decisions about her. Let me talk to her before anything else is said. I need to hear her voice."

"I understand that. But she's at catechism; we will call again later when she gets home. For now, I have called for other reasons."

"Catechism! You have enrolled her? What else is going on over there? I want her back in the States with me."

Mary sounded unperturbed, "You know that wouldn't be wise right now. We are in a lovely little town on the coast; in a house where Sandi has her own room and children in the neighborhood to play with."

"You moved to the coast and have a house? Which little town? This was to be a brief vacation. I want her home, now!"

Mary responded with cool authority. "I appreciate how much you love Sandi. But we must consider her well-being in our decisions. Some bad ones have already hurt her. We both should have seen this coming, and now must protect her from further hurt."

"Mary, be careful with your judgment about what's good for Sandi. She loves me – you know how close we are. And she needs me."

"My judgment! Look what's happening, Lauren. And I'm far from alone in my beliefs. If I were, you wouldn't be facing the problems you have."

Lauren visualized the righteous expression on her face; she had seen it often.

Giving Lauren no time to respond, Mary continued. "Sandi is getting adjusted to things over here. Everything takes time. But believe me, I have been with her from the day she was born and will fight for what's good for her. I know she loves you; but let's get your situation cleared up completely before we even talk about other arrangements. I will call soon and see how things are going."

"I need your phone num…" Lauren was cut off by the buzz of the phone.

She sat, stunned and frightened.

Gerry Fields and his deputy were ready to cut a deal when Will Jones arrived. But not reading them, Will started his argument.

Gerry interrupted at the mention of pelvic exam. "It won't fly and isn't necessary. Let's be serious, we all know what's been happening in the news; let's not make more waves than necessary. Bart and I have already talked about reducing this to a misdemeanor for both defendants."

Will smiled, "Sounds good to me."

After Will left, Gerry and Bart looked at each other. "Stupid shit," Gerry said. "'Pelvic exam' – jurors would have loved that one."

Will Smith phoned Lauren with the news several hours after Mary's call. And for the first time since the raid, she felt hopeful.

Lauren hung-up the phone and turned to Dan. "It worked. You did it. They made a deal and the charge has been reduced to a misdemeanor. At least they can't sentence me to more than a…." She stopped, "My God, Dan, a year is a hell of a long time. I can't – I mean I've got to get Sandi and bring her home."

"Hmm," Dan looked worried. "You're right. We need to talk. With an election coming up – D.A.'s, judges, every official will try to capitalize on the case. I've been thinking about attorneys."

"Oh God, Dan, so have I. I have no confidence in Will Jones. And I can't – I won't – take a chance of his blowing my case. For one thing, I don't believe he has the clout Claire and I need when we're in front of a judge." She shook her head, "But I don't know any other lawyers. It's surprising considering everything, but I've never had to deal with them before."

"I'll do some checking." Dan rubbed his chin. "Matter-of-fact, I'll call Robert Farmer. He often covers the courts for The Oregonian – and he gave input for my Esquire article."

Dan picked up the phone, and within minutes he scribbled a name and number on a pad.

After hanging up he said, "James McCaffrey's his choice. He turned a sole practice into a large firm. Only handles high profile cases, which are usually circuit court level. Ours is a misdemeanor, but the issues of this case merit a high caliber attorney. Robert is calling him about taking it."

Within an hour James McCaffrey phoned Lauren and setup an appointment for the following morning.

The office was on the tenth floor of the building, with a panoramic view that stretched from Portland to Mt. Hood. The room conveyed good taste as well as success: thick beige carpets, linen smooth wallpaper, and centered above a leather couch was an original Diego Rivera.

James McCaffrey looked every bit the head of a distinguished firm. His thick hair was graying and age had softened the definition of his chin, but his eyes were sharp and youthful. He wore a dark gabardine suit, white shirt, and black tie with subdued navy stripes. His shoes looked shinier than new.

What best defined him was his voice. Deep and theatrical, Lauren imagined its effect in a courtroom.

"Miss Thompson." He shook her hand; then turned to Dan. "Mr. Carter, Robert Farmer gave you high praise, and I appreciated your column in The Oregonian."

Next, he introduced the young man sitting across the room. "Let me introduce my son, Frank McCaffrey – a senior at Reed College. He comes here to get some ideas about the reality of practicing law. Plans on going to Law School next year."

The son had dark good looks, and Lauren noted that he was at the edge of an office dress-code. He wore baggy beige cords, Armishaw saddles, a white shirt that was unbuttoned at the neck, and no tie.

"When confidentiality isn't an issue, Frank has been sitting in on my cases – learning. Of course, this is always with the client's permission."

Lauren smiled at Frank, "I'm learning too, but I'd rather be doing it from another perspective."

Chapter Twenty

While waiting for her court hearing, Lauren and Dan didn't leave home other than his driving to the store for groceries and newspaper. Lauren feared missing a call from Mary; and when they walked to the river, she would leave windows open, staying alert for a ring.

It was a hot July. Early each morning they would head down the trail to their beach; where they set-up chairs and a table. She read the newspaper while Dan waded into the water, throwing a stick for Maddie to chase. Then he sat beside her and read. Afterwards they returned to the house and Dan put on bacon and eggs.

Constantly, they talked about Sandi and plans of getting her. Their hope was that Lauren's sentence would be light so they could go to Ireland soon, find her and bring her home.

But Lauren's fears were escalating. She made calls to Mary's sister and other relatives. No one gave information, and each made it clear that they didn't want to talk to her.

She and Dan stuck to a daily routine. Lauren knew it was what kept her going. She had never felt so helpless. Sandi was gone, she didn't know where, and she wasn't free to find her.

The phone rang at eight. Thinking it was Mary, Lauren ran to answer. It was James McCaffrey, saying he had some interesting news.

"What?"

"Be in my office in an hour and you'll find out."

Lauren hung-up the phone and told Dan. "What does "interesting news mean?"

"Coming from him, I'd say it's something good."

As they walked into his office, Lauren was surprised to see Claire and Will Jones.

Picking-up her thoughts, McCaffrey said, "As you see, I have asked Dr. Karriden and Mr. Jones to join us. What we have learned will affect both cases.

"Have a seat; I've got lots to tell you."

He waited, and then said, "As you know, the raid happened two days after Geraldine Francini was raced to the hospital from your clinic. And we assume this is what helped the police decide it was time to shut you down."

Claire interrupted. "You're right about that. But I hope it's clear that we didn't do surgery. When I arrived at the clinic, she was lying at my door. I called for an ambulance right away."

James nodded. "This is what we understand. My investigator, George Cabot, has been busy and read the report from the surgeon. Who, by the way, believed what you told him. He wrote that he knows your reputation, and you would not have caused the condition Geraldine Francini was in when the medics brought her to the ER. Her injuries appeared self inflicted.

"However, George interviewed Sister Calligan, a nun at St. Theresa's, who came to the hospital shortly after Geraldine arrived. This nun could be a powerful witness for the prosecution, and is prepared to blame you for a botched abortion. If the court believes her accusations, you might spend a full year in jail – or worse, which we won't surmise at this time."

James pulled a picture of the nun from his file. Lauren thought how she could have been a model for Michelangelo. Her face could fool angels, let alone jurors.

"And this is the transcript of George's interview." James pointed to typed pages. "Exactly what the sister was ready to say under oath. I can summarize it in two sentences: A thirteen-year-old, Geraldine Francini from St. Theresa's, went to your clinic for an abortion. It was bungled, ending with her being taken to the hospital."

James put his hand up, stopping both Claire and Lauren's response.

"George gave little credence to her words. It was just the first step of his investigation. Checking records at Good Sam Hospital he learned that they had performed an abortion; a necessity due to Geraldine's condition when she arrived. The hospital did what is required; they reported the incident to the police. However, they noted that there was no reason to disbelieve your statement, Dr. Karriden, that Geraldine had been dropped off at your clinic after an attempted abortion. And that you had called an ambulance. Their report went on to say that her timely trip to the hospital had most likely saved Geraldine's life.

"However, George learned much more than this." James' voice was solemn. "After the abortion, when Geraldine returned to St. Theresa's, Sister Calligan suspected that word had gotten out. She decided to instill fear in the other girls, at the same time as having Geraldine do penance for her sins. The good sister accomplished this by forcing Geraldine to confess her pregnancy and abortion to an auditorium of St. Theresa peers – ranging in age from eleven to eighteen."

James drew a deep breath. "Horrible; especially in light of Geraldine's history. Her father is in prison for rape, and she was the victim. Having no other relatives as her mother died during childbirth, Geraldine was placed in St. Theresa's three years ago.

"The ugly result of all this is that Geraldine committed suicide two days after her confession to the student-body."

No one spoke. And Lauren thought how of all the heartbreaking stories she had heard, this was one of the worst.

James broke their silence. "The reason you didn't read about the suicide is that they have kept it hushed; especially from the press. By law, there had to be a death notice in the paper – and this simply stated that Geraldine died.

"But be assured: there is no question that we will have impeached Sister Calligan's testimony by the time cross-exam is over."

He faced Will Jones, "We have a strong hand for making a deal. Bart Miller isn't going to be anxious to put his star witness on the stand after he learns what we've got. Our cross-exam of Sister Calligan, forcing her to explain her ideas of fair penance, could place your client and mine in line for sainthood."

Will Jones, looking as if he appreciated the inclusion, turned to Claire. "I concur with Mr. McCaffrey. The best thing we could do right now is deal."

Turning from Will, Claire spoke to James. "I want you to make a deal for me, as well as Lauren."

James shook his head no. "Mr. Jones is your attorney and will represent you."

"This isn't a game we're playing, Mr. McCaffrey. This is my life. You have done the necessary research to save our asses, and you're the one who should present it to the DA."

"Dr. Karriden, I never treat cases lightly. It is not a game; it is a matter of legal ethics."

James faced Lauren, "With your permission, I'll talk to Gerry Fields – see about a deal on your pending sentence. He knows what goes on at police headquarters, and that Geraldine's hospital emergency precipitated the raid."

"Permission! You've got to be kidding. I'm overwhelmed, and all I can say is thank you."

James McCaffrey wasn't surprised when Claire returned by herself within the hour. He was relieved. It served Lauren best for him to argue both cases. He had already phoned Gerry Fields, and asked for a meeting the following morning.

McCaffrey knew it was better to meet with Gerry in the morning rather than the end of a busy day. Each side was in a better frame-of-mind for dealing. At eight-thirty he and Deputy D.A. Barton Miller, sat facing Gerry's desk.

Gerry crushed out his cigarette and looked at James. "Okay, why the meeting? You've got to have something big up your sleeve."

McCaffrey nodded, "You're right. There are some things you need to know about one of your witnesses."

Gerry shook his head. "I could see this coming. What?"

McCaffrey watched their frowns deepen as he told them what George Cabot had learned.

Gerry winced, "I'd like to hire your investigator for the State. Jesus! Putting Sister Calligan on the stand would be like trying the Catholic Church."

He took a deep breath and leaned back in his chair.

"I grew up Catholic; was taught by nuns most of my way through school. This is ugly stuff – even for this office to hear, let alone jurors.

"Goddamn it, Jim." He took a cigarette from his shirt pocket and lit it. "What do you want?"

At three that afternoon, James McCaffrey, Gerry Fields, Dan, Lauren, and Claire waited in the courtroom. It was quiet. Lauren focused on the long hand of the clock above the door to the judge's chambers, watching each minute creep toward the next.

It was almost three thirty when Judge Crouse entered. As he sat, she thought how everything surrounding him symbolized power: the State Seal on the wall, flanked by US and Oregon flags, the large oak desk, and the judge's gavel. Beneath his robe he wore a starched white shirt and black bow tie.

And Lauren noted that his jaw was firm-set and his eyes seemed that of an angry hawk. She flinched; he may not have accepted her plea.

He looked directly at her and then Claire – his expression cold.

"You two ladies just got lucky. During my years of sitting as a judge I have made an effort to respect attorneys who are in my courtroom. You have been served by three of the best in the State: the district attorney, his deputy, and your attorney James McCaffrey.

"It is due to their competency and fine reputations that I will accept the plea; though I do so with reservation." His frown grew darker. "I strongly suggest that you follow the terms of this agreement. If you don't, you will come before me again.

"It is the order of this court that you serve one year of closely supervised probation. Specifically, those terms provide that neither of you will engage in any activities connected to abortion, including giving advice or referrals. Also, you will not leave the State without this court's permission, and will report to a probation officer once a week. In other words, you are on a very short leash. Do you understand this?"

The judge glared, and Lauren wanted to glare back. Instead she looked down at her hands, avoiding eye contact. This man enjoyed his power and would relish sending her and Claire to jail for the full year.

"You will speak to your lawyer about what this requires. Is that clear?" He looked at them as if they were already in contempt of court, then rose and walked back into his chambers.

Lauren shuddered to think of her sentence had a jury found them guilty.

Dan, Lauren, Claire, and James ate in a curtained booth at Zen's, four blocks from the courthouse.

James frowned. "This is the first time I've dealt with Judge Crouse in a court matter. Only knew him from the few times he joined some of us for morning coffee. Fortunately, he didn't have any choice but to accept the plea. You can thank Sister Calligan for that."

"I thank you, Mr. McCaffrey," Claire said, "and want you to remain my attorney. Let's hope it won't be for anymore criminal work."

The late afternoon paper was on the stands by the time they crossed the new bridge to Sauvie Island. The headlines read, Abortionists Sentenced.

Dan drove as Lauren read.

"Listen to this! 'Abortionists Receive Slap on the Wrist. Anne Thompson, alias Lauren Martin…" Lauren's voice rose, "Alias, like an ex-con…" 'and Claire Karriden were lucky. Their crime has been reduced to Attempted Abortion, a misdemeanor, which means that their sentences cannot be longer than a year. Of this, these two criminals won't spend a day in jail.'

"Jesus, Dan, you'd think Claire and I were ax murderers – and that we've been allowed to skate."

"Don't!" Dan said. "Don't read more of that crap. The important thing is that you won't go to jail, and we'll talk to McCaffrey about a plea, allowing you to go with me to bring Sandi home."

Lauren didn't respond, thinking how Judge Crouse wasn't about to do any favors – especially one that allowed her to leave the country.

She looked out of the window, across the field of burgundy colored dahlias. She could almost see the shimmer in the air. It was over 90 degrees. She thought of their beach, and Maddie retrieving sticks from the cold water while they sat in cool breezes. Sandi hadn't been with them. And now... Lauren wondered what it would be like when Sandi came back. She hadn't even seen Sauvie Island.

"Dan, nothing will ever be the same. I've been found guilty of a crime that the news is equating to murder. By now Sandi's friends in Portland have heard it, and Mary will read about it by morning.

"I've been naïve – thinking you and I could get Sandi and take her to New York." She mumbled, as if to herself. "If Sandi comes here she'll be hiding out. Her school... her friends... her life... everything would be..."

"Stop, Lauren. Sandi is resilient; give her credit. And don't lose track of what we want for her. Do you want Sandi to fit-in with them? Narrow-minded and cruel? I want her to grow-up with the same values as you – and the strength to stand up for them.

"We'll bring her here and then to New York – make her part of the world we want for her." He turned and looked at her. "Okay?"

He was right. Lauren moved close and kissed his cheek. "Thanks, Dan. I love you."

Lauren wondered if for the rest of her life she'd feel a lump in her throat every time the phone rang. This time it was from New York.

Lauren watched Dan, and understood the call was serious.

Before hanging up, he said, "I can't, but I'll be in New York in two days, and will talk to Shultz. He can do the job."

After the call he sat in the large cushiony chair that Lauren had chosen for him. He lit a cigarette and looked at her – bothered.

"I let them know I couldn't be there tomorrow. You and I need to sign adoption papers before I leave. Then I'll go to New York."

Lauren nodded, "Within a month we'll be a legal family. It will be nice. But Dan, there's something else." She hesitated, and then said, "They want you in Korea. Right? "Yes. But I'm not taking the assignment. I'll go to New York and meet with Tony Shultz." He's smart, a good reporter, and can handle it."

She shook her head no, and then said, "Now I have a suggestion that I'm reluctant to make. You're needed in Korea, not someone else. You've been the one reporting it for two years and know what's happening.

"Dan, I'm sure you know by now that I'm not fragile. I'll be all right. And let's face it, what's happening in Korea affects thousands of lives. You have little choice."

He didn't say anything, and she added, "Besides, you want to go."

"God, am I that easy of a read?"

"Only by a woman who spends her time reading you."

She paused, and then said, "But don't get me wrong. I'll miss you and always want you here with me. And importantly, I want you here in a month when you are Sandi's legal parent.

Chapter Twenty-One

Almost a month later the phone rang in the middle of the night. Lauren got out of bed and ran.

"Mary?"

"You sound breathless? Did I calculate correctly? 'Tis early morning over there?"

Lauren rushed words, "Oh Mary, I miss Sandi. I need to talk to her, hear her voice. Please put her on the phone."

"I can't do that right now. She's at school"

"School! It's summer, and you've put her in school?" Lauren's voice rose. "I want to talk to her. It's been over a month. You have to give me a phone number; let me know where you are. You have no right to do this; not to her or me."

"To you! You're not my concern, quite honestly. I'm doing what I must for my granddaughter."

"Mary, stop! Sandi's my daughter. And if necessary, I'll stop you through the law." Lauren added, "Remember – you wouldn't be in Ireland if it weren't for the money I provide."

"Ah yes, that is sadly true, and 'tis tainted money. But I can remedy this. Believe me we can exist without your money. I'll take a job scrubbing floors before I allow her to go back to a situation that would continue to do her harm."

"Harm! Being away from me – that's harm. And about support, I have always supported Sandi and always will."

Afraid Mary would hang-up, Lauren backed off. "Please listen, Mary. I'm at Sauvie Island. It's private where we live, and she'll love it here until we move from Oregon."

She hoped Mary hadn't read about her probation.

"Lauren, as long as I breathe she will not return to Oregon and suffer consequences of your reputation. And don't be so sure of her wanting to return. She's beginning to talk of memories; of effects your – err – profession had on her as a child. We, my sisters and I, have found a wonderful psychiatrist for her."

"Psychiatrist! My God, Mary, you have done this without telling me. But then, why should that surprise me! What else are you doing over there? I want Sandi here! I…" Lauren backed off… "Dan – both of us will come for her and…"

"Dan? Hmm. Why haven't you already come for her, Lauren? But then, of course, that may be impossible. What's happening? You must have received a sentence you're not mentioning? Oregon's a long way from here, thank the lord; and I'm not able to keep-up with the news.

"Oh, Lauren. You must know that I am doing what I have to do. I was happy living in our old home; never wanted your money. Our world changed when you went to that clinic. Now I say Hail Marys everyday because I became complicit when I moved to that house. And look at the emotional cost. Sandi is paying the price. I fear she'll need a doctor for many years."

"Stop! Sandi doesn't need a psychiatrist. She needs me, and I want her here. And as to your suggestion that I received a sentence, I'm on probation. In simple terms this means closing-up the office, which Claire and I knew we had to do anyway." Lauren weighed her words, "And for a while it will be difficult for me to leave. But believe me, I will do what's necessary to get Sandi back.

"I have tried to talk to you, placing unanswered calls to your sister. You have made it impossible to tell you anything. Dan and I were married soon after you left. We plan on having another ceremony with Sandi as soon…"

Mary broke in, "You got married without telling Sandi! Why do I find this typical of you? Do you have any idea of... Never mind. Why should I be surprised? When have you ever worried about how your life affects her?"

"Good God, Mary, you know that's not true. Besides, how can I tell her anything when I'm never able to talk to her?" Lauren took another deep breath. "She loves Dan and he loves her. He's in the process of adopting her. Give me a number so I can call her when she returns from school. I'll tell her..."

Mary's voice rose above hers. "And undo all we have been helping her overcome. No, I won't do that. She is putting her past behind her. Just go on with your life. Do what you want, but don't try to see her.

"And Lauren, I can do without your support. It isn't the fancy schools she needs; it's an environment where she can grow up with the clear knowledge that certain rules must be followed. Rules she can feel proud of – given to us by the Church and lived by many."

"Mary, those rules are yours, not mine – and not what I want for Sandi. But you know that. Just remember that Sandi is my daughter; I decide what is right for her. And I don't want her being told that my profession is immoral, or whatever term you use. I have saved lives, something you don't understand."

Lauren could hear a quiver in Mary's voice. "Don't approach me with more of your blasphemy if you ever want to speak to my grandchild again."

"If I ever want to speak to her! What in God's name are you saying? No more arguing. Sandi is my girl, and I'll take legal action to have her returned to me."

The phone went dead, and Lauren immediately called the telephone operator.

"I need to put a trace on a call I just received from Ireland."

Lauren dialed James McCaffrey, catching him as he arrived at work. She launched into details of Mary's call.

When she finished, McCaffrey asked, "Dan will be home soon – correct? Hope he's ready to board another plane. The adoption's complete, so he can go to Ireland as a legal parent."

"Yes. Thank God, Dan will be coming home. But the reason I called is to ask you if you can arrange a hearing before Judge Crouse. With your help I'd like to ask for a short reprieve from probation. I want to be the one to go to Ireland. I made a promise to Sandi before she left – and she's waiting for me to come for her.

"And I'd like to see you bring her home. But that's not likely to happen. However, I'll call Judge Crouse right away. Then I'm going to contact the American Embassy. Mary Sullivan is not a legal guardian. And Sandi isn't a citizen of Ireland. Her grandmother has no legal right to keep her there. And we might be able to bring her home without you or Dan needing to go. Mrs. Sullivan has no legal right to keep her there."

Lauren sighed, "From my understanding, church is more powerful than law in Ireland."

"But not international law. It honors our laws as well as Ireland's."

That night Lauren didn't sleep. Anxious, she wanted to see Judge Crouse right away – get started on her trip to Sandi. She also worried about Dan. She couldn't phone him, and it had been a week since she had heard from him.

Then near midnight Dan phoned, but she strained to hear him.

"I'm on a field phone in Panmunjom covering a meeting between UN and Communist who're trying to secure the 38th parallel. It's a joke. That's artillery you hear in the background."

The blasts had to be close. His voice crackled from static that came and disappeared as he described the scene around him. She was able to make out something about a new partner – a photographer.

She interrupted, "Dan, it's almost impossible to hear what you're saying. Before we're cutoff, let me say I miss and love you."

"Jesus, Lauren, I didn't intend to spend this time on me. Are you all right? It's been a month and the adoption papers must be..."

A thunderous explosion cut into his words and Lauren yelled, "Oh my God, what's that?

Come home." She pushed the receiver hard against her ear. "Can you hear me? When will you be home?"

His voice crackled, "That's why I called... I can't... just... longer... " There was a brief clearing and he repeated, "Just a few weeks. They've asked me to stay longer."

Lauren shouted no but knew he couldn't hear over the static.

When it cleared, he rushed words. "When I leave they have to have a new reporter – that's hard in this hellhole, but one will come in two..."

This time the blast took his voice, and the phone clicked off.

"Dan," she yelled; then waited for a clearing.

More than ever she understood that their worlds were a million miles apart. Bombs, bullets – death!

After minutes she got a dial tone and placed the receiver back. She worried when he didn't phone back, but finally returned to bed – where she lay wide awake.

Within minutes Maddie put her paw on the bed and whined.

"Girl, it's been a bad night."

Lauren ran her hand through her soft fur. "He loves us, right girl?" Maddie curled onto her mat, as Lauren finished her thought, "And he and Sandi will be back with us soon."

She woke as the sun rose lighting her room and walked to the window. The rain was gone, and the sky was pure blue. She thought how the world was resilient. Today she would turn things around.

Without hesitating she rang the operator, and had her dial Mary's sister, Margaret – who launched into a prepared statement.

"I talked to Mary last night and she asked me to tell you that if you don't want to provide for Sandra, then don't. Her banker, who has known our family from his schooldays, told her of your effort to trace withdrawals from her account. Now she hesitates to accept any of the money; which, she wants you to know, has only used for Sandra's care. Not for her own needs."

Lauren thought how McCaffrey's detective hadn't wasted any time.

"Margaret, we resorted to tracing money because I need to know where Sandi is. She's my daughter; surely you can understand how I feel."

Margaret's voice was sharp, "I understand that your life has made Sandra's terrible. When Mary arrived, I didn't know how you earned money, or why she left Oregon. Now, whatever Mary's actions may be, I support her. And let me tell you clearly, I don't want more of your phone calls and I won't talk to any detectives who come snooping at my…"

Lauren's voice rose over hers. "Your sister is guilty of kidnapping and when you help her you're an accomplice. I will do everything in my power to…" She stopped. Giving more information would push Mary deeper into hiding.

"Your power to do what? This is Ireland. I'd advise you to back off. That child of yours has suffered enough."

The phone went dead.

"Who is it?" Claire answered after six rings.

"It's me," Lauren said. "Thank God. Calls are seldom good. When Jane phones, she lets it ring once, hangs up, and then I phone her back."

"I can't believe that reporters haven't discovered I'm here," Lauren said. But today I want out of here. Need a good friend to talk to."

"So do I. Coffee will be ready, and I'll throw on some breakfast."

Within thirty minutes Lauren drove into her own garage. The media had given up and left. She wanted to keep it that way, so she didn't enter her house. Instead she let Maddie run down the path in the direction she had taken as a puppy. Within minutes she turned back and caught up with Lauren, who was close to Claire's house.

Claire had been watching for her and opened the door as they arrived.

"Wow, have I missed you," Claire said, and they hugged.

"There's so much to talk about – things I won't say on the phone. If there's a way to tap it, reporters have done it."

Lauren waited until they sat at the kitchen table sipping coffee. "First, where's Bill?"

"You mean ex-husband Bill. Thank God he's gone. By the time we got back from the honeymoon, I was wondering how to get him out of my life. The only thing positive about the arrest is that he left.

"My money was disappearing even faster than Jane and I can spend it; and that's pretty fast. It seems that Bill has a gambling problem."

"I'm sorry, Claire."

"Don't be. He's a liability, and I'm glad he's gone. But enough about him; I'd like to take on that mother-in-law of yours, or whatever you call her. Especially right now; I'm ready for a fight."

"And this is going to be a big one," Lauren said. "As always, there's so much going on. Cutting it short, I'm trying to get permission to leave for Ireland. I know I can bring Sandi home. I've been to see James McCaffrey, and he's setting up a meeting with Judge Crouse."

"Good God, Lauren, you think that judge is going to let you leave Oregon, let alone fly half way across the world?"

"We'll soon find out. I want to leave within a week."

Claire shook her head and smiled. "You just might pull it off, and I wish I could go with you. I'd handle Mary. As I said, I'm angry and need to release it – no one is more deserving than she."

"You're right, and I'm planning on being well armed if I go. The Church governs Ireland. Can you imagine how they'll look at me?""

"Just about the same as Portland has seen us this past year. This brings me to something else I need to discuss, though I know it's not the best time. So first, you sit here and enjoy the view as I fix some breakfast."

Lauren looked out at the sweeping view of the city, and remembered how she felt the first time she came to see Claire. She had wondered how it felt to live at the top of Portland Heights.

Now, looking at the weed-free lawn, she thought how hers was the same, and only a block away. It also was trimmed and edged, with a path that separated it from the wild rhododendrons, shrubs, firs, and pines that filled the hillside.

"It's nice, this view." Lauren started to get up. "Let me help you."

"Too late, I had it in the oven, just had to fry eggs."

Claire carried the plate to the table.

Looking at the eggs, ham, and a berry tart, served on Spode China, Lauren said, "Everything you do is special – this is elegant."

Claire smiled. "It takes no more time to serve breakfast on china than on plastic."

Lauren laughed. "With all else, our career has been lucrative. I have more money than I ever dreamed was possible."

"Leave it to you to come right out with it – no self-delusion." Claire smiled. "I would have seen most of those girls with or without the pay, but you're right, it's provided a grand lifestyle."

"But you're right, Claire. You have never turned anyone away for lack of money." Lauren looked at her with admiration. "What are you planning on doing after probation? There's much I'll miss about our clinic, but most of all I'll miss seeing you every day. You're in a class of your own and I've been lucky.

"You know Claire, as soon as I'm free and Sandi is back with me, Dan wants us to move to New York. Have you ever thought of moving there? I'd like that."

"New York? And leave this?" Claire nodded toward the hills. "Besides there's Jane and the grandkids."

Claire paused, and then said, "But there's more. It's time I share my secret. The women still call. At first I refused them; then – you know how it goes. They're always desperate, and some... well I've been helping them. I talked to Fred Atchison, who has done occasional abortions in his clinic, and he…"

Lauren interrupted, "Fred, the chiropractor?"

"The same. He has rooms in the back of his building."

Lauren said nothing but shook her head in disbelief.

"I know, Lauren. It's risky. But to be honest, I need the money. Jane, with that house, and the girls – they depend on me, as does Carol. I have kept her on the payroll. My God, if anyone deserves it, she does.

"And I have a secret that I haven't shared with anyone. I've put a down-payment on a large piece of property in Florida – far away from here. I'm going to build a place for Jane and the girls."

"So, facts are, it's not just because women keep calling. As you pointed out, our work has been lucrative. Quite simply, I have to continue."

Lauren nodded and they sat without speaking. She thought about her own future: leaving for New York with Sandi and Dan.

She felt a chill, and then said, "It's all far away. I wonder, Claire, if New York will happen…If we – Sandi and I – will ever go."

Chapter Twenty-Two

When Lauren returned home that afternoon she called James McCaffrey. Time was passing, and Sandi was waiting – trusting she would come for her. Of all the promises in Lauren's life, this was the most important.

McCaffrey sounded surprised, "You beat me to the phone. I was just going to call and tell you to meet me in the judge's courtroom tomorrow morning at eight. I caught him in time. He and his family are leaving in three days for Hawaii."

Lauren felt a flicker of hope when Judge Crouse took the bench. Unlike the last time she was in his courtroom, he wasn't glaring. Instead of anger, his squint appeared nearsighted as he motioned for her, James, and the court-reporter to be seated. It occurred to Lauren that there were no prosecutors, members of the press, or critics in the gallery to influence him.

James remained standing. "Judge Crouse, my client, Lauren Martin, has requested this hearing. She is concerned for the welfare of her eight- year-old daughter, Sandi. And she has good cause for this concern.

"Before she explains, I want to say that I respect my client's integrity. So totally, that if you grant her request I will personally guarantee that she will follow every condition you set."

Lauren noted the Judge's expression as he listened to James. It was of respect and gave her a measure of hope.

Wearing a black suit, no make-up other than pale lipstick, and her hair pulled into a tight chignon, Lauren was somber as she stood to plead her case.

"Judge Crouse, I know that your world and mine are quite different, but there are some things that I believe we share. You have children, and recognize the depth of concern we parents feel about their well-being. You know what it's like if that is threatened. My eight-year-old daughter, Sandi, is in a situation right now that could change her life forever. When I spoke to her last she was crying, and begged for me to come and bring her home. This is what I promised to do when she left for a short vacation with her Grandmother."

The Judge interrupted, "Mrs. Martin – Carter, whichever you go by, I understand that your daughter is in Ireland, being protected from scandal related to your profession – including your arrest. Is that correct?"

"In part, yes."

Lauren stood straight. "Judge Crouse, I wasn't ashamed of what I did. I know that you were elected to uphold the law, and I recognize that I worked outside of it. But I truly believe that I saved girls, some as young as twelve, and women who faced situations that could destroy their lives. Many were referred to me by reputable doctors, who understood this. I saw girls who suffered from brutal acts – rapes, incest. And I helped them with or without payment."

Watching the judge's expression, Lauren recognized that she had taken the wrong tack and before he responded she changed directions. She emphasized her words, "Judge Crouse, about my girl, I, and I know her father would feel the same, want her to grow up with a set of values that are intrinsically good."

The judge put out his hand stopping her, and snapped, "I assume that Dan Carter is the father of your child. Correct?"

Lauren shook her head. "No, he isn't."

"So, Mrs. Carter, should I assume the father is Mr. Martin?"

"No, Judge. That's my maiden name. Her father's name is Ben Sullivan."

"Hmm." The judge shook his head with disdain. "So who is her father?" Lauren hesitated, not prepared to tell him about Ben. But the judge waited.

"Ben died during the early months of World War Two. He was on an aircraft carrier headed for the battle of Guadalcanal. I was three months pregnant with his child, Sandi." Lauren didn't intend it, but her voice quivered.

Judge Crouse's expression softened. "I'm sorry, Mrs. Carter." He cleared his throat. "Please continue with what is happening to your daughter. How is her well-being threatened? Is she facing danger?"

Lauren shook her head yes, and then told the judge how Sandi went to Ireland with her grandmother for a short visit. She watched him while she described each event of the past month. Unlike before, he appeared concerned.

"Your Honor, Mary is hiding Sandi. And the last time she phoned, she told me I would never see her again. I know she is serious. And I also know my Sandi; she's waiting for me to come for her.

"Judge," Lauren heard herself begging, "I had always said I would quit my profession if it affected Sandi. I am guilty of being terribly naïve – I should have quit sooner. And now my punishment is far beyond any the court can give. My daughter is aching and I can't go to her.

"I am not afraid of jail, except for how it would affect her. Please let me go to her. I will serve any extra probation you order. But now, I need to go to her and bring her home."

For long seconds the courtroom was quiet.

Then Judge Crouse spoke, "There are few times that I have changed conditions of probation." He cleared his throat. "This is one of them. You are correct, Mrs. Carter, my wife and I would do everything imaginable to help our children. And I feel what you are saying, even though I still have to wonder how you could have put your daughter at such risk."

He shook his head and then said, "That aside, I feel your fear. But also, and very important in this situation, I have great respect for your attorney who vouches for you."

He looked directly at her, emphasizing the seriousness of his words, "I am going to give you three weeks to go to Ireland and bring your daughter home; but with the condition that you make every effort to protect her from the notoriety that your crime continues to bring.

"Do you have a plan for that?"

Flooded with relief, Lauren answered, "Oh Judge Crouse, thank you. And yes, her well-being is my greatest concern. I do have plans. We will live in a vacation home which has become a refuge from reporters; few people know about it. And I'm fully prepared to home-school Sandi for the rest of my probation. As you probably know, my husband is a journalist and has homes both here and in New York. He and I plan on taking Sandi to live in New York when my probation ends."

The judge addressed James. "Mr. McCaffrey, as I have stated, I have great respect for you. And I hope that Mrs. Carter fully recognizes what it means to have you vouch for her. But regardless of that, I would not change the rules of her probation if not for their potential of harm to her daughter. I trust that you will prepare papers for the Irish courts that will secure Mrs. Carter's rights."

He turned to Lauren, "I will give Mr. McCaffrey several days to prepare papers, and then on Monday of next week you will leave for Ireland. By the first Monday of October, you will report to your probation officer. That gives you exactly three weeks to go to Ireland and bring your daughter home. Is that understood? "

"Yes, and again I thank you, Judge Crouse."

"Thank your attorney, Mrs. Carter" Then the judge emphasized, "And, I must add, I appreciate that your daughter's father gave his life for this country."

Lauren looked at him and thought of Ben. She shivered. He had played a part in the judge's decision.

The only way Lauren could reach Dan was through the New York office. She spoke to his secretary, who said she would try get a message through to him. It worked, and he reached Lauren within the hour.

"You all right?" He asked.

"Yes, but excited, worried, missing you, and have something big to tell you. I'm going to Ireland."

"You're what!"

"I saw Judge Crouse this morning and leave for Ireland by Monday."

"You had a hearing this morning and will be going to Ireland! I know you have magic powers, but how did you pull that off?"

"Thank James. He vouched for me. I have three weeks to go and bring Sandi home. James is contacting a magistrate this afternoon, arranging to have Sandi's name included on my passport. Her own is probably locked in a vault.

"I have to be the one to go. I told her I'd come for her."

"I'm going with you. I'll rush my story so it…."

"No, Dan. I can't wait. It will take time to find Sandi. I already have a ticket and will leave on Monday. I'll fly to Gander, Newfoundland;

that will take at least twelve hours. From Gander to Belfast will be another twelve. Time is the key. If Mary finds out I'm coming, she'll go deeper into hiding. Probably into a convent, and it would take more than a court order for me to get inside.

"Dan, I know I'm changing our plans; I have to."

"I should have left earlier. I'm sorry, Lauren."

"Don't be. You had no choice."

Then she thought of how quickly things were changing "Oh my God, Dan, I was terrified when you phoned – just two nights ago. Where are you now?"

"Seoul. I came in to call New York and dictate my story – if that's what it's called. We're in a goddamned hell-hole over here – as you heard on Tuesday.

"Now, today, when my secretary said you were trying to reach me, I knew I would leave no matter what. The mess over here isn't going to get anything but worse. And you come before my story – before anything. I need to come home."

"Dan, I want you here – safe, so please come home now. But as I said, I need to leave right away. And, if everything goes as I plan, the three of us will be together in week."

"Jesus, Lauren. You be safe. I should be with you."

"I'll be more than safe – I'll be ecstatic when I find Sandi, and we're headed for home."

Chapter Twenty-Three

As soon as Claire heard the decision she went to a phone booth, fearing that her home phone was still being tapped. She placed a call to Liza Haines, who had come to the states in 1940, and attended University of Oregon where her uncle was a professor.

During Liza's sophomore year her boyfriend drove her to Claire's clinic.

After Liza graduated and returned to Ireland, she wrote Claire, "You helped me when I needed it the most, and made such a difference in my life. Now I want to do something to help girls and women over here."

She and Claire kept in touch. Liza became active in an underground system for women, and sent Claire her phone number with a note, "This is in-case any girls from America need help while over here."

Claire needed it now.

Liza was ready to help, and told Claire to phone back in two hours. Claire did, and was impressed. Liza told her that Lauren needed to board a plane and arrive in Belfast in three days.

Lisa gave her detailed information.

Claire was impressed and got hold of Lauren right away, telling her that she had exciting news and suggested they meet at Thiele's. "We could each use a good meal, and I need to get out of that house."

They met within the hour. For privacy, Mrs. Thiele gave them a table in her office.

As soon as they sat, Claire said, "I just phoned Liza. She can't meet you in Belfast, but has arranged for Sean O'Sullivan, a barrister, to come to the airport."

"O'Sullivan?"

Claire nodded. "You've got it. Ben's cousin."

"My God. I never heard Mary talk about him."

"Mary," Claire shrugged. "From what Liza says, Mary wouldn't approve of him anymore than she does us. He's far from a family favorite. Liza describes him as an Irish reject; but one she wished they had kept. He became a barrister in Ireland, but left because of politics and now practices in London.

"Liza contacted him today, and he'll be at Aldergrove Airport in Belfast in three days to meet you. I'll phone her back with your ticket number and the time you'll arrive. Get this – he's cancelling clients to do this. Liza said he's enthused about helping you. Not just because he's related to Sandi, but he considers us – you and me – heroes. A notion we don't often hear.

"I told Liza that I think you can leave from Canada day after tomorrow in the middle of the night. She knew there's only one flight from there to Belfast. He'll look into the schedule and be waiting when you arrive.

"Oh yes, and she told him not to worry about finding you. She remembers you from a non-surgical visit to our clinic, and told him to look for a gorgeous redhead.

"And Lauren, the best news is that Liza believes that Sean O'Sullivan, Mary's nephew, knows where you'll find Sandi."

On the following day Lauren booked planes to Newfoundland and Belfast, and exchanged five hundred dollars to pounds. Next, she phoned James McCaffrey to see what was happening about getting Sandi's name onto her passport. McCaffrey had tried to get hold of her. She needed to go with him to Oregon's US Passport Office to change it.

When they reached the office, Lauren saw that the executive in charge had a no mentality. Even when they presented Judge Crouse's official request, the man shook his head "no."

James stood straight and looked him in the eye. "Call the courthouse, if you wish. But have this done by tomorrow afternoon, or we'll file an affidavit of malfeasance to take before Judge Crouse."

The man appeared ready to argue; then pursed his brow and mumbled, "It will be done by this time tomorrow."

James looked at his watch, "Let's make that three p.m. tomorrow."

After leaving the office, Lauren asked, "What's an affidavit of malfeasance?"

James smiled, "I'll have to see if there is such a thing. If not, there should be."

On the night Lauren was to leave she packed a light bag with a couple of change of clothes. And then dressed as if going to work at Thelie's: flat shoes, a beige blouse and black skirt. She wore a trench coat but tossed a pair of wide-rimmed sunglasses back into a drawer, deciding she didn't want to look like a spy out of a war movie.

She left Maddie at Claire's house; then Claire drove her to the airport.

Chapter Twenty-Four

Due to tail-winds and clear skies across much of the Atlantic, Lauren's plane landed at Aldergrove early. Upon arriving she walked to the counter and learned that the plane from London wouldn't arrive for an hour.

It had been twenty-four hours since leaving Portland. She was stiff from sitting and needed a brisk walk. So, after putting her suitcase in a locker, she went outside. As in Portland, Belfast was cold and dark clouds threatened a downpour. But she could see fields not far from the airport, and walked past the busses, cabs, and cars, toward them. Stretching after sitting for so long, she breathed in the damp, cold, but fresh air, and kept walking.

She had gone too far when she realized the sky had grown even darker, and the storm hit with unexpected fury. She started to run toward the airport as thunder rumbled and clouds burst. She pushed against the wind and hard rain. By the time she reached the airport her hair and trench coat were dripping.

Her shoes squishing, Lauren walked to a hook near the lockers and hung her coat. Then she went into the woman's room. Grabbing paper towels, she soaked some of the water from her hair, then let it hang damp on the shoulders of her blouse. Looking into the mirror she wished she had a rubber-band to pull it into a ponytail. When it dried it would be wild and curly.

Then it hit her that she was concerned about her hair as if it mattered. But as she stepped away, she thought how it would be nice to have dry shoes – and simultaneously she remembered having packed a pair of loafers.

She was pulling her suitcase out of the locker when she heard him. "You have to be Lauren Martin."

She turned. and thought how his eyes were dark like Sandi's.

"Sean O'Sullivan?"

"Yes. You're my round-about American cousin."

He looked at her hair. "A leak on the airplane?"

"That would be a better excuse than taking a walk. But I needed fresh air." She rolled her eyes, "and got a shower with it."

"A shower! That was a downpour. Welcome to Ireland. Liza should have warned you to bring an umbrella." He picked up her bag, "But I see you traveled light."

"I'm hoping that I won't be here long." She paused, "Not that I wouldn't like time to get to know you – Ben's cousin. Thank you for meeting me."

"My plane was early, and I've been looking for you. Liza told me I'd recognize you by your full red hair." Looking at her hair, he added, "I'm glad she also said tall and beautiful." He reached for her coat. "Let me take this."

She shook her head. "No. You'll end up as soaked as it. I'll get a bag for it."

Ignoring her refusal, he took the coat and headed for the desk, where he folded it into a bag, and then returned.

"We'll drop this at a laundry, before getting a bite. I haven't eaten since early this morning, and would just as soon talk over fish and chips at a pub instead of what they serve at Aldergrove."

He looked at her shoes. "We'll also pick up another pair of shoes. You have time; your bus, the first of three, doesn't leave until tonight."

"I'll be on a bus tonight! We've got to talk. Don't worry about

213

shoes." She pulled loafers and a cloth from her suitcase, took off the wet shoes, wiped her feet, and slipped into the dry ones.

When they stepped outside, it was still pouring rain. A cab drove to the curve. Sean asked the driver to stop at a laundry. Lauren thought how he had a nice easy way of taking care of things.

The pub was designed like an English Inn – a brick building with black painted window boxes, trim, and door. An English Flag, with its red and white cross, hung from the pergola.

The owner met them at the door and gave Sean a robust handshake. "Mr. O'Sullivan, it is good to see you."

Sean chuckled, "I never hear that in Dublin."

"That you wouldn't, even though things have been a bit quiet lately." He looked at Lauren, "And you must be a friend from London."

She smiled, "Never been there. I just got off a much longer flight."

"American. You'll be welcomed in Belfast." He shook her hand, "We appreciate what your boys have done for us."

They walked to a booth and a waiter arrived with a Guiness. "Nice to see you Mr. O'Sullivan. And what will the lady have?"

"An Irish Toddy." As Lauren ordered, she remembered that Mary had introduced her to them.

"Good choice in weather like today's." The waiter said, and then headed for the bar.

Sean tasted his Guinness. "This is the best product of Ireland. But that's not what we're here to talk about. We've got a lot to cover before you catch a bus at seven."

He stopped and smiled, "But I do need to tell you that Liza was right. Every eye in this place followed you since we walked in. A beautiful redhead doesn't go unnoticed in Ireland."

"I hope that's meant as a compliment, not a warning. Mary thinks I'm not allowed to leave Oregon. But if she learns I'm here, she'll get my picture to the police, while taking Sandi into hiding beyond..." Lauren stopped. "I don't need to say more."

"It was meant as a compliment. And at this time no one knows you're anyone other than a pretty woman with very fuzzy hair."

Lauren laughed as she touched her hair. "You're right – fuzzy is good."

Then she said, "I was concerned that I wouldn't recognize you, but it was easy. You look like Ben – or what Ben would have. . ." She stopped and shook her head. "You don't know who Ben is, but you look like him."

"I do know who Ben is. And as for my looking like him, I'm an O'Sullivan – one of the clan. We all have a strong resemblance; especially our attitude – we're a cantankerous bunch. I'm as tetched as the rest. What separates me is my feelings about Church and State, which of course is the most important part of an Irishman's life.

"Few O'Sullivan's will claim me. As you must know, I'm persona-non-grata in most of Ireland." He looked around the room and added, "And that includes a good part up here as well as England."

She nodded, "I've heard that England isn't much more receptive to my profession than Ireland, or, for that matter, the U.S."

He laughed. "England professes limits between Church and State, but these limits vary – and don't exist in laws concerning abortion." He nodded, "Very similar to the States."

Lauren studied him. "I don't know why I never heard of you till now. Ben would have appreciated you."

"I heard about him. He died too young, and will remain an unsung hero along with so many here in Belfast. It's a sore point with me that few Irish joined the fight. In 1940, at seventeen, I left home and joined the RAF, ending up flying in the Battle of Britain. Injured before America entered the war, I came back to Ireland. My family nurtured me back to health, while thinking I was a fool for enlisting."

He stopped. "But let's get to you. I've got news, and you don't have time for the Battle of Britain."

Lauren nodded. "Not now – but will have someday when you come to visit me and my husband, Dan. Now, I need to know where Sandi is.

"Sandra is on the west coast, in Galway.

Lauren leaned forward. "Galway?"

"Yes." Sean reached into his briefcase, pulled out a map of Galway, and spread it before her.

"Mary is working at the Great Southern Hotel as a cook." He had circled it, the bus depot, and St. Francis parish school. "She works an early shift, and then volunteers at Sandi's school in the afternoon.

"We'll leave here early enough for you to purchase tickets at the bus station. You'll be boarding in about three hours, and it will take you to Cork. You'll have an hour's wait. There is a middle of the night bus passing through, and it will arrive in Galway by eight thirty tomorrow morning.

Liza will be in a black Vauxhall, waiting for you at the far right corner of the station. And by the way, Liza usually arranges for other volunteers to be drivers. But she admires you and wants to be the person who drives.

She'll let you off a block from the parish. You need to be at the playground at 9:10, when the girls are there for recess. Liza knows the details. You'll go through the gardener's entrance on the east side; the door will be unlocked. Walk down the garden path, follow the voices of children, and you'll reach the playground.

"That's it. Sandra will be there, but has no idea that you're in Ireland. She and you will have quite a reunion, but it's going to have to wait until you're out of the parish. We're hoping you'll be in Liza's car before word gets to the Bishop. But I'm certain that won't happen. The minute you're on that playground, he'll be informed and Mary will be summoned."

.Lauren squinted in disbelief. "Everything you've planned is amazing, and I'm wondering how you and Liza have arranged all this. Gates open for me! Sandi will be on the playground! You know her schedule. How? Who else is helping?"

Before Sean could respond, the waiter returned to their table and asked for Lauren's order.

She deferred to Sean, "You know the menu."

"You're right. We'll have halibut and chips," he said. "And I'll have another Guinness."

Lauren ordered tea. Then, when the waiter was out of hearing range, she said, "My God, I'll be with Sandi tomorrow morning. And you and Liza have made this happen. But there has to be someone else, someone I want to thank."

Sean hesitated and then said, "I'm thinking that you, more than most, have lived a life of keeping secrets. And I know that you'll protect those who are helping you now. So, I trust that you won't ask for his name, or reveal any of what I tell you. He is a priest – and we go way back to catechism. However, as he dove deeper into religion, I grew further away. But our friendship isn't based on philosophy – not that we haven't discussed it.

"Life is filled with uncanny coincidences and this is one of them. He knows my mum, and knew what was going on from the time Sandra and Mary arrived in Dublin; including their secret move to Galway."

"Now, this gets even harder to fathom – especially if you've lost faith in miracles. Of all parishes in Ireland, Mary surreptitiously enrolled Sandi at St. Francis, where my friend was a priest. I say 'was,' as he transferred to another parish a short time after Mary joined. But he knows what is happening.

"Mary told the head priest at St. Francis that she and Sandra were on the run from a horrible situation. They were hiding from you – a convicted abortionist. In Ireland, that's the same as saying convicted murderer. And I'm certain the head priest, Father O'Connor, believes it is God's providence that brought Sandra to his parish".

The day before Sandra enrolled in classes, Father O'Connor had a special prayer meeting for the priests and nuns at St. Francis – protecting the soul of Sandra O'Sullivan. He explained that Mary O'Sullivan had brought her to them, not wanting Sandra to return to the house of an abortionist.

"My friend expressed his opposition to this, causing his transfer to another parish. It was during this time that he confided to me – knowing that Mary is my aunt.

"I was figuring how to handle the information without involving him – or causing a ruckus that would force Mary and Sandra into deeper hiding. This is when Liza contacted me. She and I have worked together before – and knew my connections to both Sandra's family and the church.

"Let me add, my friend the priest has had problems with the Church's over-reach into State affairs. His strong sense of justice sometimes gets in the way of his vows." Sean shook his head. "The truth is, he was always less rebellious than I." Sean smiled, "And if there's an afterlife it will pay off for him. We went to parochial school together, and on to Trinity. I entered the School of Law, but he chose Philosophy and then the seminary.

"Which is right for him; he was always much more devout. However, he never pretended to believe in the church's over-reach into State affairs. And he really thought that in becoming a priest he would have more voice in changing its over-zealous tenets.

"Over the years he's grown more disillusioned, especially because of the church's involvement – I call it intrusion – in personal liberties. Truth is, I suspect he'll be leaving the priesthood one of these days. And if word gets out of how he's helping you, it may be very quickly."

Lauren put her hand out, "Word won't come from me! The church needs more like him – and please thank him for me."

"That I'll do," he said, then looked at her plate "Are you going to taste that? You'll never find fish and chips as good anywhere; that includes London. The halibut is caught fresh from the Atlantic off our coast."

Lauren heard his pride. "I wish I had more time to see Ireland"

He nodded, "It's a beautiful country, and you'll see plenty of it before you get back on the plane to America."

Lauren smiled, "Yes! And once Sandi and I get out of Ireland, I don't expect to ever come here again. I'm certain it's beautiful, and that its people are as warm and funny as I've always heard. But my profession brings out the worst in them. You're well aware of that."

"Correct. And defensively – as an Irishman who will never return home – I need to say that Ireland isn't alone. As you're aware, the US hasn't been broad minded toward abortion – and for the same reasons: Church and its influence on politics."

"Touché. But still, I'll stay out of Ireland."

"And someday I'll be coming to the U.S. Want to visit some relatives, and will probably make it out to Oregon."

"If you want me to show you around, you better come quickly. When my probation is over, Sandi and I will be moving to live with my husband in New York."

"That will be even better. I'd love to see New York through the eyes of one of the world's renowned journalist."

Lauren smiled. "Thank you. And Dan would enjoy showing Ireland and England's renowned barrister the many Irish pubs in New York."

She looked at her watch. "Should I be picking up my coat?."

"They should be dropping it off here any minute. In the meantime, either you eat the fish and chips, or I'll take it from you."

"She laughed. "No way, this may be my only relaxed meal in Ireland."

Chapter Twenty-five

The girls were dressed in green and white uniforms, and the nuns' habits stood-out in dark contrast. Lauren, carrying a briefcase over her shoulder, stepped through the door and looked for Sandi. She wasn't concerned about the nuns who rushed toward her.

"Mom." Lauren heard, and then saw Sandi.

The other girls stopped what they were doing and watched Lauren twist past the nuns who were trying to catch her. One grabbed her arm. "Wait. No one is allowed to enter these grounds without…"

Lauren shoved her hand away and kept going. In response the nun blew a screeching whistle, loud enough to stun anyone within ten feet, except Sandi and Lauren.

Lauren reached out as Sandi fell into her arms, crying. "Mom, you're here."

Pulling her close, Lauren answered, "Yes, and we're going home."

At first everyone watched, caught up in the emotion. But this changed quickly. Priests, hearing the whistle, rushed onto the playground. Everyone stepped aside as the head priest approached Lauren.

"I am Father O'Connor, and you must be an acquaintance of Sandra?"

"I'm her mother, and I'm taking her home."

"Hmm. We had no word of your coming. We don't allow our girls to leave without proper permission. For now, you need to come inside where we can talk privately."

"No. We don't need to do that," Lauren said. "I have papers that I'll show you right now, as I will be leaving right away with Sandi."

As she spoke she realized that they were surrounded by priests, nuns, and girls – all listening. She sighed as she started to open her brief case. "These papers prove who I am, and my right to leave with my daughter. Would you please look at the documents, and let us leave without a bigger scene?"

"We cannot do that. You must be aware that we don't allow our children to be taken from our premises by anyone without thorough proof of identity and rights. So please bring your briefcase and step inside. Make it easier on yourself and Sandra."

Then, surprising Lauren, Sandi spoke – her voice was soft. "Mom, I can't leave until I go to homeroom for some of my things. And…." she hesitated, "there's something else. I need to say goodbye to Grandma."

For the first time since arriving, Lauren searched for words. Then, looking at Sandi, she saw her pain – and how much she had grown in the months they had been separated. None of this was easy. And Lauren thought of how Mary had been with Sandi from the day she was born.

She put her arm around Sandi's shoulder. "Of course."

They followed the head priest to a room inside. The first thing Lauren saw was a large gilded cross on the wall across from the entrance. That and a small window with a view of the front grounds, kept the room from being totally austere. There were no paintings to break its dark gray walls. The only furnishings were a long wooden table and stiff, straight back chairs. Not designed for comfort, it felt like an interrogation room.

Lauren squeezed Sandi's hand, as the priest motioned for them to take seats at the opposite end of the table. He sat in front of the gilded cross.

Within minutes the nun who had stopped Lauren outside, entered. "I'm Sister Grace. I had our secretary phone Mary and a barrister, who will be on their way here."

Not sitting, Lauren said, "I'm assuming this will take a while. It will be a good time for Sandi and me to pick-up what she needs to bring with her."

The priest raised an eyebrow. "Your assumptions about leaving might not be correct." Then he nodded, "Sister Grace will go with you. But I don't believe our wait will be long, as Mrs. O'Sullivan will come quickly."

Lauren started to respond but didn't. Instead, she and Sandi walked with the sister to a classroom. They entered as a girl was reciting a Gaelic poem, Pangur Ban.

They listened and then the nun praised the student, before walking with Sandi to the closet.

Lauren knew that most of the girls had seen what had taken place on the playground and were curious. But Sandi looked relaxed as she took her coat and book-bag off the hook. Once again Lauren realized that Sandi had changed – seeming much more mature than when she left for Ireland.

By the time they returned to the meeting, the barrister had arrived. The priest introduced everyone, using O'Sullivan as Sandi's last name. And he introduced Lauren as Mrs. Martin.

After the introduction, the barrister asked, "You, Mrs. Martin, are Sandra's mother. Correct?

Yes. And Sandi's last name is Martin. And we're in a hurry to start our trip home."

He smiled without humor. "We'll talk about that. But our records show that her family name is O'Sullivan. I presume this is correct."

"Her father's name was O'Sullivan. But her name is Martin. I have legal papers with me that you may read. They are clear about Sandi's name, and that I will be taking her home to America. We are waiting so Sandi can talk with her grandmother. However, all legal matters have been taken care of through my attorney at home."

Lauren took the papers from her briefcase and passed them to the barrister.

The room was quiet as he studied them. Then, as he started to comment, Mary arrived.

Lauren's first reaction was pity. Mary looked older. Her skin, always smooth and clear, had blotches of rosacea, and her hair was streaked with gray. She obviously had left in a hurry as she wore a stained apron and wisps of hair stuck out of a loose chignon.

The nun pulled out a chair for her and she sat on its edge – distressed. Lauren knew Mary well – she was suffering.

Everyone in the room waited. Finally, she spoke, her Irish brogue thicker than ever. "Oh child, you don't know what you are doing. I have brought you here to save you – to save your soul. And now…"

Mary stopped and faced Lauren, "You have come all this way to take her to … you know what you are taking her to."

"Oh Mary, stop. You're wrong." Lauren drew a deep breath. "And I don't need to listen to this – not after what you have done. I'm taking Sandi home."

But surprising Lauren again, Sandi stood, walked to Mary, and sat facing her.

"Grandma, mother has come for me as she said she would. I've been waiting. You know that I haven't wanted to be here. I begged you to take me back home – or let me call mother and tell her where we are.

"I knew she would come for me, but I was afraid she wouldn't be able to find me. I tried to use the office phone or to mail letters... but it wasn't allowed. They told me that you had to give approval."

Sandi shook her head. "Now I want to go home. I wish you would come with us. But I know how you feel about mother..."

Mary looked broken. "Oh no, Child, 'tis not that I don't like your mother; it's that she has committed crimes – terrible ones. And I don't want you..."

Lauren stood, "Oh my God. Mary, stop! Hear what you are saying. I won't just sit and listen." She walked to Sandi. "It's time to go. You'll phone your grandmother from home, and she will call you. But we're going back to Oregon."

Lauren faced the barrister. "Let me be clear. You have just read the papers I brought. You're aware that I can legally leave with Sandi. And I don't want to be forced to press charges against Mary or anyone for illegally trying to interfere."

She took Sandi's hand. "It's time to go."

They started to leave, but as they walked through the door, Sandi stopped again and turned toward Mary.

"Goodbye, Grandma. You know how I've begged for you to let me go home to be with mom. I don't want you to be sad... Now you can go back to Dublin and be with your sisters."

Mary's expression changed. Her face was contorted – frightened. "Oh child, you're so young. You don't understand – I pray for your soul."

Lauren squeezed Sandi's hand, wanting to get out of the room quickly.

When they were in the hall she kissed Sandi on her head – searching for words.

Then Sandi looked up at her and said, "I prayed you'd come for me. God was listening."

Liza smiled as Lauren and Sandi approached the car. "You two look pretty calm. I've been waiting to race out of here."

"Calm? I'm elated," Lauren said as she opened the front door for Sandi. Then after all three were seated, she closed the door and nodded to Liza, "I like your suggestion, let's get out of here."

Several blocks from the school, Lauren leaned back and put her arm around Sandi's shoulder. "Now we can relax. Thank you, Liza. But that's too simple; how can I ever thank you for all you're doing for us?"

"Let's call it even. Claire made a huge difference in my life, and you have done the same for many. Doing something for you is payback; besides, it makes me feel good."

Liza smiled and added, "Now let's celebrate. What about some Irish cooking? A friend, who thinks as we, has offered us a place to spend the night. She and her husband live in Dublin. But she grew up here in Galway and inherited her family's home. She often offers it to women who need help.

A Tudor home built in the nineteenth century, Lauren loved the feel of it. It was comfortable, with signs of family in every room. Portraits, both proud and distinguished, chronicled styles from the 1870s on. And furniture, including the huge dining-room table, had been built solid with expectations of an expanding family. Everything gave Lauren the feeling of being lived in. Fresh and used towels were in the bathrooms, a half-finished puzzle was on the coffee table, clothes hung in closets, cans of food, spices and baking ingredients were on pantry shelves, and there were enough dishes to feed several large families at the same time.

Liza had arrived a day earlier and prepared a deep dish pie filled with chicken, potatoes, green-beans, carrots, leeks, herbs and spices. She called it wash-day stew.

Lauren was impressed. "With everything else you do, you cook! I normally don't ask for recipes as I don't do much in the kitchen. But this one I want. If it turns out like yours, Dan will be so impressed he'll want me to start cooking."

Liza chuckled. "If you're born female in Ireland, you start cooking by the time your mother's belly starts to swell again. I grew up with six brothers and two sisters. Cooking is about the only thing I have in common with the women in my family."

After dinner they did dishes and went for a walk. By the time they returned it was late, so Sandi and Lauren went to their bedroom. It had twin beds that were covered with hand-made quilts. Toys appeared to have been tossed into baskets that lined a wall. The closet had stacks of boxes on shelves, but no hanging clothes. Lauren figured they kept it clear for guests.

"Our own room," Sandi said, while stretching onto the bed and leaning against a stack of pillows. "Every wish I made is being answered. You're here."

Lauren sat on the edge of Sandi's bed. "I always knew I'd bring you home, but it got more complicated than I had planned." Lauren took a deep breath. "But now we're safe and together.

"And Sandi, I've got so much to tell you. For one thing, Dan will be waiting for you when we get home. He wanted to come with me – was going to fly home from Korea. But I didn't want to wait. I needed to get to you as soon as I could."

"I've missed Dan. I kind-of feel like he's my dad."

"And he feels the same." Lauren hesitated, "Sandi, Dan is now your legal father. He and I were married, and he filed adoption papers. We are a family."

"You and Dan are married?"

"Yes. And Dan is waiting for us."

"I always felt Dan was part of us… and now..." Sandi shook her head, "he is."

Lauren stood and then bent, kissing her forehead. "I feel this is going to be the happiest time in our lives. Although, I'll have to say, right now I feel about as happy as I could ever be. They each got ready to sleep. Sandi wore Lauren's slip as a nightgown, and there were extra tooth brushes in the bathroom.

It was cold in the room and within five minutes Sandi was under the wool covers. And Lauren turned out the lights and got into her bed. But even though she hadn't slept since leaving Portland, she lay awake.

Then, within a half-hour, Sandi whispered, "Mom?"

"Yes. I can't sleep; I'm too excited."

"Well…" Sandi hesitated, and then said, "I want to tell you something, I think I know why it took you so long to get me."

"Sandi, I am sorry. I thought I'd be with you in two weeks."

"But I know what happened after we left. I heard Grandma talking to Aunt Margaret. She told her that you were arrested. And I was scared – I thought you were in jail. That's when Grandma took me away and wouldn't tell me what happened to you – even though I told her what I heard. I was afraid."

Lauren heard the quiver in her voice and wanted to go to her, but didn't. It was time to talk. She searched for the right words.

"Sandi, first let me tell you that I've been all right, except for constant worry about you. Nothing frightened or hurt me as much as not being free to come get you.

"And I didn't have to go to jail – which I'll explain later. However, I wasn't free to come to you. And then Mary hid you from me, so I couldn't even talk to you! I didn't know where you were."

Lauren thought how Sandi knew this, and it was time to go forward. "We'll soon be home. My dreams and prayers have been answered."

"Mine too, Mom." Sandi came over to Lauren's bed and stretched alongside of her.

"Sandi, you'll be surprised by changes when you come home. We still have your old home, but we also have another one. You'll love it. The house is on Sauvie Island. The kids who live there take a bus from the island to a Portland School."

"Mom. I hope you know that I don't need to go to another school. I don't care about people like Jamie and her mother. I'll like being in our old home – or anywhere. I'll be with you." She paused, then added, "And Dan too. People know about Dan; he has articles in the Irish paper."

"You've read them way over here."

"I did until Grandma moved me to Galway. At the parish I never saw a paper." Sandi took time, and then said, "I've thought about both you and Dan – how special you each are. And now, Dan is like – I mean is part of our family."

Lauren kissed the back of Sandi's head. "Thank you, Sandi. You're the most special."

Sandi relaxed against her and they fell asleep.

Lisa took them to the bus station in the morning. And by five a.m. the following day they arrived at Aldergrove. In two hours they would leave for America.

Lauren walked to the phone booth and placed a collect call to Dan. After a few rings he answered, "Love of my life."

The operator chuckled. "No, but I believe she's hoping that you'll accept the charges?"

"I'll even give you a tip. Put her through."

Lauren was listening, and said, "Dan, Sandi and I are coming home."

"She's with you?"

"Yes. Right here at Aldergrove Airport."

"When do you leave? I'll get a ticket and meet you in Gander. I want to fly home to Portland with the two of you."

"That would be perfect. We'll leave here in one hour, arriving late tonight. We don't have tickets to Portland yet, so would you get tickets for the three of us. But for right now, Sandi's waiting to talk to you."

Lauren handed her the receiver and listened, thinking how Sandi was as excited as she had always been when meeting Dan in Portland. Then, Lauren was surprised by what she said.

"This time when we meet I have something for you. Something I've kept with me everywhere I went."

Lauren thought how it had to be in her bag, the one she had gone to her homeroom to get.

As soon as she hung-up, Lauren asked, "So, I'm dying to know the secret. Can you tell me what's in that bag?"

Sandi's smiled as she nodded. "It's my treasure. I've tried to keep it near me wherever I was, while hiding it from Grandma." Sandi took a deliberate breath. "And now, yes, I'll show it to you."

She reached into the bag and pulled out the small music box. "My ballerina will dance again when I'm with you and Dan – it's a promise I made. It's been my charm. When I held it, I made wishes. And now they're all coming true.

Before Lauren responded, Sandi added, "And mom, you know what the other package is?"

As Lauren was shaking her head no, Sandi reached in her bag and pulled out a bundle of papers, tied together with a rubber band.

"These are letters I wrote to you every day from the time Grandma took me to Galway."

"Tears filled Lauren's eyes as Sandi handed them to her. They were on school notebook paper, neatly folded.

"I knew that you'd find me, Mom. You'll read it in my notes. I thought maybe you could feel me when I was writing – so I wrote each day."

Sandi had left in late spring. Now it was September, a time when the sky is blue every day and the air is crisp.

Entering the house, Sandi had no time to look around as Maddie jumped, twirled and wiggled, then smothered her with sloppy kisses. Laughing, Lauren opened the door and Maddie led Sandi down the path and to the river.

Dan laughed, "I thought Maddie saved her energy for me when I come home, but she's never knocked me down with kisses."

Watching Sandi run with Maddie, Lauren thought how this was another moment to remember. There were so many of them, and it occurred to her that with all the lows she had gone through recently, nothing was as powerful as these moments.

After a totally carefree week, Lauren had to face reality. Dan would be returning to New York in two weeks and then to Korea. Also, the school year had started. It was time to go into the curriculum office and gather home-teaching texts.

But as happened often, Sandi surprised her.

"Home school? Why?"

"Well, I'm assuming you won't want to return to your last school, and going from here it's quite a ways to the nearest Portland school – unless we do home-teaching. As you know, school started last week."

Sandi looked puzzled, "I have planned on going to regular school. Why wouldn't I go to the one nearest to here? I love this island. And I've seen a school bus running near. I've just assumed that you wanted to take a week off to be together before Dan leaves."

She hesitated and then added, "Mom, don't worry about me. You read the letters I wrote, and know how I felt" Sandi looked as if she was deciding to say more. "To be honest, I still think about how I let Jamie, her mother, and those other kids say things about you. And I feel bad. I'll never be friends with people like that again."

Once more, she paused. "Mom, I never wrote about my older cousin, Mary Lynn, who I like. She's the one who told me that Dan wrote articles that were in Irish papers, I mean all the way over there. That's when I began to understand what he does.

"But more than that, Mary Lynn told me about you. She had heard her mom and Grandma talking, and she didn't agree with them. She told me that you help people, I mean girls who were in trouble – I mean pregnant. She told me some things, and then said I'd learn more later. I kind-of know what she was talking about.

"And she told me that I should be proud of you. And I am. I admire you and Dan more than anyone else in the world."

Feeling over-whelmed, Lauren thought how Sandi was only nine. Again, she recognized how going through such a horrendous year had changed her. She was confident, and almost too wise for her age. She would make a difference – a remarkable difference with her life.

Lauren also thought of Ben and felt a chill.

Dan would be leaving in two weeks for Korea, and Lauren knew that each day together was the best of their lives.

In late afternoon when Sandi returned from school, they all walked Maddie to the beach for games of fetch. Later, Dan would barbeque dinner on the back deck, where they would relax talking into the night – with Maddie stretched on the deck next to them.

Lauren recognized the irony of feeling so happy while on probation.

On the day before Dan left for Korea, Sandi told him that her teacher had shared one of his articles. "She told the class that you're my dad, and that you are a famous journalist. And then she asked me to explain what journalists do."

Dan looked surprised, "And what did you tell them?"

"I was a little embarrassed, as I don't know a lot about what you do. But I said that you write articles about things like war, and people read them in the paper – even as far away as Ireland." Sandi looked serious, "And I also said that I don't hear you talk much about what you do."

Dan nodded, "That's because the most important part of my life is being with you and your mom. I enjoy being home, and don't want to think of other places.

"And when I leave this time, it's going to be hard." Dan looked at Lauren, "This has been the best three weeks of my life."

Lauren knew this was true – she felt the same.

But there was something else. She thought of the last time he was in Korea; his voice had been drowned by the blast of bombs.

Chapter Twenty-six

Life Magazine's photographer, Francine Colbert, made it clear that Dan was the one she wanted for the pictorial she would be doing. She read his work, and knew he was the best.

By the end of their first day working together, Dan was impressed. She had New York savvy and was a talented photographer. He never had to explain what he wanted. They complimented each other's work. She expressed through photos the dark reality of scenes he described. He understood that words could never capture the pained eyes, gaping mouths – all the expressions that defined the horror of war – as well as a skillfully aimed camera. Francine had the instinct, seeming to view her whole world from a lens.

After Francine and Dan did the article for Life Magazine, she stayed. Her editor agreed that there was too much happening for her to leave. With China's support, the North was gaining power as it pushed deeper into Southern Korea.

During all his years as a reporter, Dan had never gone into the depth of a fighting war with a woman photographer. But now he and Francine went into enemy territory, including torched villages, recording the terror. Francine didn't just catch scenes that defined the war, she searched for them.

They worked well together, sometimes needing to cover each other's back. And their relationship grew tighter without his giving it much thought.

But it became clear to Dan when, after three hard weeks, they both were leaving for home. Dan had a deadline in New York and left a day before Francine. She walked with him to the jeep he would drive to Seoul, where he would catch a plane home.

He smiled at her. "See you again, but hope it's someplace warmer and safer."

She winked. "Hey, no question about that. You're my soul mate."

It was the first time either had referred to their closeness. He didn't answer and turned to step into the jeep.

"Wait, don't go yet," she said.

He turned back, questioning, and she pulled his face to hers and they kissed.

Then, backing off, she said, "Go on. I'll see you in some other hell-hole that no one but us crazies would volunteer to cover."

Her touch lingered as he drove away.

"Jesus Christ," he mumbled, and then thought how he had been over thirty-years-old before falling in love. And now, crazy as it was, he felt a loss.

But this was Korea, a million miles from home.

He rounded a corner and was stopped by two marines carrying a third, who appeared seriously wounded. They needed a ride to the battalion aid station, about three miles down the road. His day trip to Seoul turned into two days by the time Dan took the detour, and then waited for four injured soldiers who needed to be driven to a better equipped medical facility.

By the time he got to Seoul he had missed the plane to Fort Lewis. Luckily, there was a flight to Camp Pendleton the following day and he phoned Lauren.

Two days after Dan arrived home, Life Magazine hit the stands.

He and Lauren dropped Sandi off at school and drove to Thiele's for breakfast. On the way they picked up several copies of the magazine. As soon as they got seated at the restaurant, Lauren opened her copy, and saw the photographer. Without commenting, she read the headline,

Armistice in Abeyance as World Waits for Promised Peace.

World War II: The war to end all others. What went wrong?

By Dan Carter

We don't have to go far back in history to understand why war sometimes seems inevitable. An answer can be found in Korea's recent background.

Shadowy, behind the print, was an image of an American soldier – little more than a kid – wearing camouflage fatigues and carrying an M1 rifle, his eyes were wide with fear – or innocence. Lauren decided it was both.

It was a good picture.

Turning the page, Lauren saw photographs of Syngman Rhee, General Ridgeway, UN representatives from Sweden and Switzerland, and scenes of the ravaged villagers in the vicinity of Panmunjom. Touching, it put faces on unnamed Koreans who were caught in a cross-fire.

Lauren turned to the next page but stopped – caught off guard. It was a full-page photo of Dan and the photographer, Francine. They were in front of an adobe clay hut with a thatched roof. She was holding a Korean baby, while Dan was starting a fire in a pit.

Francine appeared tiny; oversized by the army fatigues she was wearing. Her brown hair was pulled from her face, emphasizing the smoothness of her long forehead, and arched brows. Romanesque lines that suggested class, Lauren recognized that she was more than beautiful.

"This is Francine." Lauren commented, more to herself than Dan.

"Yeah; as you can see, she does incredible work."

"Yes, I see," she said.

"Jesus, I didn't know that picture was going to be in this," he said, and then pointed to the pit. "They actually heat their one-room huts by fires like this. The heat is drafted through circular tiles – a tube that runs under the floor and up a chimney on the back of the house. It's quite amazing. We were invited in for tea; it was twenty degrees out and comfortable inside. I describe it in the article."

Lauren looked at Dan, he was talking too fast.

Then she studied the picture. "She's lovely."

"Francine? She's a good partner. Captures in one photo what I try to express in a thousand words."

Lauren didn't reply, not wanting to say something she would regret.

"When you come to New York we'll have her over. You'll like her."

"She's in New York?"

"She lives there; has for most of her life."

Not commenting, Lauren turned the page. And when breakfast was served, they still didn't talk.

Then, on their drive home, Lauren tried to relax and push the photograph from her mind; but she couldn't. She looked at Dan, who was quiet – too focused on driving. Normally he would be talking, describing scenes behind scenes.

Arriving home, he said, "Let's walk down to the river with Maddie."

"Sounds good to me."

Maddie ran out the door and headed for the river. As they followed her, Dan put his arm around Lauren's shoulder.

During his four weeks away, the weather had changed. Lauren felt gusts of chilled air, and noticed that the roses had darkened and dropped, becoming part of the mulch that crunched beneath her feet. This, and the gray sky, fit with her mood.

She uncovered the beach chairs and sat.

Dan stood behind her and kissed the top of her head. Lauren was waiting; she knew him – he was going to tell her something.

His voice was soft. "If your silence is something to do with Francine, you and I need to talk. She's a partner; I work with her and respect her. You have to know by now that no one could ever take your place. You are and will always be the love of my life."

Chapter Twenty-Seven

Ten Months Later

Two days after Lauren's probation ended, Carol phoned.

"Congratulations! You're free to go anywhere in the world. And as you know, Claire is doing just that. She left for France at five this morning. I couldn't drive her to the airport as she, Jane, and the grandkids have ten pieces of luggage. She hired a Volkswagen Bus driver to get there.

"Was she excited! Not just because she was free from probation, but mostly because she was free from Bill – the divorce was final three days ago.

"But that's not why I'm calling. I've got a favor to ask. Claire intended to take care of it, but in the rush of getting out of here, she couldn't."

"You know the limits of what I can do. But for you and Claire, I'd stretch them – to a degree."

"Thanks, Lauren, but this is within your limits. Claire wouldn't ask if it weren't. Unfortunately, it can't wait till she returns."

"Carol, I don't trust phone lines, and miss seeing you. So why don't you come here and we'll talk over lunch."

"Sounds perfect. I'm on my way."

"Good. I'll whip-up something fancy like a tuna sandwich."

It was sunny and warm, so Lauren served lunch on the deck. They ate as Carol described Claire's day in divorce court.

"The jerk asked for half of everything including her home which, as you know, she's lived in for over twenty years. Even the judge looked outraged. I was watching him and wondered if he'd give Bill twenty years in a psych ward instead of a divorce.

"You would have loved Claire. She did everything but wear an apron to court – the perfect housewife. And I swear the judge bought it. Old Bill was given the ranch in Baker, which is mortgaged to the hilt so he'll have to sell it immediately. Other than that, he was lucky to leave with the pants he was wearing."

Carol laughed and then sat back, relaxed. "I love this home; I can feel the fresh breeze coming from the river."

"Yeah, I love it too; especially now that it's filled with Sandi. Who, as you know, is the reason I refuse to do anything that could affect her. But I'm repeating myself. Tell me what's happening?"

"It has to do with money – but much more than that. Claire was paid a sizable amount which for good reasons she won't accept. She planned on returning it yesterday, but you know what her life is like. A young girl got hold of her – desperate as they always are – and Claire helped her. She didn't have time to return the money, and barely had time to get packed and leave with the girls this morning.

"She tried to reach you last night, but you weren't home. So, she'll phone you from Paris. But something needs to be done right away. It's a desperate situation, and she asked me to talk to you today. The money needs to be returned. But more important, the young patient, Nan, has to be protected. Nan confided in Claire. It's serious – Nan had been repeatedly raped.

"I know we've seen it all, but this is one of the most frightening situations. The girl needs to be protected. Claire promised this – and even if she hadn't, we need to stop what's happening."

Lauren sighed. "Always! We always want to stop what continues to happen. And, of course, I'll help. But who are we talking about?

Who raped the girl, and gave the money? A judge, a mayor? Higher? Maybe a senator?"

"I know that nothing is a surprise anymore. But hold onto your teeth with this one."

"You're right. Nothing surprises me."

"Well this did me." Carol said. "The money came from Father Riley, the bishop at St. Theresa's – the same parish where Sister Calligan resides. But Claire knows that Father Riley is not the rapist. He's protecting someone else in the church."

Lauren appeared unfazed. "Hmm. We've helped pillars of enough churches to have turned our clinic into a church annex. But you're right. As far as I'm aware, we've never received money from a priest. However, priests are men, not Gods. So, this doesn't surprise me."

Carol nodded, agreeing, and then said, "Claire talked to Nan, the young patient, and learned that this goes beyond parishioners. Nan was brought to us by the school nurse, who was directed by Father Riley."

Carol reached down and pulled an envelope from her purse. "The nurse gave this to Claire. It's filled with a lot of money. Claire wants it returned. But what's most important, she wants to know who raped Nan – who now needs protection. And the rapist needs to be punished."

"How many days ago did Claire see Nan?" Lauren asked as she took the envelope."

"Two. She's worried. When she couldn't reach you last night, I promised to talk to you today. She said something needs to be done right away."

"She's right; time is important. I'll take this to Father Riley this afternoon. I have to wonder if Sister Calligan is aware. You and I know what happened to Geraldine Francini – that is, we know how she died."

Lauren thought and then added, "I wonder. There's a huge possibility that the man who is molesting Nan, had other victims. We never knew who caused Geraldine's pregnancy."

Lauren got up, "I'm going to be out of here in ten minutes. I'll stop by Sandi's school and tell her I have an appointment – and then head for the parish."

As they started to leave, Carol stopped her. "Wait! I almost forgot to tell you something important. Nan told Claire that she has a brother, and the most important thing in her world is to be with him again. She never knew her father, and her mother died when she was nine. This is when social workers took over, and placed Nan and her brother in different facilities.

"Claire promised that she would help find him. I know she will when she returns. But that's three weeks away, and if there was ever a time that Nan needs to find him, it's now. When you meet with Father Riley it would be great if you tell him."

Lauren nodded. "I will. I'm hoping that after the bishop and I talk, he'll be looking for every way possible to help Nan.

As Lauren drove to the parish, she asked herself why a bishop would condone, and more, pay for an abortion. The answer was clear. Having an abortion was a sin, but being a priest and a rapist was a far greater one – it was pure evil. Father Riley broke his covenant with the church in trying to protect it against this evil.

Lauren thought how she was not going to allow this protection.

Approaching St. Theresa, Lauren saw that it was built like an early Spanish mission. There was a large white cross that rose above the front wall. The grounds were protected by a tall wrought-iron fence.

Before admittance Lauren spoke into an intercom, giving her name and reason for her visit. She had come to see Father Riley. A caretaker opened the gate, and she saw that the splendor of the garden stretched toward ivy-covered brick walls.

He walked her to the front entrance, and opened the door. She stepped into the foyer which was striking in its simplicity: there were Spanish Colonial wooden benches, chairs, and a desk, on shiny tile floors.

Within minutes a nun bustled in. "I'm sorry for keeping you waiting. You say you have an appointment with Father Riley?"

"No, I said I am here to see him. I'd appreciate your pointing the way."

"Sorry. But you can't see him without an appointment."

"Let's backup to your first assumption," Lauren said. "Let's assume I have an appointment, and he will want to see me."

The nun became assertive. "He simply isn't available. You'll have to come back after scheduling an appointment."

"I assure you that he'll make time for me now. Where is a phone? I'll call and tell him I'm here."

Frowning, the nun walked to the desk phone. "What is your name? I'll see what I can do."

"Tell him Anne Thompson needs to see him – now."

The nun dialed a number and relayed Lauren's message. Within minutes she led Lauren to Father Riley's office.

His secretary smiled but was less cooperative than the nun. "Father Riley, not expecting you, will not be available for at least an hour."

"I suggest that you reach him and let him know that Anne Thompson is here and cannot wait."

The secretary's smile dissolved. "Then I suggest that you leave. Do you have any idea of Father Riley's responsibilities? No one comes here and expects to just walk in and see him."

"But as you see, I have. Either tell him now that I'm here; or later you will need to tell him that I've gone to the police, having no other choice. And give him this."

Lauren handed her the sealed envelope of money.

The secretary, caught by Lauren's reference to the police and recognizing the priest's handwriting on the envelope, looked at her with curiosity. Then relented, "This is definitely against regulation, but I will break into the meeting and tell Father Riley you're here."

She handed the envelope back to Lauren and left the office.

Within minutes the priest appeared. He looked nothing like what Lauren anticipated. In his early forties, he had thick, somewhat unruly black hair, and dark expressive eyes.

He reached to shake her hand. "I wish I had known you were waiting. As a matter of fact your partner, Dr. Karriden, was a subject of our discussion this afternoon. And though I'm somewhat apprehensive, I know it's important that you and I talk."

He opened the door to his private office. "Coffee? Tea? Anything to drink?"

"No, Father, but I'll confess – excuse the loose usage of the word – you have somewhat disarmed me. I was negative when I arrived, and no one has given me any reason to feel otherwise until now.

"It appears that you're aware of why I'm here. I hope your meeting was going in the direction it needed to take. And that you recognize how I feel about what has been happening."

He motioned for her to sit, and then he sat facing her. Before answering, he rubbed his forehead as if dealing with an ache.

Lauren watched, wondering if this was theatrics.

Finally he answered, "Much the same as I felt when I called and requested Dr. Karriden's help. I can assure you it is one of very few times when I have taken sides with the devil, so to speak."

He hesitated before continuing. "But as history repeatedly demonstrates, there are times when expedience is needed to avoid catastrophe. Or said another way, the church is forced to weigh choices between two evils, and is guided by the one that leads to the greater good. And in this case, a child's future is involved."

Lauren read his discomfort and waited.

He pressed his lips together, and then lowered his voice. "As you know, I believe that abortion is a mortal sin. But we felt we were weighing this against a greater sin that involved the destruction of an adolescent child's future. "

Lauren raised her eyebrows. "It sounds as if you're defending my profession. But that aside, pardon my bluntness Father, but I don't think you're being honest. You and I know the reason why Nurse Kelly brought Nan to Dr. Karriden's clinic – and I don't believe it was to protect Nan.

"Extolling the virtues of the church by saying, or worse, believing that what was done was for Nan's better good, may sooth your soul, but it does nothing for mine. I believe that a horrible crime has been taking place at St. Theresa."

Lauren paused, giving effect to her words, "The decision for Nan to have an abortion was made to hide the fact that she was raped by a priest at this parish. And we have reason to believe that Nan is not his first victim. More specifically, there was another girl who came to us over a year ago."

Father Riley's expression made it clear that she was correct, and Lauren pushed-harder. "Nan and she are why I'm here today. I can't sit back and not report the crimes, knowing that this deviant fraud will hurt other girls"

Father Riley stopped her, "Wait!"

From the change in his expression, she guessed what was coming.

"Miss Thompson, you're a bright and persistent woman. But," he challenged, "I believe Dr. Karriden received her payment two days ago."

Lauren pulled the envelope from her purse. "Yes, Father Riley, but she won't accept it. Neither she nor I are ashamed of our profession, knowing that our patients have come to us in desperate need. We have our own values, and won't accept money as a bribe. And if necessary I will go to the police."

The priest looked both caught and embarrassed, and put his hand out stopping her. "I have no doubt that you will." Heaving a breath, he added, "But that aside, is what I have been doing. There is nothing worse than defending something that I know is wrong."

His words allaying her anger, she waited for him to say more.

"I was told about each of you when you were on trial: you are confident and act on your convictions. You're ethical in your own way. I haven't met Dr. Karriden, but you speak well for her. And you are correct; my actions invite contempt."

He shook his head as if denying what he needed to add. "I've been appalled by what I have learned. During the six months that I've been here I haven't been aware of this – that is, until four days ago. And the news keeps getting worse. Now … hmm … now I have to protect…"

Lauren broke in, "Protect what, Father Riley? Your church?Or deeper, your beliefs, as I protect mine. They are part of who we are. Hmm. But whatever you've been protecting, it hasn't been the children here at the parish. It appears that you have helped to hide a horrible crime: the rape of a young girl," Lauren accented each word, "by one of your priests.

"And making the situation even worse, Father Riley, I believe the rapist impregnated another child – one who lived at this parish. I assume you know about her, and what happened. If not, ask Sister Calligen.

"As far as I know, the rapist has gone unpunished. Every day of no sanctions allows him to do more harm. I would like to turn him over to the police and have him imprisoned. Unfortunately, I know what a trial and press exposure does to the victim.

"But something serious needs to happen so this rapist will never be able to harm another person. Every minute he goes without serious sanctions, he's free to harm other young girls. I know you fear how the priest's crimes will affect your church. But you're fear should be for the children he will continue to hurt if something isn't done right away.

"I want to see him stripped of all power, and disgraced. And I want him to feel the same pain and shame he has inflicted on his victims. Most of all, he must never be in any situation that allows him to harm another person."

"Miss Thompson, he never will. Trust me, the church will handle it. We are taking action. The meeting I came from was about this very matter. His penance will be tough and long: he will be defrocked, and then watched closely. The church has its own power, and we will use it."

He spoke from his heart, but Lauren wondered if living a life of shame within the protection of the church could ever equal the punishment decreed and enforced by the State.

But she stood, knowing that she had done as much as she could – for now.

Then, before leaving, she asked, "And what about Nan?"

"Those who work with Nan are planning what must be done. She will receive outside counseling as we protect and care for her. Holding ourselves responsible, we will make certain that no such thing happens to any of our girls ever again."

"Good. And there's something else I need to ask for. Nan has a brother. As you are aware they were orphaned three years ago. After their mother died the State separated them, and Nan has felt painful loss. Dr. Karriden talked to Nan, and promised that she and her brother will see each other soon. I want to make certain that happens. The best of all situations would be if they can grow-up being close – he is the only family she has. I'm willing to pay any expense to see this happens." She once more handed him the envelope. "This will be a beginning."

Now he smiled, and the weight in the room lifted. "You know, Miss Thompson, you're quite an amazing woman. You wouldn't consider changing your vocation and joining our church?"

"Hardly. Though I've pretty much been forced from my career, it speaks for my beliefs; not your church." She smiled back at him, "And I don't think many of your parishioners would welcome me."

She dropped the smile. "Now, what about Nan's brother?"

"I will find where he is and make certain that a meeting between them is arranged. And I'll let you know when this happens." He looked at the envelope. "Also, I think it's fitting that this money goes toward Nan's future. We'll start a savings for her."

"And, Mrs. Carter, our church is open to all people, including those who, according to our beliefs, have sinned. It's not the role of a priest to judge. We have all learned that there are times when some things that we consider evil, turn out to be for a better good."

Before Lauren could respond, he put his hand out stopping her.

"I am not saying that we ignore evil. But my words are true. We would welcome you into this parish. You've convinced me that some sins might actually be on the same plateau as virtue. I'm quite aware that you have worked with many church members who understand what I am saying."

Lauren shook her head. "Saving souls is your role, Father, and I'm glad that you find mine in a redeemable class, even though I have no fears about heaven."

The Father nodded. "Hmm. That's a freedom that I don't know. But, in all truth, I understand the total freedom that some people, like you, must feel. And I can even envy it."

He shrugged; then said, "But that's digging too much into my soul and is not what we're here for. Now, let me guarantee you once more: I'll see that Nan is helped and cared for. And I'll make certain her brother is located, and work to bring them together as family."

Lauren turned toward the door, and he hurried to open it.

"This has been a memorable morning." He added, "Actually much more than that. And I wish you well."

"And, Father Riley, I wish the same to you" She put her hand out, "And I trust that you will watch out for Nan and all the other girls residing here."

They shook hands on a promise.

Chapter Twenty-eight

Dan had left in the fall and returned to a sticky hot New York summer, where pub doors stayed open and musicians soloed through the night. The view from his open window equaled the beauty from Lauren's in its own New York way – geometric lines of skyscrapers, higher and more commanding than any other in the world.

The article took longer than Dan wanted, and he couldn't return to Portland as soon as planned. But after writing and editing – making certain the story was press-ready, he was assured of an uninterrupted month before returning to Korea. He had been there for eight months – too long.

When he finally returned to Sauvie Island he again recognized that life couldn't get better than this.

Sandi had grown. Dan saw the same fine quality in her that he had always seen in Lauren. He thought of how they epitomized the expression "lovely as a breath of fresh air." They were that – and a billion miles from the bloodied hills of Korea.

The month went fast. It was the closest he ever came to chucking his career, or at least, the Korean part of it. At the same time he recognized that his work was integral to who he was.

Several days before Dan was scheduled to leave, Lauren made a suggestion. "I know you'll be busy preparing for your assignment in Korea, but it would be so wonderful if Sandi and I could fly back and spend a few days with you – see what your life is like in the city. I know you'll be working during the day, but I'm thinking you'll have some evenings off."

"A few days? Make that a week. I'll fly back today and do some work. You and Sandi leave on Friday. New York is waiting for you. You'll see what I mean. You belong there."

She laughed, "That's interesting, I would say you belong right here."

"You'll see what I mean. We need both places."

As she and Sandi waited at La Guardia, Lauren understood that this was a totally new world. And, so far, she didn't like it. Everyone, even mothers with little children, seemed focused, cold, and rude – huffing past each other in a rush. There was sense of urgency, and Lauren thought if anyone stopped quickly he would be knocked down and plowed over.

She stepped closer to Sandi, squared her shoulders and stood tall as if on guard; and wondered if all of New York would feel this hostile.

Then Dan walked toward them, smiling, and she relaxed.

He flagged down a cab and they went to his flat in Greenwich Village. It was exactly as Lauren thought it would be. Book-laden and messy, it was one large office with a bedroom and kitchen partitioned off. The bathroom was the only separate space, and it was also filled with books – on the floor, towel shelf, and top of the toilet tank.

Reading her, Dan laughed. I know where everything is. But I intended to clear the couch before you got here."

He picked up some books, making space. "Sandi, this is your bed. You can look straight out this window and see other old buildings with flats. And since it's summer we'll leave the window open and you'll hear the sounds of the village: yelling, laughter, tinkling pianos, and saxophones playing the best jazz in the world. You'll go to sleep happy."

The walls throughout the flat were covered with copies of art, mostly abstract: de Kooning, Pollock, and Picasso, and others that had been signed by local artists. Also, Lauren noted, there was a photo by Francine. She glossed over it, not wanting to read the inscription at the bottom. Not now, when she needed Dan to assure her that she belonged here, in this world that was so different from the one she knew.

His flat was within walking distance of theatres, restaurants, bakeries, bars with jazz or blues, poetry readings, and shops filled with incredible art.

On their first full day they walked Fifth Avenue from Washington Square Park to the heart of Midtown – where Sandi and Lauren shopped in stores more chic and expensive than any in Portland. Later they took a cab back to The Village, and ate at a sidewalk-table of a bar where Dan knew most everyone.

Within three days they walked through Central Park, went to a Broadway production of Death of a Salesman, and took a subway to Coney Island, where they ate foot-long hotdogs and waded in the warm surf.

Dan watched Sandi and Lauren as they took in his city.

"Now you can see why I need to live in New York. The beauty of Oregon is breathtaking, but it doesn't jingle my imagination. Here there's drama on every corner – constant stories, taken from the streets and frozen by word or lens into another truth."

Lauren's opinion had totally changed from her short time at the airport – even though everyone on the sidewalks seemed in a hurry. Now Lauren liked the excitement of their rush, and most everything else about the city, except the weather. It was humid and hot. But New Yorkers accepted the heat with their own panache. Women sat with legs, shoulders, and midriffs bared. Smooth and tanned, freckled and pale, fat or thin, it didn't matter in The Village.

To Lauren this lack of self-consciousness was part of its freedom. She, Dan, and Sandi sat at outside tables, with fans circulating the thick air. They were offered drinks containing multiple kinds of alcohol, fruits, and vegetables. They tasted food from everywhere in the world and Lauren wondered why New Yorkers weren't all waddling instead of racing down city sidewalks.

Dan watched her. "You have the right instincts for New York."

"I do. You're right." She swept her hand across the sky, toward the towering buildings. "And I wish we didn't have to leave. As soon as we can, I'd like to drive back here with Sandi and Maddie. I'll leave all else at Shangri-La, for when we need some fresh air."

"Sounds good to me," Dan said.

Later when Sandi couldn't hear, Dan said, "I've been thinking. We'll keep my flat. It will be ours – yours and mine – a New York retreat. At the same time I'll buy a home near Central Park, where we can walk Maddie, and Sandi will have a large room. And I've been thinking how it would be nice to include a nursery."

"Hmm," Lauren smiled, "Yes, it's time."

On the day before Lauren flew home, she met Frank McCaffrey, James' son. Now, after graduating from Reed, he was a freshman at Yale Law School.

Dan decided to skip their lunch. He would be leaving for Korea within days and needed to spend time at his office. He invited Sandi to come along.

"I want you to get an idea of what I do when I'm here. And I'd like to show you off – your mom too." He shrugged, "But she has other plans."

Lauren rolled her eyes. Dan used to joke about Frank's crush on her during the years when he observed and worked at James' office.

Frank had driven with some classmates to meet Lauren at a restaurant near Dan's flat.

He introduced her, and then added, "Lauren is one of Portland's greatest draws – certainly for me."

Not taking him seriously, she laughed. "Good. We want you back in Portland."

After lunch she and Frank left the others and spent a couple of hours walking from So Ho to Lower Manhattan. Frank's view of New York was quite different from Dan's.

"I feel the energy of this place, and enjoy the inbred sophistication that has to come from surviving here. The pure scale of everything is amazing, whether it is buildings, art, noise that never ends, or bodies on the street. Wealth, poverty – everything is expansive. And quite honestly, as soon as I can, I'm heading back to Portland and staying there."

Lauren thought how Frank was only twenty-one, as smart as his father, and would have a similar take on the law – though even more liberal.

And as she walked the same streets that she had seen earlier in the week, she became more impressed by Franks take. He zeroed in on the pathos and lunacy of street people, and the sadness of the poverty.

"After being here, I plan on practicing poverty law. It's at the heart of what we see on these streets. Of course, it's not only in New York;

but as everything else in this city, it's magnified."

"I hope you return to Portland," Lauren said. "You'll be an asset to your dad's firm. But as far as poverty law – well I'm not certain about how many low-income cases the firm handles. And Portland certainly has its homeless. I say this, knowing I'm guilty of closing my eyes too often."

He looked at her as if checking her seriousness. "Yeah, like you haven't helped hundreds of women who couldn't pay a cent – while risking your own freedom. Of all my dad's clients – his many success stories – you and Claire Karriden are the one's I'm most proud of."

"Thanks, Frank, but most credit goes to Claire. I learned everything about the practice from her. And it was her policy not to turn anyone away for lack of money.

"But back to you," Lauren said. "I really do hope you will return to Portland."

"I will." His answer was simple.

The afternoon passed quickly and it was time for him to head back to school. As they walked toward Dan's she told him about going to Ireland to get Sandi.

"But you probably know most of this. You were coming into the office 'observing.' And you know Claire and I were on probation."

"Yes. But I haven't heard much since leaving for here. Actually, I feel privileged today – spending this time with you. I don't think you ever noticed who my attention was on every time you came to Dad's office."

She smiled. "Well it's not every day that an infamous abortionist came to your dad's."

"A lot of infamous clients came to Dad's office. Your career isn't what fascinated me." He paused, and then said, "You were the most beautiful woman I had ever seen. And," he grinned, "still are."

Lauren felt uncomfortable but made light of the comment. "Hmm. Thanks for the compliment, and for not adding "older" woman. Now tell me about Yale. Knowing you, you're doing well."

He dove in, telling her about case-law that they were studying, and describing the professors. As he talked she realized that he observed law in the same way he did New York City. It was clear that the professors he respected the most explained law from a human perspective – the impact of laws on real lives.

Time passed quickly as they walked the mile to Dan's.

"Here we are," she said. "It's been great hearing about school, and seeing New York from your view. I agree with you about Oregon. As exciting as this city is, I prefer Portland."

He smiled, "And as I said, you're Portland's greatest draw."

"Yeah, right. But keep it up, I appreciate the flattery. Facts are, I've had a great afternoon, and look forward to seeing you when you head back to Oregon."

Lauren turned to go inside, but he touched her arm. She turned back, questioning – and he bent to kiss her.

"Don't, Frank," she backed off, "Dan is…"

Interrupting, he touched her lips with his fingers and said, "Dan is a lucky guy." Then he turned and walked away.

Watching him, she thought how life was never simple.

She headed upstairs to the empty flat, where she sat waiting, trying to read, looking outside at the Village streets – all the while being drawn to the photograph on the wall.

Finally, thinking that it was time – she didn't want to return home without knowing – she walked over and studied it. It was of a hand: long and lovely.

She told herself to turn away, but instead she read the flowing script: To my deserter – The recruit didn't work out. He's not you. Love, Francine.

As soon as Lauren read the words, she wished she hadn't.

When Dan and Sandi returned home, they all went out for dinner. It was the last night of her vacation. Sandi talked about her day with Dan. And, of course, she was impressed.

Later, when Sandi was in the kitchen, Lauren looked at the photograph and said, "I read it."

He shook his head, just slightly – letting her know that she was wrong. "It's a nice photograph. We worked well together."

She heard the past tense and accepted it.

Chapter Twenty-nine

1957

Maddie raced ahead like a puppy, while Sandi and Lauren walked down the icy path to the river. Snow had closed schools for the day, and then the sky turned blue, making it a perfect day for a walk.

But they were halfway to the river when Maddie jumped in – paddling after a tree limb. Sandi and Lauren yelled as they ran toward the beach, begging her to turn around. And Maddie paddled to the shore with the limb in her mouth.

"Good – good girl," Sandi cooed.

Then within minutes she and Lauren were both screaming and laughing. Maddie had dropped the wet branch at their feet. Then, as she had done so many times with Dan, she started shaking off the water – saturating Lauren and Sandi.

The more they yelled, the more Maddie shook. Finally, already soaked, Sandi bent down and stopped her with a hug. "Okay girl, it's time to go home."

Maddie knew the word home and started up the path.

"She's probably expecting a treat when she gets there," Lauren said as they followed. "And she'll get one. Thank God she didn't freeze to death in that river."

Sandi picked up her pace. "Yeah, like I'm freezing to death now."

When they walked inside Lauren gave Maddie a treat, and then wiped her with a towel. This is when she saw the gray in her fur. She pulled her close and whispered, "I love you, Girl."

The moment was bitter-sweet, and Lauren thought how it would be a good day to relax inside.

After changing clothes and eating, she went into the living room to light the logs that were in the fireplace. Maddie followed her, and stretched out when the fire started to crackle. Watching her, Lauren realized she was smiling and called Sandi to come see.

Like so many others, the day became one that Lauren would never forget. Sandi sat next to Maddie and leaned against Dan's chair, while Lauren sat on the couch facing her. At first, they talked about Sandi's classes, teachers, students – general things.

Then Sandi took off in a totally different direction, "You know Mom, some of the girls know about Aunt Claire's clinic."

Lauren felt heat rush to her face and waited to hear more.

"A friend of mine went to see her… and… well… Aunt Claire helped her."

Sandi paused as if expecting a comment. But when Lauren didn't respond, she said, "Mom, she told me you worked with Aunt Claire. And, well, you and I have never talked, but I already knew this.

"By the time I was in eighth grade, I heard about Clarie Karriden – her name is pretty well known. And I remembered a lot – like Jamie and what she said. I was only eight and didn't know anything. But neither did Jamie – she was quoting from her mother. And when I came home from school crying, well – later I blamed myself for why I had to leave for Ireland.

"Then when I was there, I heard Grandma talk to her sisters and to a priest. She said you were an abortionist. At that time, I didn't know what it meant, but I knew it was something bad."

Sandi stopped and waited.

"I should have told you way before this," Lauren said. "When we came home from Ireland, I thought you were too young. Then as time passed it seemed too difficult to talk about. But I should have known that you would hear things. Our clinic has never been a secret – too many doctors have sent patients. And more women and girls came to it than I can count.

"Sandi, I hope you'll understand someday that I feel my work helped women. Many, some very young girls, came to us in desperation."

Lauren looked thoughtful, "But I never meant to hurt you – to put you through those months in Ireland."

Sandi wrinkled her forehead, puzzled. "Mom, there's so much I don't know – things I think about – questions about that year, and more. I mean like how long did you work with Aunt Claire?

Lauren took another deep breath. "Seven years."

"You started when I was a year old!" Sandi thought for a minute. "Grandma knew, right?

Lauren shook her head, "Yes."

"And when Jamie said all of those things, you were working with Aunt Claire." She thought, and then said, "Mom, I almost lost you when Grandma took me to Ireland. Remember how I begged not to go. And then, from the time I left without you, I blamed myself – wishing I hadn't told you and Grandma about Jamie and her mother."

"Oh Sandi, I was going to be there for you in two weeks – we and Grandma were going to vacation. Then…" Lauren paused; Sandi didn't know about the raid or probation. "So much happened over here, and I wasn't able to leave. It was the worst time in my life, not because of what was going on here, but because of what I was putting you through.

"I'm not sure how much you know about the clinic. But I assume you're aware that abortion is against the law. Do you understand that, and why?"

Sandi shook her head. "Mom, I'm almost sixteen. Of course, I know it's not legal. But it seems that everyone acts as if it's also illegal to have babies without marriage. At least that's the way people treat pregnant girls.

"Do you remember Fredricka Crawford? She was a year older, but rode the school bus with me up till a couple of years ago. That's when she started looking pregnant, and kids whispered as if she had committed a crime. She was forced to leave school, and hasn't come back. I don't know where she went. But I feel guilty that I wasn't a better friend. I watched how she was treated. I could have said more – helped her, but I didn't." She paused, then said, "Being pregnant isn't a crime, but it might as well be."

"You're right Sandi, and it's been like that for as long as I remember. I'm proud that you understood what she was facing. You were pretty young then, but what's important is if she was on the bus now, you'd be there for her.

"And, Sandi, you've answered my question about abortion being illegal – you understand how I felt about helping girls who came to our clinic. But I hope you also know how sorry I am that my work ended up hurting you. That year – when you were gone – was the worst time of my life.

"When you left for Ireland, I was preparing to quit; I had started refusing all but the most desperate patients. But then, before I could come to get you…well…there were things beyond my control that kept me here."

"Mom, I know what happened – at least I think I do. I heard a lot, and I saw your picture in the Irish newspaper."

Lauren shook her head. "I knew Mary would see it, but hoped you wouldn't. You were so young. I ache when I think of what you must have been going through. You begged to stay home. And Dan, who's seldom angry with me, sure was angry when you left."

"Mom, if all of that hadn't happened I wouldn't know how wrong things can be – I mean people and their beliefs. I hope you know I'm proud that you're my mom."

Lauren felt overwhelmed.

"Thank you, Sandi. Of all the things in my life that I feel good about, nothing could compare to how proud I am of you." She paused, then added, "I see fine qualities in you that I loved in your father – Ben. He was extraordinary, smart and caring; he wanted the world – our world – to be a better place than it is."

Sandi looked at her, intense. "You know, Mom, I somehow feel him. I always knew that it wasn't just the things that Grandma and you said. But for as long as I remember, I have felt he is here; I mean when I need him. Grandma would say I was like him. And I really do feel he's a part of me."

Lauren saw the expression in her eyes. "He is, Sandi. He is."

It was December, and Lauren had booked tickets for her and Sandi to fly to New York. Dan had bought a family home on Fifth Avenue, across from Central Park.

But a week before they were to leave, Lauren met Claire at Thiele's and had second thoughts. Claire hadn't looked well for the past month, and Lauren had told herself that the workload at her clinic was taking a toll. But as Claire walked into Thiele's, Lauren felt shock. Thin and unsteady, Claire seemed to have aged since a week earlier. And when she sat in the booth, Lauren was alarmed by the color of her skin. It was gray.

"I'm thirsty." Claire's voice was weak and scratchy. "It's been a long day."

She put her hand out, flagging-down Jan, who waved back and then turned toward the bar. Within minutes she came to their table with two wine glasses and a carafe of the house burgundy.

Lauren thanked her, and then faced Claire. "Before anything else, I want to talk about those long days."

"Don't bother. You already have."

"I know I have, and you don't listen." Lauren didn't back off. "Claire, this clinic is as well-known as our last. And we each know what can happen if there's another raid." Lauren knew her words were wasted, but added, "You can't help anyone if you're in prison."

"I'm not working just to help women." Claire sipped wine, then continued, "My price has gone up. It has to. Not just because of the risks, but because of expenses – and I mean personal expenses. Who ever dreamed when I was growing up in Pendleton, sleeping in a room with three sisters, that I would someday have a home with five empty bedrooms, while supporting another home for my daughter and grandkids?

"And now I'm bent on securing a special insurance for them. After that I'll consider quitting. I bought land in Palm Springs and had plans drawn for a 4000 square-foot home, with a guest house, pool, and garden with a watering system that will keep it in bloom through the sweltering summers. It will be Jane and the grandkids' retreat, especially if something happens to me. I want it paid for by the time I either retire or am arrested again."

"Not funny!" Lauren said, while thinking that something was going on that was far worse than the threat of jail. She had seen it before: the gray color of Claire's skin.

When she returned home, Lauren phoned Dan.

"Plans are changing. I don't feel I should leave; I'm too worried. I was just with Claire and there's something very wrong. I mean, she isn't well. I think we better have Christmas in Portland – at the Fairmont house. I'd like a tree, decorations – a real Christmas with family: Claire, Jane, her kids, and us.

Carol continued to work at the clinic, but made it clear to Lauren that she wanted to stop. "Not just because I worry about another raid; but Claire looks worse each day – and refused to slow down. Our hours are growing longer.

"I've told her I want to quit, thinking that would force her to stop. But instead she looked at me – like sympathetic – and said she wouldn't blame me if I did.

"She keeps going and as always takes the time to make certain her surgeries are safe. No one leaves until she has done everything to ensure their recovery. But oh-my-God do I worry. She looks like death warmed over."

A week after that conversation, Claire phoned at about ten p.m., her voice muffled.

"It happened! Carol and I are at the municipal jail. They let me out of a cement cell smaller than a bathroom, to make this call. I tried James and no one answered. A matron is standing next to me, either to monitor what I'm saying or shoot me if I try to escape."

Lauren was already thumbing through her address book. "James is in Hawaii. So, I'll get hold of Frank before coming there."

She hung up and dialed Frank. He answered with a muffled yawn and then, like his father, he took charge.

"I'll post bail at Levi's, then meet with Claire and Carol within an hour."

Before leaving Lauren woke Sandi and told her the truth – knowing that it would be all over the news by morning.

"The clinic's been raided. I'm going to see what I can do for Aunt Claire and Carol. They've been arrested."

Sandi sat up. "Is Aunt Claire all right? I want to go."

"Honey, it's best that you don't come. They wouldn't let you in to see her."

She got out of bed and started toward her closet.

"I don't want you going alone."

"Thanks," Lauren shook her head, "but I don't want you at that jail. Besides, Frank will be there, and he'll make certain that Claire and Carol are released. We'll be out of there in short-order."

"Mom, I worry about you."

"Promise I'll be home within two hours."

This is when Maddie got their attention. She had followed Lauren into the room. And though she was getting arthritic, she jumped onto Sandi's bed and dug herself a space.

"Look who's settled-in, expecting you to join her.

Sandi laughed, "We'll be waiting for you."

It was midnight and traffic was light, so Lauren made it to the jail in record time. As she was pulling out her identification to show the policeman at the desk, a uniformed guard entered the room and said that Frank McCaffrey was expecting her.

The guard walked her to a small room where attorney-client meetings took place. There were no windows in the room, and scant furnishings

– a table and five chairs. Frank, Claire, and Carol were highlighted by a bright bulb hanging from the ceiling.

Frank stopped what he was saying, and stood to pull up a chair for Lauren. She noted that he had taken time to put on a suit and tie, quite a change from the corduroy pants and open necked denim shirt he had worn in New York.

Lauren sat across from Claire. More than ever, she thought how Claire had to be ill – very ill. Much more than the stress of the night, it was the way she held herself. Unlike the fighter she had always been, she was diminutive and weak.

She had been talking to Frank when Lauren entered. Now Claire turned to her and said, "You warned me."

Lauren shook her head. "I'm not proud of that. I, more than anyone, know the need that's out there."

Claire nodded, "That's true."

Then she turned back to Frank. "This detective, who called herself Patricia Ritter, played her role well when she phoned. But within minutes of seeing her, Carol buzzed me. We had a system in place, and it was the first time Carol needed to use it. I was in surgery, and had no choice but to finish."

Carol told the rest, "I knew I needed to stall this woman, who was pushy and in a hurry. She stepped into the clinic the minute I opened the door, and it was obvious she wasn't the girl who had phoned saying that Dr. Craig had recommended us. And she wasn't much of a detective either. She came dressed like a streetwalker, wearing stiletto heels, a low-cut dress, and scarlet lipstick. She said she needed help right away, like we're an 'abortion on demand' service.

"And after I told her I didn't know what she was talking about, she smirked and said, 'Whatever you call it, I want it done.'

"This is when I told her I needed more information before we could talk. I walked to the desk, opened a drawer, and pressed the emergency button as I took out a pad of paper. Stalling, I asked questions like "where's your worst pain.

"She became annoyed and told me that I knew she was in the office for an abortion. She went further, saying she had been raped by her boss and needed help. This was laughable as she looked like she could take down a Los Angeles Ram.

"When she saw I was buying time, she went back to being pushy and said she had driven from Seattle, had cash, and just wanted to get this over-with."

Claire broke-in, "Carol raised her voice so I could hear her ask 'Get what over-with?' And Patricia Ritter yelled so the police outside could hear her. 'The Goddamn abortion, that's what. And I'm headed back to see Dr. Karridan.'

"Carol shouted for her to leave, or she would call the police. And Ritter answered that she'd save her the trouble, and within seconds I heard the police enter and head back toward my room.

"I had barely finished the abortion when they pounded on my door. My patient was panicked as she moved her feet from stirrups and managed to sit-up. I tossed a housecoat to her, and she was putting it on when they tried to break-in. That's when I opened the door."

Claire looked at Lauren, "From this point it was almost exactly like the raid seven years ago. And if the photos make it to the paper or T.V. my patient will be indelibly hurt."

A picture of Claire in her white surgical jacket, bent toward the operating table while facing the police, was in the morning paper.

Quoting her, the headline read: "Have you no decency?" But there was no mention or pictures of the patient, and Lauren wondered if Dan had helped.

Chapter Thirty

Dan's position with CBS had changed, giving him enormous power.

He returned from Korea in 1953 and started a new career. Leaving the New York Times, he became part of the fledgling Columbia Broadcasting System. Well-known and respected as a journalist, CBS asked him to join their new team. He started as an on-scene reporter in New York City. And by 1956 his face had become familiar to most New Yorkers.

As CBS became the most powerful news network in the country, Dan's role grew. He became their expert on political news, both national and international. He introduced reporters around the world and gave opinion pieces.

Lauren was able to watch him every week night, and sometimes on special weekend forums – as did millions of others across the country. She understood it was unreasonable, but as she watched him grin, raise an eyebrow, shake his head in disgust – gestures that she knew so well – she felt as if her own world was being shared. And, as during other times, she was concerned about her place in his life.

She thought of moving permanently to New York, but knew it wasn't a good choice for now. Sandi needed to stay on Sauvie Island. She was sixteen, excelled in school, liked her classmates, and constantly said she never wanted to move. Lauren knew this would change, but also knew she was sharing a perfect time in Sandi's life.

Dan respected her decision even though he wanted her with him. And, as always, he made it clear that she had no cause to move to New York because of worries about the changes in his life.

"New York or here, my world is perfect when you, love of my life, and Sandi are in it." He smiled, then added, "Madeline, too."

When Lauren returned home from the jail, her phone was ringing and she ran to answer.

"Dan?"

"I've been trying to phone you from the time I heard. I figured you would be with Claire and Carol. When did James get there?"

"James is out of town, but thank God for Frank. He took charge. It's his kind of case."

"You're right – he spent over a year with Justice Douglas. But before anything else, tell me you're okay. Were you. . ."

Lauren stopped him, "No. I wasn't any place near the clinic. I was in bed when Claire phoned.

"It's clear that the climate hasn't changed since the last bust. If anything the news is going to be worse; she'll be all over television. Even Farrell Seigart, our loyal columnist, now has a spot on our local channel. He was there with a mike when I drove her home at two this morning. His camera crew caught me as I stepped from her house. He tried to interview me, and I refused more politely than I would have if his damn mike wasn't shoved in my face.

"I wanted Claire and Carol to come to my house. Claire preferred being in her own home. And Carol has her dogs and cats to take care of. I tried to convince her to bring them here. Heaven knows she's done enough for me over the years."

"True," Dan said. "She's been part of the clinic since Claire started. Jesus, that was in the early 30's."

"For over 20 years they've been in one clinic or another. And they're both aging. Claire is in her sixties. And, oh my god, Dan, if you thought she didn't look well last time you were home, you should see her now. She's bone thin, her eyes shadowed by deep circles, and that gray color – it's as if…" Lauren shook off the words. "I know her; have seen her almost daily for over fourteen years. She has to see a doctor."

"And there's a long list of doctors who owe her. I'm flying to Portland on Friday. I've always been pretty blunt with her, and she's been blunt right back. This time I'll win. She'll see one."

Lauren was skeptical. "It won't be easy with all else she's facing. I'm not sure when James will arrive home, but suspect the meeting will be Monday morning. It's going to be a bad weekend for her."

"I'd like to be at the meeting with James, but have to fly back late Sunday. I'm anchoring a forum on Monday that'll include John Foster Dulles. The network's busy coordinating with his schedule, so I can't get out of it.

"But I'm doing as much as I can to help Claire. Life isn't as simple as when I was a freelance reporter. There's a golden rule in television – keep family members out of our reporting. Claire isn't family, but comes damn close. And most people around here know how proud I am of you, including your career.

"So instead of commentary, I'm looking for a story. I've already sent a crew with one of our best reporters – one I know personally who'll tell it from the right point of view."

"Good," Lauren said, "I just hope we can spot him from the others. Tell him to wear a big CBS on his jacket."

Lauren picked Dan up at sunrise on Saturday morning.

Sandi and Maddie were waiting in the kitchen as they entered the back door. Maddie whined, twisted and twirled. Then as Dan bent to pet her, she managed to jump high enough to kiss his face. At twelve years old this was a feat.

Lauren smiled. "Maddie tells you how we all feel."

"Well she deserves a trip to the water. Right, Madeline?"

With that, Maddie rushed to the door.

"Wait," Sandi yelled as she ran toward her room, "I need a jacket."

"Hurry," Dan called. "She's already headed for the path."

Sandi and Lauren caught up and the three walked to the river together. Once there, Dan breathed in the fresh river air, while watching Maddie wade into the calm water. As in the past, Dan thought how nothing in New York could compare to this.

When they returned to the house, he fixed breakfast. No one mentioned Claire. That would be later, when he and Lauren had time to talk.

Dan had lots to say, and not just about the arrest.

"Success comes at a price. Every time I see Sandi she's grown – and I know I'm missing too much. I want my family with me."

He read the concern on Lauren's face, but continued, "I know how you feel, and that Sandi loves it here. But she'll thrive wherever she lives, and New York offers everything – theater, museums, music, bigger and better than everywhere, and she would be part of it."

"It doesn't offer our island. She'll have time for all of those things, but right now I'm doing what she wants – staying here." Lauren paused, "Besides, Dan, you are the best part of New York. And if things go as I hope, we'll spend a good month with you this summer."

Before he answered, she added, "That is depending on what happens with Claire. I'm talking about much more than the arrest. As I told you, she looks terrible. I know you want to talk to her. But she's so worried about everything right now that I doubt if she'd go to a doctor even if... Oh, Dan, even if what? I don't want to say the words; but she looks like she's..."

Dan touched her hand. "I know."

After a brief silence she said, "I'm glad you're here. I've needed you."

She drew a resigned breath. "Now, let me bring you up to date on what's happened since we talked on the phone. Was that only yesterday?"

Lauren took the Oregonian from the shelf and spread the editorial page on the table.

"This morning I woke up to this. The paper's filled with Claire. But it hasn't been all bad. Let me show you the biggest surprise"

She pointed to a letter to the editor.

Dan looked, "Father Riley?" Who's this? A Catholic Priest?

Lauren nodded, "Read."

He read out loud, "The Catholic Church takes a definite stand against abortion. But as we do, it is wrong to remain silent about conditions that make the practice difficult to eliminate."

Dan shook his head in disbelief, read the rest, and then looked at Lauren with disbelief.

"A priest who writes about unfair laws that target unwed mothers, but not the men involved; about married women who are forced into unwanted pregnancies: and a society that ignores the suffering of others – especially when it involves poor and unwanted children."

He read Father Riley's final words out loud.

"'All God's children should begin their lives in a world that watches over them, protecting and providing. And we – each of us – must practice mercy and love: the strongest part of Christ's teachings. Perhaps then, women will not feel the need to cry on the doorsteps of abortionists. Father Gavin Riley. St. Theresa's home.'

"I fully believe that Claire is special and has magical powers, but just how did she gain this kind of clout?" Dan said.

"Don't ask, but I did have occasion to meet with Father Riley. However, this letter is totally unexpected. He's gone out on a limb. A Catholic priest placing male irresponsibility, women's desperation, and unwanted children into an equation with abortion is unheard of to my knowledge."

"Make certain James and Frank see this." Dan chuckled, "Father Riley will set the prosecution back some notches."

Chapter Thirty-one

Frank McCaffrey had become an expert on privacy rights. After graduating from Yale Law School, he spent a year clerking for Justice William O. Douglas.

In deciding whether Frank should handle Claire's case, James said, "The kid learned more in the time spent with Douglas than the years at my firm and law-school. He's as well versed on civil-rights cases as anyone in Oregon. And he has the instincts of a prize fighter when faced with a cause."

Lauren wasn't surprised. She remembered Frank's concerns on the day she had met him in New York. Unlike Dan, he had zeroed in on the homeless who lived on the streets – people seeming too alienated to question their rights.

She thought of this as she took the elevator to McCaffrey's firm. It had taken over the top two floors.

As she, Claire, and Carol entered Frank's office, Lauren thought how James had made it easy for him. The office had a view of downtown Portland, the Willamette River, and Mount Hood. All the chairs were covered with black leather that matched a large couch and covered bar in an alcove. His large desk was of rich mahogany, as were the built-in wall shelves that appeared to hold a full legal library.

Watching her, Frank smiled. "Dad felt I should start at the bottom and work my way up."

The three women laughed, and Carol asked, "After they release me from prison could you use a secretary?"

"I don't plan on your spending more time in a cell. I'm seeing the presiding judge today about dismissing your case. You didn't commit a crime – you were doing your job. And," he smiled, "I'd like to hire you after Claire's case is won."

Frank's words were reassuring, and Lauren thought how he was the right person for their case.

As if reading her, Frank said, "You're heroes to me – each of you." He smiled at Lauren, "But you know that."

The earnest expression on his face gave away his youth. But Lauren nodded yes; thinking how he cared, was capable, and, importantly, he could win.

At this time James entered the room and pulled a chair next to them.

Frank smiled, "Hi Dad. I was just getting ready to tell them about Douglas and his work on privacy rights."

"Good. Because that's exactly what you're going to be arguing."

"I was leading to that, but was waiting for you to get here."

"You needn't have. They'll soon recognize that you, not I, will be the one who serves them best."

Lauren wondered about this. Frank was smart, but he was young and didn't know his way around a courtroom. James did. But she, as Claire and Carol, said nothing and waited.

Frank broke the silence, "Well, since I haven't heard any protest yet, I'll give you an idea of the direction I plan to take." He searched their faces, before continuing, "Stop me with questions, protests, whatever.

"Much of our case will be based on whether the charge of manslaughter meets its definition. That is, whether a grouping of fetal cells, before developing life-sustention, meets the criteria of being human.

"Just as important is an argument about the legality of abortion laws: whether the government has legal authority to interfere with a woman's right to choose what she wants for her body.

"Justice Douglas is the most informed man in the country when it comes to this kind of argument. As his clerk, I spent the past year researching the reach of government authority and its breach of individual rights. The right of women to control their own bodies meets Douglas' criteria, and that's what I'll argue.

Frank added that if necessary he felt competent to argue their case in the Oregon Supreme Court or if need be, in the federal courts.

Up to this point Lauren had agreed, but now she interrupted, "I don't like the sound of that. It's as if you're not expecting to win in the lower court."

"It's a good possibility, based on prevailing attitudes right now," he said.

Claire frowned. "Quite honestly, Frank, I don't want this to become a banner case. The last thing I need is more publicity. I have grandkids, and I worry about them and my daughter. This case will be covered by the news. I don't want it to go one bit further than it must."

Claire turned to James for help. He said nothing, and Frank answered, "I'm going to be blunt. This is your second arrest, and on the last one you were sentenced to a year of probation. That will work against you. And we can't argue that you weren't practicing again – the prosecutors will kill us if we do."

He leaned forward, emphasizing his words. "Abortion is against the law. And quite simply, jurors believe they are there to enforce laws.

"But our intent will be to show that there are times when laws are unjust, and need changing. If we succeed it will mean that the abortion law is altered. We will have created 'case law'– and attorneys can use this new legal interpretation when proving their cases.

"Claire, you know that you aren't just a client to Dad and me. You're much more. But besides this, I believe these are bad laws, and in our system the best way to change a bad law is to try it in our courts.

"As I said, my argument will be based on whether or not abortion meets the elements of manslaughter; which it doesn't. And I repeat that it might need to be appealed, even as far as the US Supreme Court."

As Lauren started to protest, he put out his hand – still addressing Claire. "It's a case that needs to go there. But," Frank accentuated, "I understand how you don't want to be the one to take it, and I want you to know that I will make every effort to win in our circuit court. I'm just telling you that if it does need to be appealed, we will win. And exonerated, you will have made an enormous step toward changing laws that are intrinsically wrong."

Claire wrinkled her forehead, looking surprised. "Where have you been? During our last trial you were a quiet kid who sat watching your dad with admiration."

"I still admire Dad and look to him for direction."

He turned to James. "What do you think?"

"I think this would make a hell of an appellate case. And it might be where it ends up. But one thing should be very clear and I'm certain Frank agrees – making a change in future laws is not our goal, nor should it be. We are working for you.

"But this is a tricky business. There would be little need for attorneys if laws were always just. This case is going to fly in the face of laws designed to meet long held attitudes and beliefs. And sometimes we are forced to look to appellate courts for justice."

Lauren started to speak – to argue that time was important, that Claire couldn't wait. But what could she say? That something was terribly wrong – tell them to look at Claire's eyes, the color of her skin, the way she held herself.

Catching her look, Claire squinted, "What?"

"Nothing, or at least nothing to talk about now."

Claire sounded irritated, "Well then, we'll talk later." She turned back to face Frank. "It sounds as if our case is in excellent hands. I've always trusted your father, and now that trust includes you."

"I agree," Lauren said, "but let's hope this is accomplished within the year, rather than years of fighting in one court or another."

Frank shook his head, "I agree. But, if it is appealed we want it in the Warren Court."

He looked at his watch. "We have our work cut out; it's time to get busy."

The walls of the courthouse – aged and fusty – took on dank odors when winter rains came. Slight shifts from age and earth had created imperceptibly fine lines, and vestiges of their wintry history were more sensed than seen.

As planned, on Tuesday morning Lauren walked with Claire to Arraignment Court. The door was unlocked and Claire took a seat next to James and Frank, who were waiting at the defense table. A judge entered, and James asked for reasonable time to prepare his case.

The judge assigned a date – two weeks off, and told James that Judge Cook would be presiding over the case. Then Claire was released on her own recognizance.

After the hearing, Frank showed Lauren and Claire the back exit of the courthouse. It was often used to avoid the press. As they left through it, Frank invited them to coffee. Lauren begged off. She wanted to talk to Claire alone.

As they walked, Lauren recognized that Claire needed help walking. She seemed weaker than when they had walked into the courtroom.

As soon as Frank was out of earshot Lauren said, "I'm going to be blunt. I'm too worried not to be. You don't look well, and I hope you'll do me a favor – call a doctor."

Claire squeezed Lauren's hand, "I'm okay, Lauren. Don't worry. Yeah, I don't feel well – the raid, all of this, has taken its toll. I have to face what's going to happen. You and I both know that I'm not going to escape prison – the climate hasn't changed from our last raid.

Sandi looked frightened. "What happened in court today?"

Lauren sat on the couch next to her before answering. "Claire was arraigned, but nothing will happen for a while. How are your friends reacting to all the notoriety, especially as cameras are aimed at me as much as Claire?"

"Actually, Mom, most of them are pretty intrigued, like I've got this famous family: Dan, you, and my Aunt Claire."

Lauren smiled. "Seriously, I know you have to be fending off some tough comments."

"Not from real friends, and I have quite a few. They know what happened earlier in my life, and we've talked about you a lot. They admire you. And Mom, you know I do."

Lauren was touched but continued. "The problem, Sandi, is that things are going to get worse. There's going to be a trial, and your friends – you – are going to hear about it. Aunt Claire might go to jail. I know you're totally aware that abortion is against the law. This trial is going to get ugly.

"You're my greatest concern in the world. And though Claire has been my best friend for many years, I don't want to see you hurt or embarrassed any more than you have been. So, I'm thinking you might be better off in New York. As you know, for years Dan has wanted you there."

"Mom, Dan has wanted us there."

"And I'd join you on most weekends, but I feel I should be here while Claire is in the courtroom."

"And I want to be here too, I don't want to be away from Aunt Claire either. Besides, no one's going to hurt me. My friends are great. But what's important, and you must know this – I don't want to be far away from you. That's what would hurt."

Again, Lauren recognized power behind Sandi's principles – and she was only sixteen.

"Okay, Sandi. And thank you."

Chapter Thirty-two

It was a winter-dreary day, with no promise of sunshine. In a perverse way Lauren was glad; the darkness fit her mood. She and Claire stepped from the car and Dan drove to park in one of McCaffrey's private spaces.

The rain stopped and parka hoods were shoved back, revealing the eager faces of reporters. They nudged and crowded each other, making it difficult for Lauren and Claire to reach the courthouse entrance. As before, Lauren appreciated the guards who opened the door for them, while stopping the press.

She and Claire took the elevator to the fourth floor and then headed to Judge Paul Cook's courtroom. Frank was already sitting at the defense table. No one else had arrived, so he was able to talk freely.

"I chose this table as it's furthest from the jury. This way we can view gestures and whispers of the prosecutors, while they can't see us without turning.

"You'll soon meet Mark Barton, the deputy district attorney who'll be prosecuting your case. After graduating from an eastern law school he practiced as a deputy district attorney for five years in New York. Evidently was good. He came to Oregon to be near his family. Gerry Fields hired him on the recommendation of one of his assistants who knew Barton in college."

As if timed, Mark Barton entered the courtroom. Lauren thought how he looked too polished – it occurred to her that he looked like Clark Kent. Dark-rimmed glasses, post-puberty smooth skin, and hair that was Brill Cream perfect.

Dan followed him in and sat next to Lauren. He had taken several weeks off, not just to be in the courtroom for Claire, but to be home when Sandi returned from school – making certain the trial wasn't having negative effects on her.

He and Lauren had thought how his being in the courtroom would create a stir, but decided that was all right. His fame has some positives. The press seemed tame compared to the trial years earlier. Even columnist Farrell Seigart showed a certain respect.

But there was an effect that Lauren hadn't thought about. It became clear that Dan Carter was related to Anne Thompson. But that too was all right, as the relationship helped Claire.

Being the first morning of the trial, the attorneys gave instructions to a panel of perspective jurors. Mark Barton and Frank were well prepared, knowing they would be influencing the final twelve.

As the morning passed Lauren grew more concerned about Claire, who was much too frail to be the focus of this trial.

Lauren was relieved when the judge stood.

"It is time for lunch break. Those who are part of this trial are to return to this courtroom by a quarter after one."

Surprising Lauren, the sky had had turned a lighter gray, with streaks of pure blue. This was Oregon. She felt a surge of energy, filling her with a sense of the past – freedom after long dark days. She recognized how this conflicted with the truth, but still, just for a moment, she turned her face toward the sky.

Then she put her arm around Claire's shoulder – wishing she could pass the energy to her.

Dan had left the courtroom early. As planned, he drove to the backdoor of the courthouse and helped Claire into the car.

Knowing they would be arriving, Mrs. Thiele had set-up a room that excluded the press.

Claire took a long breath before talking. Her voice had always had a deep and gravelly edge, but now the edge was thin and wispy. "Jane wanted to be at the trial, but stayed home with the girls, who aren't attending school. She hired a tutor who quit after a day, complaining that keeping them in books was harder than herding cats."

Dan suggested that Jane call Reed College and find a student to tutor them.

"It's as liberal a school as you're going to find anywhere in the country, and it's my bet they'll view you as a hero. Besides being supporters of yours, they'll have the girls quoting from Salinger to Camus in a week's time."

"Great," Claire said, "But who the hell are Salinger and Camus?" She didn't smile. "Seriously, I want them to stand-up to all of this. A lot to ask, but I'll be damned if I'll apologize for what I do. And I hope someday my girls will see what we have done." She looked at Lauren. "We've helped a lot of women over the years."

The strength of conviction that had always been a part of Claire wasn't there. She was breathing too hard – as if forcing air in and then out.

And then, Lauren saw tears.

Quickly, Claire wiped them, and tried to pull herself taller. "Pardon me. I've been preaching to the choir. Yes, Jane could use one of those students, and it would help if she's also a marathon runner."

No one spoke as they dabbed at their lunches. After a few minutes Claire put her fork down. "I feel so worn out."

Lauren drew in a breath, and then said, "Claire, I sound like a broken record, but I'm concerned. You need to see a doctor; I've never seen you like this."

"Matter-of-fact, I have never felt so. . ."

Claire didn't finish the sentence, and Lauren felt panic.

"Knowing you, you haven't said anything to anyone. I want you to see a doctor, I mean now!

"Do I look that bad?" Claire's smile was wan. "I've just been tired lately and…" Once more the sentence dangled.

Lauren pressed, "Claire, I'm worried. I want Frank to tell the judge you're sick and need to go to the doctor this afternoon."

Claire appeared to weigh the suggestion but didn't answer.

"We need to get in right away. I know the same docs you know, and I'll call one," Lauren said and then recognized Claire's expression: as always she would take care of her own needs.

"Okay," Lauren sighed, "But you promise me we'll go right away – like later today."

"We?" Claire raised an eyebrow.

"Of course, I'll drive. Don't forget it's easier to get past the campers in your yard when you're with someone."

"That's true," Claire nodded and then, with effort, she stood. "It's time to get back to the courtroom."

Lauren decided to phone Dr. Frederick and ask him to meet them at his clinic that evening. Over the years he had called seeking help for his patients. Now they needed him.

Lauren didn't hear a word of Mark Barton's voir-dire. Instead she was watching Claire. She could only see her back, but knew that something was terribly wrong – Claire seemed to be sinking into her chair. Feeling panic, Lauren stood and rushed toward her.

Judge Cook reached for his gavel at the same moment that Claire fell forward. And by the time Lauren reached her, Claire was on the floor, with Frank bending toward her. As he took her pulse, Lauren yelled for someone to get an ambulance.

The bailiff used the emergency phone, while the court reporter ran to Judge Cook's office and called for the courthouse medics.

Within five minutes Claire was being carried from the courtroom.

Chapter Thirty-three

"What the hell?" Claire asked as she opened her eyes and heard sirens. "Where's the ambulance?

"You're in it, heading for the hospital," Lauren answered.

Claire tried to raise her head, but the paramedic told her to lay back and relax.

He weighed over two hundred pounds, was over six feet, and in total control.

"We're busy saving your life, so keep your head down."

"Yes Sir," Claire croaked, barely above a whisper, "Now tell me what's going on. Last thing I know, I was sitting in the courtroom, and I hope I'm not being rushed to the county jail."

He chuckled, "You might prefer that from where you're going. A doctor is waiting, to read the reports I'm taking to him – then the nurses are gonna poke you with more needles."

"Turn this thing around and take me home."

"They don't let me control anything but fevers and rapid heartbeat – and you don't have either one of those."

"At least loosen these straps and let me sit up."

"Wouldn't even if I could; I can tell you're feisty and would get up punching."

Lauren giggled, and Claire turned toward her. "You're here."

"Yeah, hitching a ride with you and Sam. He's been taking good care of you. You scared us in that courtroom – even Judge Cook."

Claire looked up at her with warmth, then reached out as far as the straps allowed. Lauren took her hand and squeezed. "It's an awful way to do it, but I'm finally getting you to see a doctor."

Claire's smile was weak. "I've got to tell you a secret. I went in to see Dr. Frederick last week. He took blood, some x-rays, and ran a few other tests. He's probably got results by now. I went on my own, wanting to keep what he finds quiet."

Lauren bent and kissed her. "You should have told me."

"You are family, and I didn't want to upset you."

The news of Claire's collapse hit television instantly. And by the time the ambulance drove up to the emergency admittance, a crowd of strangers had gathered outside – including reporters.

And when Claire was taken into the emergency room, Dr. Frederick was waiting.

Lauren took one look at him and knew the test results were bad. He had scheduled surgery, and there was no time for argument. Claire had cervical cancer: staged four adenosquamous carcinoma. It had spread, but the doctor didn't know how far. She was to have a radical hysterectomy – followed by chemo and radiation.

On the following morning, everyone Claire considered family, plus James and Frank, sat in her private hospital room.

Jane's eyes were swollen, and she had the look of someone in shock. She stared into space occasionally shuddering as if shaking off a chill. Claire reached out, her eyes full of sorrow, and touched Jane's hand.

Her granddaughters watched, as they sat speechless, appearing awkward – ill-at-ease with emotions that were new to them. They were being told that Claire would not survive cancer – a word describing something that touched other families, not theirs.

Lauren thought how they had grown used to surprises where their inimitable grandmother was concerned, but this was beyond all they could have foreseen. She was as important to their lives as their mother, and it was impossible for them to imagine a world without her.

It occurred to Lauren that although they, as Jane, had been hit by slights and insults due to her profession, they each had gained so much. Far more than the luxuries Claire provided, they had received the abundance of her warmth, wit, and charm. She was larger than anyone else in their lives, and had always made it clear that she adored them.

Sandi leaned against Dan as Lauren moved to sit on the couch next to the girls. She wished they didn't have to see Claire as she was now – wanting them to remember the glamorous vibrant woman she had always been. Her voice, which had been edged with velvet, was a scratchy wisp that could barely be heard.

Though everyone else in the room was frightened, Claire didn't appear to be. Lauren thought how she was too tired for fear. Her eyes loomed huge in her shriveled face.

Drowsy from medication, Claire spoke in a slow murmur. "Jane, I love you – and my beautiful little girls. When surgery is over, whatever happens, I want you to get out of town. California – go to California. Get far away from these cold rainy days and go to our place in the sun. I want you to have good lives. No more darkness. You deserve more – you always have." She squinted, focusing. "Jane, promise me you'll move. Life hasn't been easy for you."

"Oh Mama, I love –" Jane's words were swallowed up by emotion as she bent to kiss her.

Before she was wheeled from the room, Claire addressed James and Frank, trying to be more direct than the medicine allowed. "Guess it will never need to be heard in the appeals courts."

James touched her forehead. "This is a case that needs to be won; you've helped many people over the years."

Claire's eyes were closing. "However – whatever," she could barely be heard.

Then she opened her eyes, and her voice rose, "Lauren, listen, you are family and I love you."

Lauren couldn't speak. She bent down and kissed her goodbye.

They gathered at her grave site. And Jane spoke.

"You, Mother, were not ordinary. Far from it. You were a hero to each of us and to so many others who received your help and care. We your family and closest friends, understand that you gave us everything you had – endless love, support, and time.

"You affected each of us, along with the many patients who came to you in desperation. By helping others, even when your own freedom was in jeopardy and many times without pay, you proved that you understood how much your profession helped others.

"We thank you for being who you are – and always being there for us.

"Each of us standing here has a heavy heart and cannot bear to think that you, Mom, won't be in our everyday lives. We pray that there is an afterlife, and that you feel the love and thanks for always being here for each of us, and for so many others. You have given so much.

Tears smudged Jane's words, "I love you, Mom. Each of us standing here loves you. We will miss you forever."

As the girls, Lauren, Dan, and Sandi placed roses on her casket. Then Jane bent and kissed it.

Jane's eulogy proved prophetic. Flowers and cards arrived for weeks. They were addressed to Jane's home, the cemetery, courthouse, Broadway Building, and even Claire's recent clinic. They were from old patients, doctors, and women throughout Oregon and other States – many who knew or were just learning about her.

She and Anne were becoming symbols of a growing movement.

Chapter Thirty-four

James asked Frank to come to his office for a talk.

"I've got a case that I'd like you to handle. She came to us because of Claire's case. Said she was one of her patients not too many years ago, and figured we're a firm that would help her.

"Melinda Pervis, colored, three kids, lives on Alberta Street. She cleans houses full time – six in the Laurelhurst neighborhood. She's been saving money to put a down-payment on a house in that area because there's less crime. But you know the problem – most of Portland, it's segregated."

"I told her we'll do it pro bono. It's time to make serious changes in our firm, and this is the case to start."

Frank squinted, "This firm is going to do pro bono?"

"Yes, especially when civil rights are involved; now that we have the man to handle them. I never did pro bono – always had the feeling I was still building a firm."

"You have been, and I've been lucky. I was coming here from the time you had two rooms on the second floor. I watched it grow as I learned.

Frank paused before adding, "You know I'd like to do the firm's pro-bono work; but not here. I don't think many indigent clients would walk into this building, let alone take elevators to its most prestigious floors. I need an office where those who can't afford an attorney will feel comfortable walking in."

When James didn't comment, Frank remembered what he had taught: Think before responding.

"Dad, I've been privileged and have always wanted to be part of your firm." Frank smiled, "Besides, I need to start earning money. So I'm not adverse to clients who pay. But whether they can pay or not, I, as you, love a good cause."

His dad's expression touched him.

"Frank, needless to say I'm proud of you. For a long time, I've known it's not the money that makes practicing law exciting. There's nothing that feels as good as winning when you know the defendant's deserving – like Claire and Lauren.

"You, I mean 'we' will take cases that need to be tried whether or not we're paid. You're the most qualified civil rights attorney in Oregon. I'm proud and want to help with your new office – wherever it is. And on occasion I want to try cases with you."

"I found a house that I want you and Carol to see."

"You're moving? And you want me and Carol to see your house?" Lauren inferred 'why?'

Frank chuckled, "I'm not going to live in it; it will be our new office."

"Our?"

"That's what I need to talk to you about – you and Carol. Come meet me there."

Before she responded he told her the address. It was on southwest Nineteenth and Madison. Lauren knew the location. Houses had histories that went back to the twenties. A safe street, and within walking distance to Thiele's on Burnside. And also, she thought, a good place for his office if he intends to work with Portland's indigent.

Burnside runs from west to east of the Willamette River, and also divides Portland's south and north.

Notably "downtown" is on the southwest side of Burnside, with upscale restaurants and shopping. Its sidewalks are swept and maintained, windows are washed, and shop doors are manned. An historic hotel occupies a full block in the city's center, and is kitty-corner from Oregon's finest department store, Meier and Franks. Women shoppers dressed up to go downtown, wearing gloves and hats. And business men wore white shirts and navy-blue neckties.

By contrast, skid-row is in the northwest, across Burnside – with decaying hotels and neglected streets that are home to derelicts: alcoholics, mentally ill, prostitutes, pimps, and strippers from the Star Theatre.

When Lauren was a teenager the bus went through this area on the way to downtown. She remembered seeing men in soot gray frayed jackets and sagging formless pants. In doorways she saw people rolled up in blankets – sheltered from rain. If the bus windows were open, there was the stench of mildew, pee, and booze. She tried not to stare. When she caught anyone's attention, she felt hostility – and was embarrassed. She was on her way to downtown, and they were outcastes.

But now, 1957, Frank would have an office that was accessible and for them.

She and Carol arrived at the same time, and saw Frank's car parked in the long narrow driveway. They stood outside studying the house. Like all the other homes on the street, it was turn of the century Victorian. Two stories, narrow but long, Lauren thought how there were lots of rooms inside.

One thing was different from the other homes on the block. It had a veranda that covered the front and much of the side area of the house. Now rotting and unsafe, Lauren imagined that it had been a family porch, designed for long summer evenings.

The builders hadn't foreseen the home's future of neglect. The paint had worn off, leaving faded and torn strips of blue on cedar shingles.

Lauren saw dents in the glass of the large front windows – as if from bb's, and the panes were rusted. She also noted that some of shingles had fallen from the roof, and thought how the inside of the house would have water damage.

She and Carol were careful as they walked up the steps. The wood was spongy, with pieces missing, and they couldn't hold onto the iron railing as its foundation had rotted.

They made their way to the front door. And when Frank opened it, Lauren was hit by the odor of mice and mold.

"Welcome to my new office. Isn't it fantastic?" He waved his hand in sweeping motion that took in the porch.

"Fantastic. But somewhat dangerous," Lauren muttered.

"Dangerous?" Frank smiled. "Part of the challenge; watch your step and come in. I'll take you on a tour."

Dressed as if he were still the student she had walked with in New York, he wore jeans and an open collared blue denim shirt.

They followed him through each room as he talked about hiring a company to do a remodel. They would turn the living room into an reception area, and the dining room would become his law office. The wide hallway between it and the kitchen would be a law library, and the windowed parlor off of the kitchen would have a big round table for special meetings.

After their tour, Frank led them back into the front room where he had put a temporary desk and several chairs.

"Grab a seat. They've been dusted."

As soon as they were seated he looked at Carol. "Now I need the best staff I can get. I'm hoping you'll be the office manager."

Carol nodded, "I don't need to wait for remodeling, I'm ready to start."

"Good. I need help ordering, buying, and keeping builders on track. And I want the front office to be a place where women and girls feel safe; especially those who are trying to leave the streets. You'll be the perfect person for that."

He turned to Lauren. "I have a special role for you. You will become our legal assistant – advising, and so much more."

Lauren was surprised. "Legal assistant? I'm flattered, but I can't. I've got something else I want to do."

Frank didn't hide his disappointment. "You're leaving for New York."

"Not yet. Sandi has to finish school. I haven't told anyone, but I expect to be pretty busy. It's something I've thought about for quite a while."

Frank raised his eyebrows, "Are you going to tell us?"

"Later."

"Is it something I can help with?"

"Thanks, Frank. I may be asking for help later, but right now it's something I have to do on my own."

She stood to leave and looked at the stained and rotting floors. "This is going to be a great office."

Chapter Thirty-five

"Each time you and Sandi leave it gets harder. Pack your bags, buy a special carrier for Madeline and come back; this time to stay.

"It's not just me; New York is waiting for you. If you haven't noticed, you and Claire are heroes. Women keep approaching me – even the studio gets calls. Not about my work; I'm just your husband. They want you to speak at their organizations about everything from abortion rights to freedom from breast feeding."

Lauren laughed, "I've gotten more than a few letters at the Fairmont address, but they're not always nice."

She took a deep breath. "Now, after what you just said, it's even more difficult to tell you about something. It's big. But first let me tell you what happened today."

Lauren described Frank's new practice, and his job offers to both Carol and her. Before Dan could protest she rushed on, "I told him I want to support and help all I can, but I can't commit to a job. I didn't give reasons, as I want to talk to you first.

"I know this will surprise you, but I've thought about it for quite a while. Problem is, it will commit me to staying in Oregon for longer than you and I have planned – much longer."

When he still didn't comment, she said, "I am going to apply for Law School. Portland has a night school, Northwestern College of Law. I don't know if you've heard about it, but it's unique. Judge John Gantenbein is both the owner and registrar. Its classes are taught by practicing lawyers and judges, and most of the students have jobs and families.

"Almost everyone is accepted. They weed you out by your performance. In other words, they let you in and then you have to prove yourself.

"It's a tough program, the last class started with about 130 students, and at the end of four years thirty-seven graduated. Of those, twenty-five passed the bar. That's just about the same ratio as those who attended our expensive law schools that require at least three years of undergraduate work.

"You know me Dan. I'll graduate and pass the bar. I'm that confident – or whatever you'd call it. I'll be eligible to take bars across the country, but so much is happening right here. Frank's new clinic will be pro bono, and as you know, his background is in civil-rights. I've thought about that. New York or here, I want to specialize in women's rights. God knows I'm aware of them."

She waited but knew what his answer would be.

"You're right, I agree. And I know you; you'll do it, and I'm not going to – I wouldn't try to stop you." He paused again, and then added, "Of course, you'll go to law school. And you – well – you'll continue helping people for the rest of your life."

Lauren went to see Judge Gantenbein the following morning.

"You'll be one of three women entering this year. We're tough and just about two-thirds of those who sign-up don't make it to graduation. But those who do and then pass the bar, end-up being among the very best attorneys in Oregon."

He gave her admittance forms, information about the school, future accreditation with the Bar, and a schedule of classes she would be taking in September.

Then as she was leaving his office he said, "Miss Martin, I have the feeling you'll be a hell of an attorney. I, and many others, know that you aren't afraid to take risks and fight for what you believe. Those are the kind of people we look for at our school."

Lauren turned and smiled, "I won't let you down, Judge."

When Sandi came home from school, she looked at Lauren — expectant.

"I did it! Your mom is becoming a student."

Sandi's smile was huge. "Good going!"

Lauren hugged her, "Now, don't take off your coat. Just put the books on the table. I've already walked Maddie, and we're going out to celebrate. And I lucked out, as it's a rare evening when you don't have drama practice, dance class, or a basketball game. We can start now.

"And the very first thing, while it's still light out, I want you to see something."

They drove from the island toward Thiele's, but stopped at the dilapidated house on Madison. Work trucks lined the street, and Carol's car was parked behind Frank's in the driveway.

Sandi looked worried. "Tell me we aren't moving!"

"Moving? Of course not. It's where I plan on working this summer, and we could sure use your help."

"You'll be working here." Sandi looked apprehensive as they walked up the rickety steps and into the open front door.

Carol was pointing to a wall, telling a worker it had to be removed. Then she saw Sandi and Lauren. "Welcome to our new office."

Lauren saw Sandi's confusion, and quickly explained, "This is going to be Frank McCaffrey's new law office. And we're going to help set it up."

"Law office! Good." Sandi looked relieved.

"Yep," Lauren answered. "It's going to be perfect, and much more accessible to Frank's clients than an office in James' tower downtown."

Frank yelled from upstairs. "Is that you, Lauren?"

"Yes, and Sandi."

"Hold on, I'm coming down."

As he walked downstairs, he saw Sandi and grinned. "You've grown, and you're still as beautiful as your mother. Welcome to the office." He looked around. "It needs a bit of work."

Sandi nodded, "A bit."

"Come on into the kitchen; just watch your step." He looked at Carol, "You coming?"

"I sure am," she said, while putting an arm around Sandi. "I haven't seen you for too long."

On the way, Frank showed them where his law office and library would be. Then in the kitchen, he pointed to chairs in an alcove. "Have a seat. This is where we'll be meeting in future years – your mom included. I'm hoping she'll be joining our team."

He walked to the refrigerator. "What'll it be: pop, iced tea, coffee?"

After bringing their drinks, he sat at the table and spoke to Sandi, "I've been waiting to see if your mom will work as our legal assistant, and now I'm hoping for an answer."

They each looked at Lauren, who smiled. "I'll do as much as I can until fall. Then I won't have much time."

Frank had an expression she had grown to recognize – brows knit, slightly annoyed. "You've said it's not New York, so what's happening?"

"I'm going to Northwestern Law School."

"Law school?" Carol looked both impressed and confused. "Good on you, but where's that?"

Frank smiled. "Northwestern is Judge Gantenbeim's school. He's an outstanding judge, and the school reflects this. Some of Portland's best attorneys teach there. Matter of fact, Dad has taught some of its classes." He looked at her with genuine warmth. "You'll be a great attorney – and partner in this firm."

"I'd love to join you here. More than anything, I want to be in a position to defend women."

"And," Sandi said, drawing their attention, "this is where I will work someday. Wherever I go to school, I want to come back and join you."

Lauren looked at Sandi, then Frank and Carol. She was aware that this was a memorable moment – a turning point in each of their lives. And she wished that Claire was sharing it.

Sandi and Lauren went to dinner at Thiele's. As they sat Lauren thought of important times that had taken place here. It was where she had first worked, and gotten to know Claire; where she and Mary had come to relax over Sunday dinners, talking-out some of their differences; and where she brought Dan on their first day together. Now, she and Sandi talked about their plans for the future.

Chapter Thirty-six

Dan tried to come home every weekend. He, Lauren, and Sandi had dropped plans of bringing Maddie to New York and walking her through Central Park. She was too frail to travel.

To Lauren it seemed impossible that Madeline had grown old. She had lost most of her hearing and vision. Her fur, no longer silky black, was thin and graying, her back was boney, and her legs wobbled from arthritis. Lauren was thankful every time she came home and found her waiting at the door.

On this Friday morning Maddie was slow getting up, so Lauren sat and massaged her back.

"Girl, this is our day. You don't need to move till you're ready."

As Maddie had done many times before, she smiled. And as before, Lauren rewarded her with a kiss – this time whispering into her fur, "Love you, Girl."

After minutes Maddie wanted up, and Lauren helped her. With unsteady steps she walked to the backdoor. Lauren opened it and followed her down the stairs and to the path heading toward the river. She was glad that Maddie only went a short way, relieved herself, then turned back toward the house.

Lauren wondered how she kept going, but then thought how life was sometimes too good to let go.

That night, before going to bed, Lauren peeked into Sandi's room. Maddie was stretched out on the bed alongside of Sandi. Lauren walked over and kissed Sandi on her forehead.

"Thanks, Mom."

Lauren smiled as she reached over and rubbed Maddie behind her ears.

"Mom, I'm glad Dan will be home tomorrow. Let's stay home together – the four of us ...before anything changes."

Lauren nodded, but didn't speak – knowing she would cry.

CPSIA information can be obtained
at www.ICGtesting.com
Printed in the USA
BVHW030938010320
573723BV00001B/95